Rebecca's CHOICE

JERRY S. EICHER

HARVEST HOUSE PUBLISHERS
EUGENE, OREGON

All Scripture quotations are taken from the King James Version of the Bible.

This is a work of fiction. Names, characters, places, and incidents are products of the author's imagination or are used fictitiously. Any resemblance to actual persons, living or dead, or to events or locales, is entirely coincidental.

Cover by Dugan Design Group, Bloomington, Minnesota

Cover photos © Gary #4883772 / Fotolia; Corbis / Jupiterimages; Author photo by Brian Ritchie

REBECCA'S CHOICE
Copyright © 2010 by Jerry S. Eicher
Published by Harvest House Publishers
Eugene, Oregon 97402
www.harvesthousepublishers.com

Library of Congress Cataloging-in-Publication Data
Eicher, Jerry S.
 Rebecca's choice / by Jerry Eicher.
     p. cm.—(The Adams County trilogy ; bk. 3)
 ISBN 978-0-7369-2637-9 (pbk.)
 1. Amish—Fiction. I. Title.
 PS3605.I34R38 2010
 813.'6—dc22

                                                    2009031513

Printed in the United States of America

10 11 12 13 14 15 16 17 18 / RDM-NI / 10 9 8 7 6 5 4 3 2 1

CHAPTER ONE

The day dawned without a cloud in the sky, the sunrise a blaze of light. In the months that followed, Rebecca Keim would often wonder where the storm clouds had hidden themselves.

A robin greeted her right after chores and breakfast. It sat on a lower tree branch outside the living room window, its claws gripping the limb, its eyes following her movements. The sun lit up the robin's feathers and gave them a soft glow.

"Good morning," she said. "So spring is here? Did you come to tell us?"

"Who are you talking to?" The voice came from the kitchen, but soon after her mother, Mattie, came to stand in the door opening.

"A robin has come to tell us of spring. Our troubles are over it says." Rebecca chuckled at her own words.

"You wish," Mattie said. "Stop staring out the window, and let's get ready. The day is getting away fast enough already."

"I'm not going," Rebecca said, announcing her sudden decision. The robin might have had something to do with it, she figured, but it didn't look guilty at all. It tilted its head at her and flew off.

"Not going? But it's the sewing. We need you."

"It's the women's sewing. I'm not married," Rebecca said, that being the first justification that came to her mind. What she really wanted was to enjoy the day by herself—to have peace and quietness in the house and no one around.

"Close enough," Mattie informed her, then added with a chuckle, "I suppose John doesn't think so."

Rebecca didn't say anything. She turned back to the window to hide the blush as the color spread across her face. That was another reason she wanted to stay home, to think of John without anyone implying her thoughts were inappropriate. She longed to think of his face, the way his jaw could firm up, allowing a smile to curl the corner of his mouth, and have no one here to say, at just the best moment, *Stop dreaming of John.*

She supposed she did dream a lot lately, but then there were reasons for that. Life had been a little rough for them but much better lately. Last Sunday night with John had been just like old times—even better than before the accident. John showed little effects from the winter's dramatic events. Sometimes she thought she saw him limp slightly, but then that too would go away.

"Come on," Mattie said. "We have to hurry."

Rebecca shook her head and kept her face turned toward the window. "I'll do the dishes. You can go alone."

"Suit yourself," her mother replied giving in. "Let's get the kitchen work finished, then—as far as we can before I go. Dad's got the horse tied up."

Rebecca hoped her face wasn't still red, but she doubted it. A few minutes more at the window would have helped, but her mother would think the same thing if she lingered. She smoothed her hair back and walked to the kitchen.

"Your wedding day will come soon enough," Mattie said, after a glance at Rebecca's face.

"A whole year yet," Rebecca said almost groaning.

"You were the ones who set the date." The dishes rattled as Mattie transferred them to the counter.

"Maybe we could move it up," Rebecca said. The statement reminded her why she wanted to be alone. Things like this just came out. Her mouth spilled them all over the place. She wanted to be alone to think first instead of speaking.

"You'd better talk to John about that, not me. Just don't go and jump the date forward at the last minute. We have to get ready. Weddings aren't prepared for in a day."

"I know," Rebecca said sighing. "I just run my mouth too much, when it comes to this, at least. I wouldn't bring it up with John anyway. When we planned the date, it seemed like the right time. Plenty of time then."

"There's still plenty of time. It goes by fast. Summer will be here before long. Then fall and winter. You'll wonder where the days went to."

"Sounds long," Rebecca said. She paused before she turned hot water on for the dishes. "Isn't it time you go?"

Mattie glanced at the kitchen clock. "Yes, if I want to be early—which I do. I guess this does work out okay."

"I'll get the horse, then." Rebecca was glad the conversation had moved on. She stepped outside, her coat draped across her arm. The weather had already warmed up considerably from when she had been out for morning chores. Still, she slipped the coat on. The robin spoke the truth—spring would soon be here. She could smell it in the air. Winter, with its bland cover of cold, ice, and snow, was broken by the faint odors of awakening life. Soon the promise would be evident in the smell of the cherry blossoms. The lush grass would need to be cut. The trees would push out their buds, and the plowed soil in the fields would be ready for seeds again.

Rebecca found the old driving horse where her father, Lester, had left it, tied inside the barn. She led it out to the buggy. It seemed weary this morning, and for just a moment, she thought it limped. That would make for complications because a lame house couldn't be used.

A change of horses meant considerable time would be lost. The younger horse, Rebecca knew, wasn't that safe to drive anyway. She didn't mind it too much, but her mother was terrified of the younger horse's wild ways. Of late it had picked up another bad habit. It shied at the slightest objects along the road and needed constant attention at the reins.

Rebecca pulled the old driver to a stop and lifted its foot. She inspected the hoof, but nothing seemed out of order—no nail or foreign object was visible.

"What's wrong?" Mattie asked, rushing from the house.

"The horse seemed lame," Rebecca said, not wanting to alarm her mother. "Can't see anything, though."

"Here." Mattie took the reins and led the horse forward a few steps.

"It looks okay," Rebecca said.

"Maybe it will last for the drive, and Lester can look at its hoof tonight."

"You'd better not drive the other horse," Rebecca said, just in case her mother's decision went in that direction.

"I can't run this one lame." Mattie pulled the horse forward a few more steps.

"I'll watch you drive out the lane," Rebecca volunteered. "If it's too bad, I'll wave."

Mattie nodded. A horse that ran might show a limp, while one that walked didn't. It would be the ultimate test.

While Rebecca lifted the shafts, Mattie brought the horse around. They had it hitched in minutes. Rebecca held the bridle while Mattie climbed in. When she drove off, Rebecca watched for any signs of trouble but saw none. She stood still, as Mattie paused at the end of the driveway and glanced back.

With a jerk the buggy turned left at the main road and disappeared over the little open bridge toward the town of Unity.

John. She let the thoughts come. *So steady now, so certain of himself yet somehow softened by what he has gone through. Is that the reason* Da Hah *allowed John's trial—to prepare us for our lives together?*

That the answer could be yes lay well within the realm of reason, she was certain. Those days of darkness, while John lay helpless and unconscious in the hospital, when they didn't know if he would survive or in what condition he would live, had been hard.

Rebecca shivered at the thought. Had they not survived, though? Had the sky not cleared? Above all, had their love not been made stronger? She was certain of that too.

There had been days when she doubted things could ever be right again. Out in Milroy she had remembered what love had felt like. Her heart would race with wild emotion and be moved when she least expected it. She felt the desire to be near that special someone, hear his voice, and see fire light up in his eyes. Only then it hadn't been John—it had been Atlee.

At times she had figured the past would always be better than anything the present could hold, but now she knew that wasn't true. The memory of Atlee was faint, swallowed up by what had happened since Christmas. She thought of Atlee only momentarily, a fleeting glance backward.

Her heart had found its home. What had been child's play with Atlee—the walks home with him from school and their promise at the bridge—had become an adult's flame, which gripped her whole being.

Rebecca shook her head and walked toward the house. If her mother was here, she would shake her head too. She would say, "You do have it bad."

Her thoughts went back to the hospital. John had told her how terrible that time had been. He woke up alone and was unable to move the whole side of his body. He was sure, he said, he would always be a cripple. He described his terror at the thought of losing her, how he hung on desperately to even the sound of her name. John had told her in subdued tones, his voice hushed in the telling, but she had felt fully the pain of his experience.

Yet John had let go. He would not have required her to marry a cripple. That much she knew. She had gone to him alone, driving the buggy with the young horse to West Union. There she had found herself ready to marry John because she loved him.

The same love she felt was in his eyes, as well. It was there when she first saw him laying in the hospital bed. His eyes reflected a gladness, a depth of joy that sprang up when he looked at her or said her name. Yet, what had surprised her the most that night had been the reaction of her own heart. It had wrapped itself around a man.

Since then John had been a changed man. There were days when he faltered, despaired on his slow way back to full health, but he had never faltered in his touch on her heart. "You don't have to stay with me," he told her a couple of times when he felt his worst, but his eyes always spoke of the depth of his love. They spoke too of the pain he would feel if she didn't stay.

John's need wasn't what caused her love to grow. It was the door he always kept open that caused her love to blossom. Last fall things had not been so. John's jealousy came between them. John knew of Atlee, and he also knew that he himself might be facing life as a cripple. John not only loved her, but he would have allowed her to leave if she so chose and would have understood the reason why.

Rebecca was certain there would have been no condemnation—no ugly words would have been spoken, no rumors spread, nor her name ruined. John would have said no unkind words when others would have asked the reason why. *She had her reasons,* he would have said and meant it. Even her promise to marry him, John wouldn't have held it against her.

This Rebecca knew. How, she wasn't certain. She just did, and nothing had happened since to cause her to doubt. Because of John's freedom, she had fully lost her heart.

A glad and joyous state of existence, she thought and shook her head again. Maybe they ought to move the wedding date up. She drew in her breath sharply at the thought. John hadn't even kissed her since that night at the hospital. Not that she thought he should have, she just wished he would—at least once in a while.

But that could wait, she figured. Perhaps it was for the best. As her mother would say, "Your years together will make up for the wait." Rebecca figured her mother had the proof, having been married all these years. Though how her mother could understand what she now felt was a little beyond Rebecca's comprehension.

This was hers and John's alone—an emotion that grew and might soon burst if nothing was done about it.

CHAPTER TWO

Working quickly Rebecca soon had the house in order. After the kitchen, which didn't take too long, she worked on the living room mess, caused by the younger children's departure to school. By ten she had the house clean.

Rebecca glanced out to the lawn to see if the robin had returned. She was glad to see the bird with its mate out on the grass. As she watched, the two would suddenly speed from one spot to another, abruptly stop, and fiercely peck the ground. Their heads would then come up sharply, and the whole scenario would begin again.

"They like each other too," she said and chuckled, glad no one was around to hear.

From the time on the clock, she knew the sewing would be in full swing by now. Women would be sitting all over the place, bent over their quilts or working on small comfort projects off in the corners. A few sewing machines would click away, but above it all would be the murmur of steady conversation.

For a moment Rebecca wished she was there and smiled at the thought. Already she felt a little like a married woman, one who wanted to be surrounded by voices of children and the other community women. That would come soon enough, she figured. For now there was this day, which she intended to enjoy fully.

With the household duties done, the hours were her own. Mattie would be back around three, just before the children returned from school and the house exploded into a noisy ruckus again.

She decided to cut out her wedding dress. Today would be the perfect day for it because no prying eyes were there to see what she would wear on her special day. They would all know soon enough, but there was no rush. Kept secret, the knowledge seemed to gather extra joy in her heart.

John would know what color she would wear because she would tell him when they coordinated the wedding plans, but he wouldn't see the dress—either in the making or after it was finished. John had an eye for color and would let her know whether he liked the dress. That he liked her, she already knew.

"You'd look good in any color," he had said on Sunday night and meant it. In the glow of his words, she believed him. On the day they would be joined together as man and wife—for that day and for that moment—it would be true. Rebecca was certain of it.

She went upstairs to retrieve the material from the box that was supposed to be stored in the corner of her closet. She looked there first, but no box was there. She thought for a moment that one of the girls had found it and perhaps moved it while looking for her secrets. Katie, the oldest, was mischievous enough to try, and Viola would support Katie's efforts.

Rebecca ran her hand through the closet a second time, then remembered she had left it out last night. Behind her the box sat beside her dresser in plain sight. Irritated she grabbed it, took the box downstairs, and spread the cloth out on the kitchen table. Its light blue sheen almost glowed as she stood back to look at it. Her heart beat faster, and she was again glad no one else was around.

Rebecca laid the pattern on the cloth, each piece sliding carefully through her fingers. She had a momentary flash of fear as the last piece of pattern ran over the edge. It looked as if she would not have enough material. Although the store clerk in West Union had assured her more fabric could be purchased, she had hesitated because this was all they had in stock. Rebecca knew how such things went and had little confidence in promises. Her preference would have been to choose another color then rather than now.

Her heart in her throat, she made a careful change in the positions of two pattern pieces and solved the problem. Next she considered whether it might be better to mark the fabric and then cut but decided against it. Rebecca preferred to cut straight from the pattern. With Mattie's scissors she followed the outline of the paper.

The task was completed by lunchtime, and the cloth was folded and tucked back into the box. Rebecca fixed herself a sandwich and ate near the living room window. That was another benefit of a day by herself—she could eat lunch in the living room.

Her eyes searched the lawn for the robins but found no sight of them. What did appear was a chicken that walked lazily across the lawn like it owned the place, pecking the ground half-heartedly. Obviously the chicken was not hungry, but only trying out its freedom outside the confines of the chicken coop.

Rebecca opened the front door, her sandwich in her hand. "Where'd you come from?" she hollered.

The hen looked at her and emitted a soft cluck, as if it couldn't understand why anyone would interrupt such a glorious day. Then apparently it remembered its condition. The hen took off, squawking wildly and running toward the barn, its wings flapping hard and aiding the fast getaway.

Rebecca shut the door again. She figured Matthew could catch the thing when he came home from school. How it came out was the larger problem and a matter that should be looked into immediately. If the yard was full of chickens when Mattie came home, her day off would long be remembered for reasons she didn't wish it to be.

Rebecca got her coat and ate the rest of the sandwich while she circled the chicken pen looking for any wires that might appear out of place. She knew chickens didn't just escape without a way out. Rebecca knew from bitter experience that where one chicken went, the rest were soon to follow.

So she walked around the coop yard again and finally found the breach in the wire. Too stupid to know enough to wait until no one was looking, but smart enough to figure out where their companion had gone, two hens poked their heads through the opening in the wire. If they had tried one at a time, they would have been out into the yard already, but as it was, the two had gotten nowhere.

"Back in with you," Rebecca told them, pushing their heads back into the coop.

They squawked loudly in protest, which attracted more hens, all apparently interested in the dash for freedom.

"No, you don't," Rebecca told them, bending the chicken wires to create a temporary fix. More would need to be done.

She ran to the barn and found wire and a pair of pliers. Rebecca was on her way out when she heard the loud clucking and squawking coming from the haymow. The stray hen raised an awful fuss.

Sure the chicken was not in harm's way, Rebecca figured the hen must have laid an egg and was now announcing the exhilarating experience. True to Rebecca's expectations, the hen appeared at the haymow edge, loud in its proclamations and wildly flapping its wings.

"Matthew will take care of you," she told it. "We ought to eat you for this."

As if the hen understood it was only an idle threat, it gave one last flap of its wings, clucked in triumph, and disappeared back into the haymow.

Back at the chicken pen, another hen already had her head stuck in the makeshift wire repair and had pushed up dirt high behind it. Rebecca released the bird from its snare and stretched wire twice across the hole. A few twists of the pliers and the job was completed. From several steps back, Rebecca evaluated the handiwork and considered it sufficient to last until either Matthew or her father could check it. If nothing else she would check it again tonight.

It was now getting on toward one, and Rebecca pulled her thoughts back to what she wanted to do with the rest of the day. The entire wedding plans had yet to be made. Food, her mother would take care of. Table waiters were her responsibility. They would be a delight to plan but still a little difficult at this point.

With the wedding almost a year away, couples who dated now might not be by then. She supposed last minute changes could be made, so some plans might survive. Still, it would be best to wait until closer to the wedding date to announce any plans.

John had no younger brothers and sisters, just his older sister, Bethany, who had been married for years but had no children. She could serve as a cook if she wasn't family. As family she would be given a seat of honor, close to John and herself at the corner table.

Rebecca was overwhelmed with sheer delight at the thought of the day to come. She wanted to add a special touch—flowers, just a small bouquet at the table. Surely Bishop Martin wouldn't object. She had seen this done at the last community wedding, and no one raised a fuss.

John's father, Isaac, one of the ministers, might be the one who raised objections, but Rebecca doubted whether he would do so for his own sake. Isaac might be concerned about what the deacon would say. Ministers, she supposed, had to be extra careful when things of the church *ordnung* involved their own children.

Fruit, she decided, would serve as the main decoration. Set in just the right locations with just the right combinations of colors, fruit was a sight to behold and perfectly safe from any ministerial objections.

They might even hang a painting of a springtime sunrise with a Scripture verse behind their table. It would be a nice reminder of their springtime wedding. She could easily imagine John sitting beneath the picture along with the two couples who serve as witnesses on each side of him. What she could not imagine was herself with John.

That troubled her. She belonged in the setting. There was no doubt about it. John was hers as sure as this day was real. Why then was she not there?

It must be a trick of her mind, she decided, and let the comfort of the thought fill her. She desperately wanted to be in the picture, but it was simply too much for her mind to conceive yet—too forbidden for it to accept.

Rebecca forced her mind to go where it apparently didn't want to go. She thought of John when he sat on the couch beside her on Sunday nights. Then she imagined the two of them as man and wife.

Rebecca let the emotion run all the way through her and blushed at the thought, glad again that she was home by herself.

Such thoughts, she told herself and then refocused her mind on safer ground. The table waiters could wait for now. The witnesses needed to be from each side of the family, people they felt close to.

Her older brother and sister were married, and Matthew, the next in line, was only twelve. That wouldn't work too well. This meant neither of them would have brothers or sisters as witnesses. Strange, she thought, but special because they were special. A slight smile played on her face.

They would ask cousins, then, or close friends. She had no cousins here on Wheat Ridge. As for close friends, she had Wilma and wondered if Mattie would consent to that. John wouldn't care, she figured. John had his cousin Sharon. Sharon's father, Aden, was John's boss at the furniture store. On second thought Sharon might be a little young.

Sharon was seventeen now but would be eighteen by the date of the wedding, so that might work if John wanted to ask her. Next she thought about Luke Byler, who lived in Milroy and was related to John, some cousin connection she thought, but John might not want him either.

Well, there would be plenty of time to think of this later, she thought and glanced at the clock. Surprised it was past two already, she took a quick look out the front window and saw Mattie's buggy coming across the little bridge.

Rebecca could see that her mother was driving hard and fast. Even if it was past two, Mattie was home early. Although the horse limped noticeably, her mother didn't slow down even as she made the turn into the lane.

CHAPTER THREE

Rachel Byler wished she hadn't done it now, but it was too late for second thoughts, she told herself. The news that morning really didn't change anything. If anything it may have improved things, but Rachel didn't feel much better in spite of her repeated self-assurances.

It really was Reuben's fault, as these things always were. Blame it on his lazy ways. Reuben's deaconship hung over her head like a sword with two sharp edges. He cut coming and going, the man did.

Reuben had brought his load of goats home yesterday—his lousy, stinky, no-good goats that scrambled off the trailer. Their hooves cut marks all over her lawn as they made their way to the pen behind the chicken barn.

The two goats Reuben had staked out in the yard now were cutting even more marks in the lawn. Reuben said that he put them there to eat the grass. This he said with a wide smile. She was surprised that Reuben didn't just let the precious dears run loose in the yard—the better to do the job—but Rachel supposed he didn't want to chase goats around when it came time to put them back in the pen.

Rachel believed Reuben to be a lazy and completely incompetent businessman. Who could believe that he, Reuben Byler, the deacon, the bishop's run-around-man, could capably manage goats when he couldn't manage anything else? Rachel wished a hundred times she would have had better sense than to marry the man.

If it hadn't been for her father's inheritance, which she had been sure would come her way, she would have sent the soft-spoken boy off to some other Amish girl. She would at least have waited for a better choice—one she didn't doubt would have come her way. But with the inheritance to come eventually, Reuben had seemed perfectly manageable, and she had encouraged his attentions. Reuben Byler had fit well into her plans for a life with plenty of money. Without the money, it was another matter.

She was now with child again, and because she was in her forties, it made things worse. Although her age was a concern, it wasn't what pushed her over the edge. It was the goats—the mere sight of them and the fact that Reuben had purchased the animals with borrowed money. Rachel she was sure he would lose that money, and she was sure she would be the one who would have to pay it back.

How the money would be paid back was outside the realm of her imagination, unless she could get back what was hers—the money from her father's lost inheritance. Millet Miller—old M-Jay they called him—willed all the money to his sister, Emma. It was lost as far as Rachel was concerned.

There was a time she had adored her father, nearly worshipped the ground he walked on. Her father had taken her with him often when he worked on the farm, let her ride on the hay wagon, work with him while he threshed wheat with her three brothers. Abe and Jonas had married and moved away to other communities, while she and Ezra had stayed.

Ezra was younger than she was and looked down his nose at girls who worked in the fields. It was M-Jay who thought girls had as many rights as boys did. He was the one who encouraged her to come along to the fields, even when the day was hot and the work rough. He had raised her in the Amish faith, and she would die in it as he had. She knew that without a doubt. That was one thing that would never change.

What had changed was her memory of M-Jay. The issue of the money made her bitter, and the bitterness ate at her soul. At first the bitterness circled her heart but was now deep within her being. Their son, Luke, had tried to help by sympathizing with her, even helped obtain information when she needed it, but that had changed too.

The change in Luke was Susie Burkholder's fault. Rachel felt that Susie drew Luke away. Luke was convinced that he would continue to date and eventually marry the girl, but how could he be so certain? They weren't engaged, but then perhaps Luke wasn't telling her everything.

Luke had drifted far from her already, Rachel thought. The boy could be hiding an engagement from her. In a way Luke should be ashamed of himself, but not because he was hiding things from her, but rather because Susie's parents were poor—even poorer than they were.

That Luke kept secrets from her still hurt. Luke was her only son. Before Susie he would have told her everything.

In addition to being poor, Susie was a common girl in looks. Rachel wished Luke had fallen for someone like Ann Stuzman, who just turned eighteen last winter. Ann was pretty, and her father was well-to-do, but instead Luke had chosen Susie. Amos Troyer dated Ann now—Luke's opportunity was likely gone forever.

Rachel's bitterness ran deep. Luke had not just rejected her and chosen Susie, he had chosen poverty. That was the hurt that stung the most. Rachel had hoped Luke would turn out differently, had hoped he wouldn't take after the ways of his father.

Surely Luke could see what that road brought—the struggle to survive, the limited money supply, the constant scrape at the bottom of the barrel. Yet Luke hadn't seen it or so it seemed to Rachel. With the passing of time, she lost hope he ever would.

Reuben was a good man at times, she told herself. In many ways he was. He tried—just as he now tried with these goats. Yet his efforts didn't improve their income. In her mellow moments, she remembered the early years, the sweetness she had shared with him. Those were the days when she still expected money from her father to come at any time.

When M-Jay's will was revealed and everything passed to Emma except a token amount of cash that was set aside for his children, those sweet times with Reuben changed. Reuben now had the bishop's ear, which he counted as great value, but she didn't. It failed to fatten any bank account, which to Rachel was how you counted the value of everything.

Just this morning she had gone to her desk in the living room, written the letter, made sure it was addressed correctly, and then mailed it. The news of Emma's death had arrived only minutes after the mailman picked up the letter, but Rachel told herself she wasn't sorry the deed was done. Ezra had brought the news himself, drove over in his single buggy, his horse lathered from the fast drive. She had been the last on his list of stops.

Rachel wondered what Ezra's rush had been, but then perhaps Ezra needed to get back to his work in the fields. He was one of the children who seemed to suffer the least from the lost inheritance. That Ezra should bring the news seemed appropriate to her. It might well be a good sign of things to come. Surely the one who was to make the money would not be the one to bring the news that would again take away her hopes.

The news of Emma's passing raised her hopes. She didn't deny the fact, and she wouldn't ever tell anyone—especially Reuben. The money would heal all things in her life. She thought again of the letter she mailed. Would it cause problems with the money?

Rachel thought this unlikely and brushed the unpleasant thought aside. In the worst case, the letter would be written off as a prank and quickly forgotten. In no case could the letter be traced back to her. Of that she had taken great care by making sure the spelled words bore no resemblance to her handwriting. The result was more likely to be taken as the product of an untrained child rather than an adult.

Rachel's heartbeat quickened. Was she finally to realize her dream? The thought thrilled her, filled her with anticipation, and then her emotions plunged.

What if Emma had done the same as her father? Surely this wasn't possible! There hadn't been time for the lawyers to fix things—not after Luke had intercepted the letter from Emma's mailbox. She had written her letter this morning with the assumption there would be time. Now this turn of events filled Rachel with delight. She pulled out a kitchen chair and sat down, overcome with her thoughts.

Outside one of the goats broke loose from its tether and headed for the rose bush that grew beside the sidewalk. Rachel was blind to the goats at the moment. Before her eyes came the sight of money—piles of it. The huge amount filled her checking account till it bulged. In her giddiness she wondered whether the local bank could hold it all. She could just imagine the looks those haughty tellers would give her when she walked in the morning after the deposit.

"Good morning," they would say, their fancy English heads bent forward in respect to her bonnet and shawl. They would nod to her. No longer would she carry shame on her shoulders—the shame of poverty. She would now be able to look anyone in the eyes and know that she was as worthy as they were.

Reuben could then be as lazy as he wanted to be. He could have a thousand goats if he wanted. She wouldn't care. Why, Reuben could have individual veterinarians for each goat come out to the farm if he wished. What did it matter? The inheritance would be hers.

Rachel calmed herself down and immediately saw the goat greedily eating her rose. Quickly angered she ran outside, yelled at the smelly thing, grabbed it by its ears, and hauled it back to the slipped rope. What was wrong with the man? Reuben couldn't even tie a rope.

She held the goat in its proper place, tied it up, and made sure the rope was well fastened this time. The knot was better than any Reuben could tie, but what did that matter now. Everything had changed. Of this Rachel was certain. The spring day had brought more than just new life to the earth, it had brought new hope to her soul.

CHAPTER FOUR

Rebecca went out to meet the buggy and could hardly believe her eyes. The old driving horse limped as it came in the driveway, but Mattie seemed not to notice. Through the storm front, Rebecca could see her mother's firm grip on the reins, her face grim, her hands extended in front of her.

Something awful must have happened, Rebecca figured, as stabs of fear ran through her. Memories of last winter's bad news flashed through her mind. *Has John been injured again?*

Mattie brought the old horse to a stop, slid the buggy door open, and turned the wheels slightly so she could climb down the step.

"Mom," Rebecca managed.

"I know it's limping," Mattie said, stepping down from the buggy. "I had to get home quickly. The horse will be okay. Its leg's just sprained a little. Elmer looked after it at the sewing. You have to get ready to leave tomorrow morning—early."

"What's wrong?" Rebecca still stood frozen in place.

"Emma passed away. Last night sometime. Sudden, I think. The funeral's the day after tomorrow. I thought you would want to go. The van load leaves early tomorrow morning. They'll pick you up at Edna's at five."

"Emma." Rebecca felt a flood of relief and then shame because she counted John more important than anyone else.

"I know it's startling news," Mattie said, "but not totally unexpected. Emma has a history of heart trouble."

"I thought you brought news—about John—another accident."

"No, you two have had your time, I suppose."

"Leona mentioned Emma's failing health when I was in Milroy before Christmas." Rebecca walked to the other side of the horse, as her mother began to unhitch the buggy.

"John might go too. He's related. Cousins somehow. I thought maybe you'd want to talk with him before morning. There might be two loads going. Who knows with all the planning going on. The women were still talking when I left. At least you wouldn't be in different vans."

"Maybe." Rebecca loosened the tugs on her side, and Mattie led the horse forward. "Matthew isn't choring tonight?"

"No. He has to help Edna with her chores. That's why the rush. I thought you might want to drive over and talk to him before chores. Afterward would be quite late. You'll have to drive the young horse because this one is lame."

Rebecca nodded and ran through the time frame in her mind. Though using the young horse to drive over to see John didn't terrorize her like it did Mattie, it could put her home quite late. No matter the time, her mother had a point, and she had better talk this over with John.

Last year she had not spoken with John about Atlee soon enough, and look where that had gotten her. She had resolved then not to let it happen again. Even if this was just about attending Emma's funeral, she wanted to let John know of her plans.

"I think I'll go after chores," she said, making up her mind. "John's probably not going, but I'll let him know anyway. Driving after dark isn't too bad."

"Then you can pack before supper." Mattie led the horse toward the barn.

Rebecca nodded. "I can help with supper too."

"We'll see if there's time," Mattie said, before disappearing into the barn.

Rebecca walked to the house, went upstairs, and pulled her suitcase down from the top shelf of the closet. Laid out on the bed, the shiny black suitcase brought back the memory of her winter trip to Milroy. She had gone to help aunt Leona with the birth of baby Jonathan.

Emma had seemed fine, despite the rumors of her health problems, when Rebecca saw her briefly in church and during a visit at her house. How quickly, she thought, things change. Rebecca wished now she had personally asked Emma how she was doing.

Perhaps it was the relationship they used to have, that of teacher and student, which squelched such questions and made the asking seem inappropriate. Now Emma was gone. At least she had been able to have one last personal visit and receive the usual good advise Emma always gave.

Rebecca's black dress went into the suitcase first, followed by travel clothes for the days she estimated the trip would take. It struck her that this was the first time she would wear funeral clothing since her mother's father had passed away two years ago.

There were times last winter when she had felt death would come sooner for someone else—John had been injured so badly in his accident. Now it was Emma. In the order and will of the Lord, who knew what was best.

Grandpa's funeral had the feeling of the inevitable about it. He had spent his days here on earth, the preacher had said, a full life lived and now had joined his Maker and those loved ones who passed over before him.

Rebecca wondered if Emma's day would be like that. Emma had never married, and for what reason Rebecca never heard. Such things usually got around, passed by the grapevine produced by close knit societies. But with Emma the vine had never produced any information. She was just an old maid, a schoolteacher, well loved by students and parents alike. That always seemed sufficient and as far as it went.

Had Emma ever loved a man as she loved John? The question presented itself just like that—out of the clear blue and just as suddenly. Rebecca laughed. That was hard to imagine. Emma had always been kind to her, thoughtful, helpful, a motherly figure, but in love? Rebecca chuckled again. She figured her reaction was answer enough.

Emma was just Emma. She always seemed to be enough in and of herself. Rebecca had even thought once that such a life might be the right one for her. Emma's life had seemed so clean, so uncluttered by the emotions she often had. Not that she would exchange what she felt for John, but the pain and trouble John and she had already been through was enough to make one wonder if it was worth it.

Of course it was, Rebecca assured herself. A sudden thought flashed in her mind. Would there be a past boyfriend at the funeral—someone Emma used to see but parted ways with? Wouldn't that be something. Rebecca folded her dresses carefully into the suitcase.

Who would know though? If this was true, why would such a person make the relationship known? Perhaps he was now old himself, maybe widowed. What if he had lost touch over the years and would never find out Emma had passed away?

Rebecca chuckled. "You are a silly one," she told herself. She remembered that Emma would have no immediate family in attendance. Emma was the youngest in her family, and all her brothers and sisters had already died. She had nieces and nephews but no one closer than that.

"I loved her," she whispered to the room, tears stinging her eyes. "A lot."

Thirty minutes later she went downstairs, helped with supper, and then walked out to the barn at five for chores. Rebecca planned to skip supper, but her father insisted she eat, though it would delay her drive to see John until much later.

Matthew helped her hitch up the young driving horse.

"Be careful," he lectured, when she got into the buggy. Already Matthew felt his brotherly superiority, even though he was much younger than she was. "John isn't worth landing in the ditch for."

"Yes he is," she told him, risking the draw of one of his arguments. Matthew could be an irritation at times. He was, she had to admit, a smart looking fellow, even if he was her brother.

"Good someone thinks so." He chuckled wickedly and let go of the bridle as the young horse took off with a snap of the tugs.

Rebecca hung onto the reins. She knew from past experience the horse would calm down once it was on the open road. True to her expectation, it took the turn at the bridge a little slower and then trotted along nicely by the time they rattled across the Harshville covered bridge.

In the climb out of the little settlement, on the grade toward Unity, the young horse calmed down even more. So much that once in town, she had to slap the reins to hurry it up. Shaking its head in protest, it increased its speed.

Rebecca liked the horse except for its habit of shying away from things, which required her to keep a sharp eye out. Being alert to the unexpected was a good idea in any case, she figured. At the Miller's lane, she pulled left and tied up by the barn.

Because no one was around and a light was on in the house, she assumed Isaac and Miriam would be in the living room. John was probably upstairs in his room because their supper would be over by this time too.

When she knocked on the door, Miriam opened it. Taking a moment for her eyes to adjust to the dim light, she recognized Rebecca and opened the door wide.

"Oh, it's Rebecca," she said. "Do come in. John is upstairs."

"You out alone?" Isaac hollered from his rocker, as Rebecca stepped inside. Isaac's chest length beard was fully white, his face beamed with good cheer.

"It's not too late," she told him with a smile. "I have a good horse."

"Mattie's was lame today," Miriam commented. "I think someone looked after it at the sewing."

"Yes, they did," Rebecca nodded and glanced toward the stair door. She didn't really want to go to John's room. They went there on Sunday afternoons sometimes, but after dark seemed another matter.

"You want to talk with John?" Miriam asked, which really didn't help much.

"Thought I'd see if he was going to Emma's funeral," Rebecca offered.

"Call the boy," Isaac said from his rocker, for which Rebecca was deeply grateful. "Tell him to get his tail down here."

As if he heard, the stair door opened and John stuck his head out. "Oh," he said sheepishly, "so this is what the fuss is all about. I thought I heard someone drive in."

"Worth making a fuss over, isn't it?" Isaac asked.

Rebecca laughed at the remark and at John, whose shirttail was untucked and suspenders hung down nearly to his bare toes.

"I suppose so." John's smile was broad. It warmed her heart. "Always is," he added and walked over to the kitchen table. He pulled a chair out for her, then sat down himself.

Rebecca took it. Miriam returned to the living room, and Isaac lifted his magazine and continued reading.

"Emma's funeral," she said meeting his eyes. "You going?"

"No," he said shaking his head, "Mom and Dad are. Aden needs help at the store. Sharon might go along."

"Thought we could ride in the same van, if you were," she said as explanation. "I'm definitely going."

He nodded. "I could have sent word too. Would have, if I were going."

"I figured," she said and met his eyes again. "I just wanted to let you know I was going."

"I'm that special?" he teased. "You come all the way over here for that?"

"Shhh…" she whispered. "Yes, of course you are."

"You wouldn't have had to," he said soberly. "It's sweet, though."

Rebecca hoped her cheeks didn't start burning, but neither Miriam nor Isaac seemed to be looking her way.

"What horse are you driving?" John asked, getting up from his chair.

"The younger one."

"Little skittish, no?"

"He's okay," she told him. But John wasn't convinced—she could tell.

"Better get you on the road again before it gets too late," he said. His firm words made her feel cared for and warm inside.

"I'll be going, then." She stood and pushed her chair back under the table.

Without a further word, John followed her to the front door, tucked his shirt in, put his boots and coat on, and stepped outside. Together they walked toward the barn. John filled her side vision, his hands in his coat pockets.

"Take care of yourself," he said, when they got to the buggy. He loosened the tie rope as she got in. "Sorry about Emma."

"Good night," she told him, as he let go of the bridle. The young horse made his usual dashing takeoff. When she turned right at the blacktop, she saw him standing by the barn, watching her leave, his form barely visible in the darkness.

Chapter Five

The late Emma Miller, beloved schoolteacher and spinster, lay in the master bedroom, enclosed in a plain pine box coffin. Behind her rose the massive stone fireplace of her residence. For hours now relatives and family had gathered, each in turn came into the bedroom, slowly moved past the coffin, and paid their respects to the departed.

Inside the front door, tables had been set up where hats and bonnets could be placed. Benches were placed in the living room. Later the overflow spilled into the dining room. The activity in the house had the feel of an informal church service.

Men and women, after going into the bedroom, found their way back out and took their seats on separate sides of the room. Even here—when death had come to call—the rigid forms of male and female separation were not broken.

Supper had been prepared and served already, the dishes cleared away. Any latecomers had to go without food. The protocol was simple and plain, as they believed the Lord God desired.

Rachel had persuaded Reuben to arrive earlier than normal. Luke would come when he wanted to. Reuben had complained, saying his goats needed his attention yet. That had not surprised Rachel because Reuben's goats were lately the most important thing on his mind. Reuben paid more attention to them then he did to her. Not that she cared, Rachel told herself, but it was just one more reason to hate the ugly things.

Reuben had expressed his regret over the eaten flowers and promised to tie the animals more securely. Promises, especially Reuben's, meant little to Rachel. To her, he was the example of a promise unfulfilled.

28

The reason why Rachel had wanted to come early was to plan for the future. Now that Emma was gone, a little forward thinking might stand her in good stead.

While they drove up the long driveway, Reuben let the horse take it's own good time. Rachel utilized the opportunity to contemplate the place—the barn, the yard full of towering oak trees, and the great house with its *Englisha* fireplace. Such a fireplace wasn't allowed in the *ordnung*, but even the Amish bishop knew it could not be torn out, as most outside influences were when the Amish purchased a residence. Dismantling the grand fireplace would have caused serious damage to the home, and so Emma had lived with the *Englisha* fireplace.

Perhaps it was the fireplace, with its massive chimney through the roof, or perhaps it was the lay of the house on the hill that caused Rachel to make up her mind. This was to be her place. Emma had two other places—nice ones—and who knew how much money in the bank, a tidy sum Rachel was sure.

This place was to be hers, though. How that was to be managed, Rachel wasn't sure, but it would be. She was certain of it. The years of pain had been too long, and the agony of the wait too great for it to be snatched away right before her eyes. That had happened when her father passed away, and if it happened again, the pain would be even greater.

For one thing, she was older, and the vigor of youth was no longer a ready source to draw strength from and recover by. The other reason was the child she carried. That she was to bear a child at her age, Rachel had made a measure of peace with. What she could not make peace with was losing the inheritance another time.

Reuben let her off at the sidewalk, and she went inside, straight to the bedroom. Emma looked like Rachel expected. Because no one else was in the room, Rachel moved out to the living room quickly and found a place to sit among the other women.

Surely her brothers would be fair. The thought had never occurred to her before. There were, after all, only three farms and four children. Rachel glanced toward the men's section.

Ezra was a local, close with Bishop Mose, and well enough off in his own right. Abe and Jonas were from an Amish settlement in Missouri. They had moved there years ago, soon after the founding of the young community, and decided to stay. These two had Rachel worried.

Granted they were her own flesh and blood, but that seemed distant and unimportant at the moment. Both were about as poor as she was. Rachel knew this from family conversations, and from a general idea of how things stood. Reuben and Rachel had traveled to Missouri for a visit some four years ago, and it had not taken long for Rachel to form her opinion. Neither the Amish community in Missouri nor her brothers' lives flowed with money.

How was this going to work? Rachel shifted on the bench and then turned to shake the hand of Esther Yoder, who had come in earlier.

"She was a good woman," Esther whispered, bending close to Rachel.

Rachel nodded and thought Emma would have been a better woman if she'd done what was right before she passed away.

"Our daughter so loved Emma. Never had a better teacher—not in all her school years. You know how hard good teachers are to come by."

Rachel nodded again. "Yes, she was."

"The Lord takes when it's His time. Young and old. Emma had a full life in years and in children." Esther leaned even closer. "You think he's coming?"

"Coming?" Rachel knew her eyes were full of questions because she didn't have the slightest idea what Esther was referring to.

"Him," Esther whispered, the tone of her voice speaking for itself.

Rachel was beginning to think the woman was a little off but quickly dismissed the thought as nonsense—Esther was one of the most sane women in the community.

"You don't know about him?" Esther asked surprised. "I figured the family all knew."

Rachel shook her head.

"Oh."

Rachel moved closer, slowly so as not to attract attention.

"Your parents never told you?"

Rachel shook her head.

"The old people must have kept it to themselves, then. My mother knew, though. Maybe not too many did. Those kinds of things are sometime kept under wraps. Emma was once serious about someone. Around seventeen or so. Fell hard too, from what my mom said."

Rachel waited.

"He was Mennonite. Always was. His parents too. Why she got thinking in that direction—who knows? Maybe it was just one of those things. Apparently it got stopped in time."

"Why would he come?" Rachel asked.

"I don't know," Esther said. "Just wondered."

"Really." Rachel fast lost interest. A crush in one's youth was normal. What Emma had done with her love life really didn't matter to her. Then again, perhaps it did.

If Emma had married... The thought sent shivers down Rachel's spine. There could be a dozen children waiting in line—all with their hands out for money from her father's inheritance. Rachel almost smiled, filled with a sense of gratefulness.

"It's sad really," Esther continued, "that Emma never married. Seems a waste in a way. She could have had children...grandchildren perhaps. They could have been here today—here when she passed. They could have lived life with her—could have mourned her passing."

"Yes...they could have," Rachel said and thought, *God in Heaven, be praised.* In all her thoughts of Emma, this was one she had never given time to. What would have happened if Emma had married, even later in life? The complications could have been immense.

"I guess she was happy," Esther said and got up. "She had children, in a way. Many of them. Maybe that's why she taught school, poured her heart out the way she did, gave them her all. It would explain a lot. At least her life wasn't lost—not with the blessing she was."

Rachel nodded and reached up to shake the hand of Sylvia Esh, who had just come out of the bedroom.

"She was a good woman," Sylva whispered. "Our children just loved her." She then moved on.

An hour slipped by as people came and went. Then Bishop Mose slowly got to his feet. Rachel glanced at the clock. It was nearly eight o'clock, time to wrap things up.

Mose cleared his throat. "As the time is getting on, the family has requested that prayer be done now. Those who need to leave can leave afterward. Let us kneel before the face of God."

As the people knelt beside their benches, Bishop Mose led out in prayer. When he was done, Rachel got up and took her seat again. While some people stood here and there in the room, some started filing out. Luke left with some of the first ones. She saw Reuben get up a few minutes later, obviously with plans to leave. His goats on his mind, she figured.

Bitter thoughts ran through her mind. *Well, let the lousy, smelly things die, for all I care.* When Reuben moved toward the bedroom instead of outdoors, she ignored him—even when he glanced in her direction. Let him pay his respects to Emma again. She had already paid hers. It was high time Emma paid hers likewise.

With a bowed head, Reuben walked forward. Rachel saw her two brothers, Abe and Jonas, just arrived from Missouri, get up and follow. The three entered the bedroom and exited a few minutes later. Rachel was sure Reuben's grim face was just a display of deacon piety—a display for others to see. What could Emma possibly have meant to him? He certainly didn't care about Emma's money.

Reuben silently drove home and then unhitched the buggy while Rachel walked to the house. She thought to stay and help but decided the man needed all the useful work he could get. He would just go tend his goats anyway.

With money on the way, she didn't care that much about what Reuben did. Funny how Reuben's effort to support his family, deacon that he was, would soon become his hobby, now that she had Emma's money. His goats would become his entertainment, really quite fitting for a man who never could see where life's real value lay.

Luke was not around when she went in. Apparently he already had gone upstairs to bed. She dismissed him from her mind and went back to her plans for tomorrow.

Suddenly she remembered her question about Abe and Jonas. *How is this going to work? There are the three farms, the money in the bank, and four children. Did Emma leave detailed instructions in her will? Probably not. It would be more like Emma to have us all fight it out,* she thought. They wouldn't give Emma the pleasure, though—she would see to that. Abe and Jonas would be satisfied with the extra money and one farm between them. The money was still of an undetermined amount, but Rachel was sure it would be large. The sum had to be from all the years of farm income. Abe and Jonas would have more money than they ever saw before.

She decided Ezra could have the third farm, she the home place, and if things really went well, there might even be a portion of money left from the bank account for her. Reuben and she would sell the place here, pay off the debt, and move. Reuben could bring his silly goats along with him, if he wanted to.

It was an hour later, when she heard Reuben come into the utility room from the outside, that the thought occurred to her. *What if Emma had left the inheritance to* him—*the Mennonite boyfriend Esther spoke about?* The thought chilled Rachel. Fingers of fear ran down her spine.

Did Emma deliberately leave a trail to Rebecca, simply for a smoke screen…to throw us off? Was all our hard work for nothing? Did I drive Luke away by insisting that he snatch Emma's letter—the one addressed to her attorney—from her mailbox to bring it to me? Was it all for naught?

Rachel could still remember those awful words from the letter. "Then please name Rebecca Keim, of Union, Ohio, the daughter of Lester and Mattie Keim, as the primary beneficiary of all my property... contingent upon...that Rebecca Keim must not under any circumstances marry a non-Amish person."

What if Emma intended for Luke to find the letter, actually planned on me reading it, and all the while, cleverly covered up the real plan until it was too late. Is Emma to have her final revenge?

She sat down at the kitchen table, and Reuben found her there.

"I'm sorry," he said and obviously meant something else entirely. He laid his hand tenderly on Rachel's shoulder.

"God is against us," she whispered, to which he couldn't have the slightest clue what she meant.

"It's a hard time for us all," Reuben said, his fingers tightening on her shoulder. "She lived a good life, though."

CHAPTER SIX

The windup alarm clock rattled up and down and clanged out its racket, waking Rebecca well before the regular choring time. She groped in the darkness and found the shutoff button before anyone else in the house awakened. Sleepily she found a match, slid the top across a dresser drawer bottom with a flick of her wrist, and lit it.

Lifting the globe on the kerosene lamp, she transferred the flame to the wick just before the heat on the matchstick threatened to burn her fingers. In the chill of the room, she gasped as her hand almost slipped on the glass globe. One side had caught on the metal brackets and refused to budge. She tried again, holding her breath, and the globe finally slipped into place.

With her suitcase already downstairs, Rebecca quickly changed into her traveling clothes and quietly left the room, carrying the kerosene lamp in one hand. Because of the early hour, she had planned to fix a bowl of cold cereal. Rebecca wasn't surprised, though, to hear her mother's footsteps coming from the main floor bedroom.

"You really should have a hot breakfast," Mattie whispered. "You won't get there till after lunch."

Rebecca shook her head and poured cornflakes into a small bowl. "I'm okay."

Mattie slid onto the kitchen table bench. "Leona has a pattern for me. Make sure you don't forget it."

"For you?" Rebecca glanced up before she added milk to the cereal.

"The sewing. It might work a little better for some of the women than the one we have. Baby patterns are all different. She has one of Jonathon's."

"I'll try not to forget."

"Leona will help. She mentioned it in her last letter."

Rebecca nodded and glanced at the clock on the wall. If the van arrived at five at Edna's, she still had plenty of time to walk across the road. Since this was the last stop, the van might even be a little late, but that wouldn't be wise to depend on. They could wait, she supposed, but that wasn't what she wanted.

"You'll be back late the day after the funeral."

"Might be early. Depends when they start back, I guess."

"Never as early as when they leave." Mattie made a face.

"Do I need to be back early? I guess you are shorthanded. Matthew's doing Edna's chores all week."

"Might as well get used to it," Mattie said resolutely. "You are getting married, so I'll have to help if things get too tight."

"What about Katie? She's about old enough."

"Suppose so. They are growing up," Mattie said, and Rebecca knew her mother had already known.

"I've got to be going." Rebecca glanced at the clock again and got up from the table.

"Have a safe trip." Mattie stayed seated, as Rebecca picked up her suitcase and stepped out into the early morning darkness.

The air was still brisk for a spring morning. Rebecca gripped the handle, its weight already heavy by the time she was halfway down the driveway. At the blacktop she set the suitcase down to catch her breath. No car lights appeared on the road, for which she was thankful. A quick dash toward Edna's lane, and she was across the road.

Had anyone seen her? She didn't know and didn't want to find out. To be caught in the headlights, the occupants would be curious why an Amish girl was out walking the roads at five thirty in the morning with her suitcase at her side. Such a sight couldn't be considered too normal in the *Englisha* world.

A dim light was visible in the front window, so she knocked on the door. Edna's voice called out from somewhere in the house, "Come on in."

Inside Rebecca saw no one around. The light came from the bedroom, where Edna was apparently still making preparations. Rebecca seated herself at the kitchen table and waited.

"I can't believe it," Edna said, bustling out moments later. "Me, an old woman who doesn't sleep anyway, slept right through the alarm. Can you believe that?"

"Maybe it didn't go off," Rebecca said chuckling, her thoughts on her own dancing alarm clock.

"Could be," Edna said, taking a quick look out the front window. "That would be worse, though. Means I didn't turn it on. Life's got us old people coming and going. Hard of hearing or forgetful. Sure a good thing the Lord is coming soon."

"At least you're well enough for the trip," Rebecca said. She wanted to express some comfort for Edna's sake.

"*Jah*, I know. Something to be thankful for. Maybe the good Lord is giving me grace. Was down last week with something. If Emma had passed then, I couldn't have gone. Would have been a hard thing, indeed."

"Were you close?" Rebecca asked. She searched her memory for the connection between the two women.

"Growing up we were. In Milroy. It's been years, though. I got married to Elmer. He wanted to move here. Emma never got married."

Rebecca thought Edna said the last statement a little sadly. "Why?" she asked.

"She never told me. She had a Mennonite boyfriend once. Real secret about it. Didn't last long enough to get her into trouble. Nothing official of course, him being Mennonite. I just thought she took it hard, from what I could tell."

"That he was Mennonite?"

"That she loved him," Edna said.

"Loved him?" Rebecca leaned forward in the chair.

"Just him. Only him. She could be stubborn, Emma could."

"Emma told you this?"

"Not really," Edna admitted. "Well...not all of it. I knew she fell for him and never dated anyone else that anyone knew about."

"She was a good schoolteacher," Rebecca said, returning to familiar ground. "Excellent she was, at least in my eyes."

"Yes, she was," Edna said, as lights lit up the driveway. "Guess we'd better be going. Now where did I put my suitcase? I had it all packed last night."

"There," Rebecca said. She pointed toward Edna's desk in the living room, where the black suitcase sat.

"See?" Edna threw her hands in the air. "You see how bad it's getting? At least I'm well enough to go. I guess *Da Hah* does help in time of need."

"Let me take your suitcase," Rebecca offered, reaching out for it.

"I'm not totally helpless," Edna told her and grasped the suitcase.

"I'll get the door, then," Rebecca said with a smile. She waited while Edna carefully made her way, her suitcase clutched with both hands.

"Lock the door," Edna said over her shoulder.

Rebecca did and checked the knob twice, before she followed Edna toward the van.

Mrs. Coldwell, the driver the Amish frequently used, greeted them with a cheerful, "Good morning."

"I guess it is, but don't ask my bones, though. That and other things, all in the body, of course," Edna told her. She handed over her suitcase to Mrs. Coldwell, who placed it in the back of the van with the rest of the luggage.

"You sound chirpy enough," Mrs. Coldwell said chuckling.

"Thankful. Just thankful," Edna said and stepped into the van. "Good morning," she said loudly, just inside the door.

"You don't have to bust my eardrums," Rebecca heard Isaac say from the back of the van. Apparently she would travel in the same van as John's parents.

"Didn't hear my alarm go off," Edna shouted at him in the same tone of voice. "Wait till you're my age, and you'll be sleeping right through yours too."

"He already shouts," Miriam said, as Edna took her seat and Rebecca stepped inside. "It's just his preaching voice."

"Now…now," Isaac said smiling. "It's too early in the morning for all these hard feelings. We have to remember *Da Hah* and His kindness."

"See what I mean," Miriam said in Edna's direction. Several of the others in the van chuckled softly.

"At least you still have him, preaching or not," Edna said, a note of sadness in her voice. "Elmer's been gone for many a year now."

"Yes," Miriam agreed, "I have much to be thankful for."

"Guess we all do." Edna settled into her seat, and silence descended on the van, as Mrs. Coldwell started the engine.

Rebecca was sure the others' thoughts had gone where hers did—where they were headed and the mortality of mankind. As daylight came some hours later, the conversations began again. Rebecca mostly listened, as their voices ebbed and flowed across the miles.

They stopped at Wendy's for lunch and arrived in Milroy early in the afternoon. Rebecca was the last to be picked up and also the last to be dropped off. No particular reason existed other than the order of where specific homes were located.

Leona was all smiles when she greeted her at the door. The children weren't home from school yet, so it was just her and the three youngest. Leroy and James said "Hi," while baby Jonathon waved his hands and feet from the crib in the living room.

"Moved him out here," Leona explained. "He likes it better, and it keeps him entertained while I work—safer too than on the blanket."

Rebecca chuckled as Leona glanced meaningfully at Leroy and James.

"They don't mean to be rough. They're just boys," Leona said. "They've been outside all day. Tired of it, I think."

"Leroy fell down the hole," James announced, "and broke his head."

"Really." Rebecca waited. Since Leroy looked fine, Rebecca figured there was exaggeration involved somewhere.

"Hard," James said solemnly. "From all the way up. Down. Smash. Dad said he could have been hurt."

"The haymow." Leona groaned and supplied the adult information. "He slipped somehow. Didn't do much damage, thankfully. James was scared, though."

"Almost died," James said.

"It wasn't that bad," Leona told him. "It just frightened you."

"Was it scary?" Rebecca asked, sympathy in her voice.

James nodded, his eyes big.

"I think he watched him go—from the top." Leona supplied the information again.

"Down," James said. "Boom!"

"I guess you won't forget it too soon," Rebecca told him. "You have to be more careful. Falling isn't any fun. It can hurt too."

James nodded, then turned his attention to Leroy, who pulled on his sleeve.

"Play with him," Leona instructed them, "out here maybe."

As James and Leroy got their heads together, their plans with Jonathon began. Leroy supplied most of the whispers. Since Leona insisted, Rebecca took a seat on the couch.

"I've been sitting all day," she protested.

"Well, I haven't," Leona told her. "You want to attend the viewing tonight? We were there last night."

Rebecca thought for a moment, considered the option, then decided. "No," she said, "the funeral's tomorrow. I'll just go then."

"We'll take you gladly," Leona assured her, "or I can, if Stephen doesn't want to go again."

"I don't think so," Rebecca said, shaking her head.

"You sure?"

"Sure," Rebecca told her. "The funeral will be good enough. It's not like I'm a close relative."

"That doesn't matter. Schoolteacher is close enough."

"I know," Rebecca said, the matter decided in her mind. "The funeral will be enough. Starts at nine tomorrow, right?"

"Or earlier, depending on when everyone gets there," Leona reminded her. "It's not like a regular service."

"Are you going?"

"Everyone is," Leona said. "She was in our district."

Outside the voices of the schoolchildren attracted their attention. The door burst open suddenly.

"Rebecca's here," the two oldest girls shouted together and rushed up to give her hugs. Elmo, the oldest boy, grinned but walked on toward the kitchen.

"Always hungry," Leona muttered. "You're going to have to wait for supper," she called after his retreating back.

"Mom," Elmo groaned, "that's a long time."

"You'll wait. Do your chores, and maybe we can have an early supper with Rebecca here."

His face looked resigned as he headed toward his bedroom.

"You're in the spare bedroom—same place as before," Leona said with a smile. "Get settled in. I'll start supper with the girls. Maybe we can do something special tonight."

"Like cherry pie and ice cream?" Lois, the oldest girl, asked.

"I don't know about that, but we'd better get busy," Leona told her. "We'll think of something."

"Rebecca is here," Verna said. "That's special enough."

"You don't have to say that," Rebecca told the eight-year-old and gave her another hug. "It's special to be here."

"You're here because Emma died," Verna said solemnly.

Rebecca nodded. "But I get to see you and Lois too."

"We'll come with you tomorrow—to the funeral. She was a good teacher. That's what Elmo said."

"Yes, she was," Rebecca agreed, surprised at the sudden tears, which sprang to her eyes. "I loved her a lot."

CHAPTER SEVEN

Stephen brought the buggy to the front of the house the next morning. Elmo held the bridle, while his father went inside to help Leona bring the rest of the children out. Rebecca, wearing her black dress, carried baby Jonathon, Stephen took James and Leroy with him, and Leona brought up the rear, lingering long enough to lock the front door once the last two girls were out.

They all climbed into the double buggy. With three of the boys standing behind the backseat, they barely fit.

Emma's yard was already half full when they arrived. Leona, Rebecca, and the girls found their way up the walk and were immediately shown to seats behind those reserved for the family.

The service started abruptly. When all the family had been seated and the yard empty of arrivals, Bishop Mose had gotten a whispered message from one of the ushers. The bishop nodded his head, and the first preacher stood.

Rebecca didn't know the speaker or the one after him. They paced the floor in front of the coffin, at times talked directly to the family, and then addressed the whole congregation. Both men spoke of the greatness of a life lived in the faith.

"God and then family," the second preacher said. People were to set their priorities in that order. Even if one was not married, life could still be good and lived to its fullest. "Our sister has shown us the way," he said. "For those blessed with a single life, there can be much to do. God doesn't usually lead in that direction," he said, "but usually wants His people to marry and bear children to fill the earth with godly children."

"Emma," he said, "was the exception, and God had blessed her also. The life Emma lived was one of service to others, to children, and to the church."

"If one were to ask," he said, "there would be many here today whose lives had been deeply touched by the care Emma had shown her pupils." He knew this to be true because he had been told so by several parents yesterday soon after he arrived.

"Emma had placed God first," he said, "and so had been able to serve others. This is an example to those who are left behind. The time will come when we all have to meet our Maker." He paused for effect and let his gaze move over the congregation.

"Emma's life had been a life lived in holiness," he said. "Emma lived in obedience to God and at peace with the church." He knew this because Bishop Mose had told him so. Such a testimony was not a thing to be scoffed at.

He went on to say that Emma was also an encouragement to the young people of the church. Her life was a pattern they could follow whether married or single. The world was out there and called with its allurements, tempting many to sin. Yet Emma had never given in to them. She had never wavered from her commitment to God and the church.

The preacher almost closed his eyes, looked toward the ceiling, clasped his hands on his chest, and quoted, "I beseech you therefore, brethren, by the mercies of God, that ye present your bodies a living sacrifice, holy, acceptable unto God, which is your reasonable service." He spoke the Scripture in German, emphasizing *lebendes opfer* and *heilig*.

When he sat down, Raymond Weaver, one of the home ministers, got up. Rebecca knew him. He spoke a few words, then sat down with a nod in Bishop Mose's direction. The bishop got up and closed the service, without the usual testimonies about what had been said. This was a day for family and remembrance.

Bench by bench the congregation stood and filed past the coffin. Few stopped for long. Most of the older folks were not directly related, and the schoolchildren whom Emma had taught paused. A few wiped their eyes and moved on.

Rebecca went with Leona when their turn came. Thankfully Leona understood her feelings and waited as Rebecca held up the line. Emma's face was still lined with the severity she had in life, the edges only lightly softened by death. Behind that face had always been a soft heart, Rebecca knew.

No one seemed impatient behind her. Leona had taken Rebecca's arm to show her support but made no effort to hurry her on. Rebecca lingered, caught up in her memories.

This had been the face of school for Rebecca. Numbers and grammar lessons she had not always enjoyed, but this woman she had always loved. From the day she had walked in as a frightened second grader, her fears of attending school with a strange teacher had melted away. Rebecca had felt secure and at home in school.

Their bond had continued even after her eight years of school were completed. The advice Emma gave her, only a few months ago, had meant as much as that given by her own mother. In this case it had meant more—partly because Emma wasn't as close to the situation, Rebecca supposed, and so was able to give help in a different way.

Now Emma was gone. Only a likeness of the Emma she had known was left behind. Was this what the preachers talked about? Was this the clay God used to mold the first human?

Rebecca wondered whether Emma walked the streets of gold. Were there schoolrooms in heaven—something for her to do? Rebecca thought there should be because Emma was so good at her work.

Leona pulled on her arm. Just a gentle tug, but Rebecca knew it was time to move on—time in more ways than one. She was no longer a schoolgirl but soon to be a married woman and perhaps a mother herself of young girls. The thought startled her, as did a glance around her. The line in front of them was gone.

Rebecca stepped forward quickly. Self-consciousness creeping over her, she hoped she hadn't attracted too much attention by pausing too long. She really wasn't family. Outside Leona and she waited in the line of women for Stephen to pull up with the buggy. The wait took some time as the family still needed to pass through first, leading the way to the Amish cemetery.

When the line of buggies started, Stephen took his place in line, and they climbed in with Leona's girls in tow. The procession moved slowly down the county roads and then at a faster clip on the state road. Here they left spaces between their buggies, so cars could pass in sections.

At the gravesite a Scripture was read, Bishop Mose led another prayer, and then the coffin was lowered by ropes into the ground. Rebecca moved closer. The men and boys took turns shoveling dirt into the hole. They stopped when the mound had become rounded and left a simple wooden stake as a marker. Rebecca knew the family would place a more permanent stone later.

The crowd broke up, and the people made their way back to their buggies. Conversations were whispered. Leona and Stephen consulted with each other in the buggy and decided to go back for the prepared lunch. Rebecca had the feeling they would have gone home if she hadn't been along. Their duties at home, no doubt, called. When Rebecca mentioned they didn't need to return, Leona would hear nothing of it.

Back at Emma's place, the house had been cleared of the benches, and tables were set up. Women filled the kitchen, busy with food preparation. Lunch was soon served, dished out by servers to those waiting in line.

Rebecca got her plate and for the first time looked around for familiar faces. The house was full of people. Her eyes slowly surveyed the room, as she tried not to attract attention. Although she noticed a few English faces, most of the crowd was Amish. A lot of them she knew—some were unfamiliar. The two preachers she didn't know from the morning were over in the corner with their wives, and children gathered around them, plates of food in front of them.

Ready to sit by herself, Rebecca was startled by a touch on her elbow. In the tightness of the room, a touch was not a surprise, but this one was done with intention.

She turned toward the person and found the familiar face of Mary Coblentz, the Mennonite van driver she met last year.

"I've been watching you all day," Mary whispered, her hand empty of a plate. "Never had a chance to get close enough. I hoped you would be here."

"Hi," was all Rebecca managed, caught up in the memory of the conversations she had with Mary and of Mary's connections with Atlee.

"Let me get some food," Mary said. "Hold a spot for me beside you."

Rebecca nodded and found her way to an empty bench. The girl behind her fully intended to fill the bench, until Rebecca smiled and said, "There's someone coming."

The girl nodded and left a space. On the other side of the table, the bench was full of older women, some of whom she knew and smiled in her direction.

Mary, her plate full of food, easily slipped in a moment later. The women across the table gave her glances. Mary's age, Rebecca knew, caused questions, and so she supplied the women with the information they obviously needed.

"You driving a load?" Rebecca asked Mary, loudly enough to be heard across the table.

"Holmes County," Mary said with equal volume, as if she knew the purpose of the question. "Had a bishop and his wife along, a couple of young people, and a deacon too, I think. Quite a load. Going back in the morning first thing."

Mary chuckled at her own joke, and the women lost immediate interest, just as Rebecca had hoped. A van driver had a perfectly legitimate reason to be here even if she was young. The murmur of the conversation on the other side of the table picked up, and Rebecca and Mary were left alone to visit.

"You staying around long?" Mary asked, sticking her fork into the potatoes.

"I'm leaving tomorrow morning too."

"You're a little closer than we are, if I remember correctly."

"Suppose so, but not by much." Rebecca had a feeling about what would come next.

"Atlee told me you two talked."

Rebecca nodded. "He stopped me in the buggy along the road."

"Don't think a Mennonite and Amish belong together?"

"It wasn't just that."

"Surely it wouldn't be too bad. You two did love each other."

Rebecca pretended to glare. "Shhh... He's engaged he said."

"I know," Mary said, like she wished it wasn't true. "You threw away his ring too. That's what he told me."

"I didn't want it. I went to the bridge, but he wasn't there."

"He told me that. After he saw you again, I think he wishes he had gone to the bridge to meet you."

"That's an awful thing to say. What about the other girl?"

Mary shrugged. "I suppose they'll work things out."

"Atlee said they were getting married."

"You are too, aren't you?"

"In the spring," Rebecca said, smiling at the thought, "to John."

"Like him?" Mary teased.

"A lot."

"Still wish you and Atlee could have gotten together? What a love story that would have been."

"It wasn't meant to be."

"That's what Atlee says."

"You shouldn't meddle in such things." Rebecca pretended to glare again.

"That's what Atlee says too," Mary said chuckling. "So tell me about this school teacher. She was yours too?"

"Yes she was," Rebecca said, then told Mary stories of Emma and life as a student under her tutelage.

Seated across from Rebecca and the young van driver, Rachel wondered what she had just heard. Had her fears from the night before been wrong? Was there really some agreement between Rebecca and Emma? Under the table, her fingernails dug into her palms in frustration.

Chapter Eight

On the day after his parents returned from Emma's funeral, John arrived home from work to find the pile of mail still on the kitchen table. Usually his mother sorted everything and placed any letters or items for him off to the side. Today everything was still in one big pile.

Tired from his work as a salesman and all-around handyman at Miller's Furniture Store, John was ready for an evening at home and something interesting to read. He found the stack of mail held the latest copy of *The Budget* but tossed it aside. It was for older people, he figured, and he wasn't even married yet.

A farm magazine caught his attention, and he set it over to his left. He would set anything else he found of interest with the magazine. There was a bill from a hunting company addressed to him. He presumed the bill was from a purchase he had made last fall and used during hunting season. He must have neglected to pay it when the accident laid him up.

That was strange he thought. Surely his mother would have brought any bills to his attention after he was well again. He set the bill to his left, to be taken care of soon, before the matter got any worse.

There was a copy of *The Blackboard Bulletin,* one of three papers published by the Amish publishing house in Ontario. Why his parents still got a school paper when they had no children in school he had never been able to understand, but his mother liked to keep up on things. She was just that sort of person.

If the magazine had been a copy of *Family Life,* one of the other three published in Ontario and due soon, the paper would have gone to his left. Because it wasn't, he kept going.

During his illness numerous get-well cards had arrived, sometimes daily. He had gotten used to it and enjoyed the remarks and Bible verses people sent him. Some of the people he had never met—the news of his accident had spread far and wide. That was one good use of *The Budget*, he thought and grinned.

The last piece of mail in the pile was a letter. He turned the envelope over and discovered it was addressed to him, the handwriting simple and unimpressive. That was strange, but perhaps a child had mailed him a get-well card. This would also explain the timing— well-meaning but late.

He placed the letter to his left, straightened up the rest of the mail, and gathered up his stack. On the way upstairs, his mother called to him from the sewing room.

"Anything for me?"

"Don't know. I was looking for my stuff."

"Anything?"

"A late bill. Another get-well card."

"That's strange. That was months ago."

"Thought so too." John paused at the stair door.

"Let me know if I know the people."

"Will do." John opened the door and started upward. He took the steps two at a time. *My, it's good*, he thought, *to be well again! I have much to be thankful for.*

After entering his bedroom, he shut the door and threw the mail on his desk, a little piece of furniture in the corner, damaged and purchased at a reduced price from Miller's Furniture. It suited him, he had always thought.

First he changed into work clothes for the evening chores he helped his father do, then he reached for the get-well letter. Its childish block letters fascinated him. One never knew what children would do.

Seated on the desk chair, he opened the envelope and slid the letter out. It wasn't a card as he expected. The words were written in the same block handwriting as the address. He read slowly in disbelief.

> *Dear John Miller,*
>
> *You don't need to know who I am. Just consider me a friend trying to warn you. Also, this is not a prank. I have solid information from which to tell you this.*
>
> *The girl you are dating, Rebecca Keim, is prepared to marry you for money. I know this may come as a shock, but it's true. Her former schoolteacher lives in Milroy and has promised her a large sum of money if she will marry within the Amish faith. I just thought you should know this.*
>
> *Signed,*
>
> *Your friend*

John burst out in laughter. This was a good joke, he thought. This was something his friend Will would do, or perhaps one of the others from the Amish youth group might come up with such a scheme. This was intended to scare him—a good joke, sent under the guise of a get-well card.

They all knew he had been ill, he figured, and were capable of such a practical joke. Imagine, he thought with a chuckle, Rebecca with plans to marry him for money. It was completely impossible.

She had stood by him while he was in the hospital, while he was threatened with paralysis, and had never complained. His mother could give witness to that. Miriam had been with Rebecca during the time he was unconscious and mentioned many times since how Rebecca never once faltered in her commitment to him.

This was one of the reasons his parents were so convinced Rebecca was the girl for him, their second child and only son. John laughed heartily again and headed downstairs, the letter in hand.

"Look at this," he said, as he waved the letter around. "Some get-well card, my foot. It's a joke."

Miriam raised her eyebrows and took the letter. She read in silence as John waited.

"One of the boys," John said when she was done. "Maybe Will playing his stunts."

"She was at Emma's funeral," Miriam said quietly.

"Emma's funeral? She said she would be."

Miriam shrugged. "Maybe you ought to look into this."

"Emma was her former schoolteacher," John protested. "You can't think there's something to this."

"Probably not," Miriam agreed. "It would be mighty strange, I guess. How would someone find out, though? These things have to be announced through wills. I think that's how money is handled in the English world. They use lawyers and all."

"That's crazy," John said laughing. "It's someone's joke. Really, Mom, Rebecca would have told me."

"Maybe," Miriam allowed. "I guess you'll find out if it's true when you marry her."

"She doesn't hide things from me," John said shaking his head. "I've got to start the chores."

"She did spend a lot of time at the coffin. Stood there with her aunt Leona."

"I can't believe you," John said over his shoulder, as he stepped out into the utility room. "Usually you have such good sense."

On the way to the barn, his mother's words affected him more than he expected. John remembered that Rebecca did hide things from him. At least in the past she did.

The memory came back to him from across that abyss, which was his hospital stay. He had gotten angry—very angry—just before the accident. For a moment his face flushed, his insides trembled, and the mindless terror ran through his head. He felt as if he had to run over to Rebecca's place, reach out to hold on, and demand what was his, but he let go of the emotion.

Something had happened to him at the hospital. Something in the terror of those first conscious hours had cured him of his secret nightmares. He could trust this girl. She was worthy of it. If not, then he was worthy of it. He would not doubt again because of groundless fears.

An hour later he was back in the house, the chores done. His father was also back from his work at the harness shop. Miriam had the table set and supper ready. The speed with which his mother could prepare supper had always amazed him. It was just the way things were.

"Supper," Miriam announced.

It was a call for both of them—to Isaac who sat in the living room, *The Budget* on his lap, and to him, the son who belonged here.

His father groaned, got up, and took his seat at the kitchen table. He waited as John washed his hands in the utility sink. His hands dry, John took his chair and copied Isaac and Miriam as they bowed their heads in prayer.

"John got a strange letter today," his mother said, as she passed the soup bowl.

"Mom," John told her, "it's nothing."

"Probably not," Miriam agreed. "John thinks it's someone playing a joke on him."

"That sounds interesting." Isaac paused, the soup dipper in his hand.

"That's enough soup," Miriam said to Isaac. "You know the doctor wants you to cut back."

"How am I supposed to stop eating with your good cooking?" Isaac tried a smile first, then a chuckle, his ample body vibrating with his voice.

"No more jokes," Miriam told him. "You know we're both getting older. Your health is important to me."

"I suppose so," Isaac allowed, looking longingly at the soup dipper in his hand, before he let it slide back into the bowl. "Starved by love, that's what I say."

"It's for your own good," Miriam assured him. "We have to try. Doctors know what they are saying."

"So what was this letter?" Isaac asked. Obviously he wanted to change the subject but wasn't quite able to help himself. "A man could die with this little soup in his bowl."

John chuckled. "Just a prank letter. That's all."

"Tell him what it said," Miriam replied.

"I can't quote it from heart," John protested. "It was a joke."

"Show it to him, then," Miriam insisted. "I want your father to see it."

John pulled the letter out of his pocket, now crumpled from his time at chores. Isaac opened the page and read silently.

"I see," Isaac said.

"What do you think?" Miriam asked.

"John's probably right," he said.

John nodded his head and continued eating.

"What if it's true?" Miriam asked.

"Would be pretty wild, I guess. She was with us at Emma's funeral. I didn't see anything unusual." Isaac turned his attention back to his soup bowl.

"She's not hiding anything," John said. His tone matched his words.

"Good to see you trust her," Isaac told him.

"What if it's true?" Miriam repeated the question.

"Then I guess there would be trouble. Plenty of it. Don't you think so, John?" Isaac paused, his spoon halfway to his mouth, his face turned in John's direction.

"I can't believe you two," John said slowly. "This letter is a joke. Rebecca is getting no money for marrying me. I really think that."

"I think that too," Isaac said seemingly satisfied. "She's a good girl."

"I guess so," Miriam agreed. "She did hold up well during John's illness."

"That she did." Isaac nodded. "You couldn't ask for better."

Silence settled on the room, broken only by sounds of supper. The unmentioned thoughts hung over them.

That night John dreamed he was in the hospital again. He tried to awaken but couldn't. He swam through a maze of silky white ooze, reaching for air to fill his burning lungs. His legs moved, he knew, because he kicked with all his might. But the feeling just wasn't there.

Sounds boomed all around him, and he cried out. Words formed in his mouth, came out of his lungs, but no one could hear them. Terror filled his mind. He saw Rebecca's face, saw it as if awakened from a dream, all hazy and unfocused. She smiled a twisted smile like she was hiding a deep malice in her heart.

He awoke with a yell, a groan from the depth of his soul. His body was covered with sweat under the blankets—chilled to the bone.

"No," he moaned, "it's a lie. I won't believe it. This was just a dream."

He lay still and stared at the dark ceiling until he calmed down. He glanced at his alarm clock, but it showed only a little after two o'clock. He would believe Rebecca, he told himself, no matter what happened. Peace came soon after that, and he drifted off to sleep.

CHAPTER NINE

Church had been held at Henry Hershberger's place, over in the east district, and John was ready to leave. He had his buggy parked at the end of the sidewalk, a little early, he knew. Some of the young boys, just off the third dinner table, came out of the house, but there was no sign of Rebecca.

Last night Isaac and Miriam had still looked troubled. He had thought a trip over to the Keim place might be necessary to satisfy them, then had decided against it. What Rebecca would say about the letter, he was already certain of, and there was no sense in making a scene. His rush now was simply because he wanted to see her again.

He had seen Rebecca in church, from across the room, but that wasn't the same as when she was in the buggy with him—sitting close, smiling that smile that lit up her face. She had a certain look in her eyes, which she focused on him sometimes in church and would have been enough to make Bishop Martin stroke his gray beard in grave concern.

John chuckled at the thought. He liked Bishop Martin and had always gotten along with him.

"You are a *gut* boy," Bishop Martin had told him once. "Always have been. No church trouble. You are your father's son."

Words like that would warm any Amish boy's heart, so John's liking of the bishop became even deeper. Since from the time he could remember, Bishop Martin's face had been a fixture. Sometimes he came over on Saturdays or even during the week to talk with Isaac. He came with his wife, Sarah, a soft spoken woman, when the occasion warranted the mixing of church business and a social event.

There was no doubt John admired the bishop. Perhaps that was part of the reason he never strayed far from the church *ordnung*, but John supposed there were other reasons. It just seemed the natural thing to him.

The horse behind him was impatient. If Rebecca didn't come soon, he would have to move. Out of the corner of his eye, he saw her, with her shawl wrapped tightly around herself and her bonnet pulled forward. He would have recognized her, he told himself, even if she wasn't coming toward his buggy. His heartbeat quickened as he urged the horse slightly to the right, which made for an easier ascent up the buggy step.

"In a hurry?" she said, with one foot on the step and the other in the buggy.

"Yep. Had to see you," he held on tightly to the reins, his horse sensing it was time to go.

"You are a naughty one," she said chuckling. "I was helping with the last boy's table."

"Good enough reason to get you away from me," he said making a face.

"It was the little boys," she replied laughing.

"Even those you have to watch," he said and turned right at the end of the lane. The horse took off with a dash.

"He's in a hurry too."

"For a different reason, of course."

"Of course," she said and playfully leaned against his shoulder.

He wished it was cold outside, so he could offer her the buggy blanket and prolong the moment.

"I thought maybe you'd come over last night."

He nodded. "I thought of it but figured I'd wait."

"There was no news anyway," she said and glanced at him. "Just a sad time. A big funeral, though. Lots of people I didn't know. I guess your parents told you all of that."

John shrugged. "I heard them talking about cousins and such. Didn't tell me much."

"I guess there wasn't much to tell. Nice trip, though. I always like going back there. Leona's children were glad to see me."

"How's baby Jonathon?"

"You remembered his name." Rebecca's pleasure showed plainly in her face.

"I'm just that sort of fellow. A *gut mann*." He lifted his chin high and pulled air into his chest.

"A right proud one too." She made a face but broke into laughter a moment later, her shoulder against his.

John savored the moment, the feel of her presence beside him.

"It was sad, though," she said, her hands clasped in front of her, "to see Emma gone. I couldn't believe it. Leona and I just stood there, in front of the coffin, for a long time. If Leona hadn't been with me, I don't know how I would have looked. Dumb probably. Just standing there staring."

"She meant a lot to you." John's tone said he understood.

"Yes…she did. Emma and school. Those will always be the same thing in my mind."

"As smart as you are, she must have been a really good teacher." John tried for a lighthearted note.

"She tried," Rebecca said. "Tried hard to get things through my thick skull."

"It wasn't that bad, surely."

"Some things were—like math. Emma was good, though."

"Did I hear she was rich?" John said, as calmly as he could, and watched her face out of the corner of his eye, his attention only half on where he drove the horse.

"Don't know." Rebecca shrugged but didn't look at him, apparently lost in her memories. "Her place is nice enough."

"She apparently has a lot of property—a couple of farms. I wonder who it will go to."

"Relatives. The usual I suppose. You shouldn't be thinking about such things. Money isn't everything. Do men always think about money? Even after the funeral of former schoolteachers?"

"Not always," John said and wished he'd kept his mouth shut. Now Rebecca thought he was money hungry, saw dollar bills on Emma's coffin.

"Seeing her laying there seemed so wrong," Rebecca whispered. John glanced at her and saw the tears in her eyes. "Emma doesn't belong gone. She belongs with children, loving them as she loved us. She was like that. Like she couldn't help herself. Emma just brought out the best in all of us. It was that way till the last year she taught. I heard several people talking about it. Said their children loved Emma. Even the smaller ones. Emma had so much to give. It just isn't right."

"God's ways are always right," John said but felt her sorrow, "even when they hurt. He must have something better ahead."

"Maybe she teaches in heaven," Rebecca said and laughed softly. "She needs to be doing something—some work where she can take care of children. That's what Emma was good at."

"It's probably better than that," John told her. "Something we can't imagine. That's how God is."

"Just hard to see it sometimes."

"It is. We just have to trust Him." John pulled the reins in and slowed his horse down, preparing to turn into his parents' driveway. Today they would spend the afternoon here. Then he would drive Rebecca home after the singing.

Rebecca helped unhitch the horse from her side and then waited for him, as he took the horse to its stall. They walked together across the lawn, taking a shortcut because the grass was dry and no rain had softened the ground recently.

He held the door open for her. Miriam and Isaac wouldn't be home for a while yet, he knew, and now would be the time to show her the letter. Yet John's heart wasn't in the action. His gentle probe on the way home was all the answer he needed. Rebecca's look expressed her obvious lack of knowledge. His parents would just have to be satisfied with his conclusion and with his trust of Rebecca.

"I've got something to show you," he said and shut the door behind her. "Just give me a minute. It's upstairs."

"Okay," Rebecca said. She took her bonnet and shawl off and lay them on the couch.

John went upstairs to his room and found what he wanted. His shoes made an even beat on the hardwood stairs on the way down.

"Over here," he said, teasing her by hiding the roll of papers behind his back. "The sewing room." That Rebecca already suspected what he had in his hands was evident to him, as he grinned sheepishly.

"It's a Sunday," she said.

"We're not working. Not really."

He unfolded the papers and spread them out on the sewing room table.

"Your house," she said.

"Ours," he said making her blush. "I thought a drawing of the place would make it easier to visualize because the renters are still in it. The sketches are kind of rough, I know—just hand drawn."

"They look fine to me."

"You're just saying that." John made a face, but Rebecca didn't see him because her eyes were focused on the papers.

"It's hard to tell from the outside just how things look."

"That's why I made these," he said. "The tenants leave late this summer."

"You're not remodeling anything?" She glanced at him, her cheeks still red. "Nothing major hopefully?"

"Not to the house structure," he said. "Maybe a wall or two, if you want." The moment caught him up in a joyous emotion. Rebecca was the one who would make the house beautiful, he thought, not the makeover they planned.

"I don't know," she said and seemed uncertain. "I'd almost have to see the house. Sometimes you have to live in houses before you know what needs to be done. That's what Mom would say."

Rebecca's matter of fact reference to their life in the house made John glad he hadn't brought down the letter that lay on his dresser upstairs. There simply was no way this girl had plans to marry him for money. Even the thought seemed profane and unseemly. If he had brought it up, he would certainly have spoiled this beautiful afternoon.

"So I can't draw too well," he said, partly to hide his thoughts. "That's probably why you can't envision things."

"It's not that. It's just a woman thing. I can start planning, though, with this," she said smiling.

"We can repaint everything," he said, his mood now expansive. "And the kitchen is a little small. Perhaps enlarge that…new cabinets maybe."

"That costs money," she said, her face showing alarm. "Maybe we'd better just use it as it is for now. I'd be happy."

"I want the house to be nice," he said and meant the words.

"It'll be nice with you," she said and took his arm. "That's enough for me."

"I'd still like to do the work." He felt happiness swell up in him and hoped it didn't show too much on his face. "At least this gives us some ideas, so we don't have to start from scratch. That is once the renters are out."

"I'll think about it." She smiled again and released his arm as Isaac and Miriam's buggy came up the driveway.

John rolled up the house plans. "I'll take these upstairs. Be right back."

When he came back down, he found her seated on the couch in conversation with Isaac and Miriam. A few minutes later, he suggested they take a walk outside, an idea Rebecca agreed to easily. They stood to leave, and in the moment when Rebecca's back was turned, John shook his head and mouthed the words, *There's nothing to it*, in Isaac and Miriam's direction. Their relieved smiles were a comfort to him.

The warmth of the day was just enough to make the walk enjoyable. They walked across the pasture, as far as Isaac's land went. The few beef cattle his father kept were in the other end of the field.

At the barbed wire fence, John was tempted to cross it and try to get close enough to where they could see his place but decided against it. He had Rebecca with him.

"You can see the place from the other hill," he said. "Don't think we'd better try crossing fences in our Sunday clothing." John paused by the fence, his eyes gazing across the fields to a place where his house sat. He took her hand. A meadowlark lighted on a post two links down, and burst into song.

"It's special for us," Rebecca said, and her eyes shone. "To the spring. To our future."

His fingers tightened on hers. He simply nodded, too full of emotion to dare say anything.

CHAPTER TEN

Rachel's answer arrived on Monday with the mailman. It was justice done, she figured, since no one listened to her. Her pleas on Friday night at Ezra's place had fallen on deaf ears. She might as well have talked to a fence post, she thought, as to her three brothers.

Ezra had shown some interest, but Abe and Jonas laughed at her suggestions. Emma probably didn't even have a will, they said, and if she did they really didn't care. That Abe and Jonas were serious was enough of a shock to Rachel, but their refusal to even think of further research was the final insult.

"Money," Abe had said, with a dismissive wave of his hand, "it got no one any good. No day. Anyway." Abe said that he really didn't want to know what Emma had done. Now that she was gone, it was none of his concern.

Rachel could see Reuben, seated beside her, nod his head in agreement. Such a reaction was what she expected out of him. It was Abe and Jonas who should have known better. They had been raised differently.

She had told them they needed to find out what was in Emma's will before they left for Missouri. There certainly had to be one, she assured them. They didn't ask, and she omitted any reference as to how she might know this.

Jonas joined in, making the point that their last expectations hadn't turned out the best. Their father had left them with little of the inheritance they had waited for. It seemed to him, Jonas said, as if *Da Hah* just wanted them to forget the whole thing.

"We got our hopes up so high last time," he said. "We waited around for that money. I'm almost embarrassed to think of it now. It was a shame how money hungry we were. How we forgot much of our faith and all the church has taught us."

Reuben nodded steadily beside her, and Rachel's temper flared. "It was our right," she declared. "You ought to be ashamed of yourselves— all of you—that you forgot that. It's high time you acted like your father's sons instead of a bunch of little whipped puppies, hiding away in dirt-poor Missouri. You know you could all use the money."

"She's telling you good," Ezra roared in laughter, but Rachel knew it was at her expense.

"It's time someone did," Rachel retorted, but beside her Reuben didn't nod anymore.

"What's your deacon of a husband think?" Abe asked. He rolled his eyes at Reuben.

It was obvious to Rachel that Abe as well as the rest of them knew good and well what Reuben thought and just made fun of her.

"I'm the Miller—not him," she said, as if that was answer enough.

"Oh my," Ezra said and laughed heartedly. "Glad this isn't a church matter. She'd fry us at pre-communion church for sure."

Abe and Jonas joined in Ezra's brand of humor, their voices filling the room.

"I think you'd better listen to them," Reuben ventured. "They are your brothers."

"Mighty worthless ones," Rachel muttered, which provoked another round of laughter.

"Emma can do what she wants with the money," Jonas said, once things had quieted down. "She's been a faithful church member all these years. She lived a godly and humble life. Even with what Dad left her. *Da Hah* will reward Emma for it. As He even may be now." Jonas glanced reverently skyward. "Who is to say the same would be true for us? For me? It might corrupt my soul and lead me away from the faith. Who knows what temptations await me. What if I had a farm paid off and money in the bank? I might start thinking about an automobile or perhaps joining a liberal church."

Jonas gave an involuntary shudder. Reuben nodded vigorously again.

"It would do me only good," Rachel pronounced. "Much more than someone else. The money has to go somewhere, you know."

"May that be in God's hands," Reuben said, using his deacon tone, which so irritated Rachel. "We had best leave it alone."

The others had nodded and wouldn't change their minds even when she protested vehemently. Abe and Jonas had left on Sunday, right after church dinner, their van drivers in a hurry to make the trip back.

Rachel thought a talk with Luke might help. Perhaps he had some ideas about what to do, but Luke had left for the youth singing and supper around five. He wouldn't be back till after midnight. She assumed he was on a date with that Susie of his. No amount of talk might persuade Luke anyway.

Rachel was suspicious about Luke and Susie being engaged, but Luke didn't talk much to her anymore. He wasn't disrespectful around the house—just kept any conversation they had to the basics. If he wanted to marry Susie—marry poor—then so be it.

Last night her inability to control the situation made her pace the floor in the hall just outside the bedroom where Reuben couldn't hear her steps. Emma's will affected her directly. Good news waited for her, perhaps at the lawyer's office, if she could just obtain it. On Sunday afternoon she could have brought up the fact she knew which lawyer was involved. That might have produced cooperation from her brothers, but it would also have produced questions she couldn't answer—questions that might have led her into a swamp of intrigue where she didn't desire to go.

That Luke knew was bad enough. Reuben had gone to bed around ten. He glanced at her as he went into the bedroom but said nothing. She ignored him but was unable to sit still for long, let alone think of sleep yet. She had paced the floor until sometime after midnight and then, exhausted from her frantic thinking, slept fitfully all night.

Now the letter was in her hand. The return address stated it came from Bridgeway & Broadmount, attorneys at law, in Anderson, Indiana.

Its contents could contain only good news, she was certain. This was the key to her bright future. Her hands trembled as she opened it.

"To the relatives of Emma Miller," the letter began.

> *In accordance with instructions left by the late Emma Miller, we are contacting you and other relatives. It is requested, at your earliest convenience, that you contact this office for a reading of the will of the deceased.*

Rachel exhaled. She hadn't noticed she was holding her breath. No doubt Ezra had received a similar letter. Even if he hadn't, this would still be all she needed to press the matter. Abe and Jonas would just have to miss out. She and Ezra would visit the lawyer's office at once.

Ezra would not refuse—she was sure of that. He still had enough of the Miller sense to know better. With Abe and Jonas gone, he might not have his nose quite so high in the air. Those two were a bad influence wherever they went.

She hitched the driving horse to the buggy, then checked where Reuben might be but could see nothing of him. He was likely in the back field, away from his goats for a moment, at work with the cattle. Rachel scribbled a quick note and left it on the kitchen table. *I've gone to see Ezra.*

If she came back in time to fix lunch, then well and good. Otherwise the man could fix his own lunch. Let him experience the true effects of poverty, which he so loved, without her around to dull the sharp edges.

She stopped at the first phone shack she came to. Holding the reins of her horse, she went inside. Her fingers trembled with excitement so much she could barely hit the correct numbers. Before the call went through, she glanced up and down the road just to make certain no other Amish people were approaching and in need of using the phone. There was no reason for her conversation to be overheard by anyone else. Her moment of triumph was sweet, and she had no need of meddlers.

"Bridgeway & Broadmount, Lisa speaking," the voice said at the other end.

"Yes, Lisa," Rachel answered, knowing her voice trembled but not caring, "this is Rachel Byler. I'm calling in response to a letter I received from your office today. I need an appointment."

"What is this in reference to?"

"Emma Miller's will," Rachel said and tried hard to keep the excitement out of her voice.

"Oh, yes," the voice said, "of course. How soon would be okay?"

Rachel thought wildly. "This afternoon perhaps."

"How about three thirty here at the office? Mr. Bridgeway will be through with court by then and has no other clients coming in."

"That would be fine," Rachel said. She barely trusted her own voice. The moment was so close, so near at hand. There was simply no way she could have gone through another night without touching what was hers.

"We will see you then," the voice said, and the call ended.

Rachel dialed another number and made arrangements with a taxi driver the Amish used for the trip into Anderson. If Ezra consented to go along, they would stop at his place last. She would pay for the entire trip herself if Ezra didn't go. It wouldn't be too expensive, especially with what she knew would soon be in her checking account. Her world was about to change.

How much is it going to change? she wondered. She certainly wouldn't have to worry about details like payment for a taxi trip. She felt satisfied and got back into the buggy just as Eli Mast, from down the road, pulled up to use the phone. Rachel smiled at him, as she knew the Lord smiled on her. *Da Hah* had even arranged for a time alone, where she could use the phone uninterrupted. There could be no other explanation, as busy as the phones were sometimes. This was just a little sign sent from heaven to comfort her until the real comfort arrived.

Ezra didn't need a lot of talk to convince him to go to the attorney's office. He had received the letter, he said, and would be ready when she arrived with the taxi driver. She got back home in time to fix Reuben's lunch—a shame she thought bitterly—then decided this must be in the plan. Reuben needed help. She would be kind to him, poor man, now that heaven was kind to her. Reuben couldn't really help the way he was born.

At the lawyer's office, they were ushered in, after only a little wait. Rachel glanced around. The surroundings were still as imposing and overwhelming as they had been so many years ago, when they had gathered here to read their father's will. Mr. Bridgeway welcomed them in and invited them to have a seat with a sweep of his hand.

"I am glad you could come," he said. "Are there not more relatives?"

"Two more brothers," Ezra told him. "They have returned to Missouri where they live."

"You didn't know about the will?" he asked.

Ezra and Rachel shook their heads.

"That's strange," Mr. Bridgeway said, raising his eyebrows. "I'm just following instructions. Emma was pretty specific. Let me read the will first."

With a rustle of paper, Mr. Bridgeway read, speaking the words slowly. Rachel's mind went into a whirl, and her arms and legs turned cold. After the first two sentences, little seemed to register. The awful news came through clear enough.

Emma had left everything except a small pittance to Rebecca Keim from West Union, Ohio, to be transferred after her marriage to an Amish boy. If Rebecca married outside the Amish faith, all the property was to be given equally to...and Mr. Bridgeway read off the names of Abe Miller, Jonas Miller, Ezra Miller, and Rachel Byler.

An executor of the will was named—a Manny Troyer. Rachel had no idea who he was.

They each were given copies of the will, and Mr. Bridgeway said he would mail copies to Abe and Jonas. He would also contact Mr. Troyer and give him some other instructions he had from Emma. Somehow Rachel found the strength to follow Ezra outside. Shuffling slowly out to the taxi driver's car, she hadn't felt this weak in years.

Thankfully Ezra insisted he drop her off first. Apparently he noticed Rachel's condition and even offered to help her into the house. She shook her head and numbly wrote out the check for the trip—it would cut deeply into their scarce funds.

"We have to do something," she whispered before Ezra left.

He only shook his head, and left her standing in the driveway. A bitterness grew in Rachel's chest, a fire with flames that torched every corner of her soul.

CHAPTER ELEVEN

The matter might have disappeared because Rachel, for once, had no idea what to do. Given more time perhaps she could have come up with a solution. As it was, the news was broadcast thoughout the Amish communities two weeks later in a manner that couldn't be easily ignored.

It happened by a confluence of events. Rachel, if she had known, would have called them divine. Others, perhaps, would have believed differently.

Margaret, Emery Yoder's wife, who usually wrote the weekly article for *The Budget*, had travel plans to visit relatives in Pennsylvania. In her and Emery's absence, their daughter, eighteen-year-old Ruth, was left in charge. Normally such a young girl would not be trusted with such a burden, but Margaret had reasons for her decision.

Ruth had always expressed a great interest in writing and had excelled in English class during her school years. Ruth had even submitted a short work of fiction to the Amish publishing house, Pathway, this past winter. The submission itself was no small accomplishment in Margaret's eyes, not just something to whisper about to the women at the sewing. She held this opinion even when the article was returned with a rejection slip.

The rejection slip contained much praise for the short story. It described the high regard in which the editor held the article. The editor explained that he had no present use for the material, that Pathway Publishers had just recently run other articles on the subject.

This had encouraged Margaret greatly and set Ruth to work again.

She made some changes to her story, used the editor's comments from Pathway as her guide, and submitted the story to Christian Light Publications, a conservative Mennonite publishing house in Harrisonburg, Virginia.

Margaret said that even though it might be unusual for Mennonites to publish material from Amish writers, they might consider it. She supposed Ruth's story, about the blessings of a single's life, to be of enough quality and depth that even the Mennonites would want to publish it.

Ruth thought so too. She continued to think so even though Ben Zook asked to take her home in two weeks. This was a nice turn of events for the eighteen-year-old-girl—not just because she liked Ben but because both Margaret and Ruth thought this showed how when one accepted the circumstances of life as they were, God could change things for the better.

This little detail had been left out of the new submission. They figured if Christian Light wanted to know of Ruth's present relationship with boys, they would ask. Apparently this decision was the correct approach because a nice letter came back almost right away. The letter thanked Ruth for a well-thought-out and written article and stated the board of Christian Light would review and consider it for publication.

In this surge of euphoric emotion, Margaret left Ruth to write the weekly *Budget* letter. Ruth, in her debut letter, paid special attention to the events of the community and felt fully prepared for her task. In the course of writing the letter, something was inadvertently added. Perhaps Ruth's recent preoccupation with the subject of the single lifestyle made her more receptive to what Ezra's daughter, Clara, told her about Emma.

What Clara whispered on Sunday struck Ruth as noteworthy. Emma, the single woman who taught school for much of her life, who lived an outwardly normal life, had done a mighty strange thing. She had left all her property—three farms, Clara said, and lots of money besides that—to an unrelated pupil of hers. Her name was Rebecca Keim, and she was from West Union, Ohio. Clara knew this because her dad had said so, and he had a copy of the will because Emma was his aunt.

"You might have seen her at the funeral," Clara then whispered. "She stayed long at the coffin with her aunt Leona. Probably knew what was coming."

Clara said that the strangest thing about the will was that Rebecca had to marry an Amish man to get the money. Clara made a face and said, "It wouldn't take money to make me stay away from an *Englisha* boy."

"Maybe Mennonite," Ruth had whispered back. She felt the need to defend Emma because Emma lived her life single, and the article submitted to Christian Light spoke highly of such a choice.

"Same thing," Clara said, and she was firm on the point.

All this had given Ruth reason to think, bringing her mind to a sharp focus. It was the focus on Emma's single lifestyle that bothered Ruth the most. If her mother had been home, she would have consulted her. But she wasn't, and *The Budget* letter needed to be in the mail. Her mind wrestled with the matter.

There were so many threads in the story Clara told. They all tied in with her article and yet threatened it at the same time. Emma had been such a good person, everyone agreed on that point. Ruth knew this from her own school experience and from what others said. She had never gone to Emma's school, but Emma's reputation and word of her methods had reached her school.

Yet, now Emma had done a strange thing. There was no doubt about it. This action threatened to increase the misconception of the weird old maid—an image so typical and easily associated with a woman who chooses to remain single throughout her life—a tragedy, Ruth thought, and no doubt unjustified.

In a zealous fervor, she wrote her *Budget* article. The motive was both to defend Emma's actions and propagate the finer points of her own article. As a result, she spilled the beans, as they say, and the results went far and wide. Once published in *The Budget,* the matter could no longer be ignored, even if one wished to.

Rachel first became aware of Ruth's work when Reuben, deep in *The Budget* the first night of its arrival, grunted mightily. Rachel bitterly thought he sounded like one of his billy goats.

"Now that's a stupid thing to do," he said. "Doesn't Margaret have any sense anymore?" Then he found the name at the bottom and grunted again. "Why'd she let her do it?"

Rachel found enough interest in this outburst to draw her attention, although little else associated with Reuben did of late. She had yet to recover from the shock she received at the lawyer's office and doubted, in her private moments, whether she ever would. There were some things in life, she told herself, from which one did not return to normal.

"Let me see," she said and held out her hand.

Reuben looked like he was on the verge of saying something—as if that would do much good, she thought—then changed his mind. He gave her one page of the paper. The rest he kept and continued reading.

Rachel found the place Reuben had commented on and read the article.

> The funeral for our local long-time schoolteacher, Emma Miller, was held this past week. Family and friends attended from too many places to mention. Emma was highly regarded by all. Her former pupils and their parents had much good to say.
>
> Emma lived the life of a single woman and never married. While many consider such a choice to be

strange and often forced by circumstances beyond the individual's control, Emma considered none of these things to be against her. She apparently was single by choice and in good standing with the church all of her life. Emma displayed an excellent example of a godly life to all who knew her.

Reports have surfaced that Emma left all her worldly possessions to Rebecca Keim from West Union, Ohio, on the condition that Rebecca marry an Amish man. While this might also be considered strange, it could well be in line with the godly life Emma lived, in which she considered both a single life and a married life to be of equal value.

"There is a God in heaven," Rachel said. Her face lit up with hope. She clutched the page of gray paper against her chest with both hands, unaware of the ink stains the grip left on her fingers.

"It was a mighty stupid thing to do," Reuben said, looking up from his own section of the paper. "There can be nothing but trouble from such things. They should be kept quiet. Instead, it's been broadcasted from the rooftops. Only *Da Hah* knows how such things ought to be said. Humans ought to stay out of His business."

"He is doing His business," Rachel said, a smile on her face.

Over in his chair, Reuben glanced at Rachel as she got up and walked out to the kitchen.

Across the state line on Wheat Ridge, Miriam found the article after supper. She handed the page silently to Isaac. He read it and went back over the words twice.

"So it's true," he said, as he returned the page to Miriam.

"That's what it says."

"Maybe she doesn't know."

"You just trying to protect her?"

"Don't think so," Isaac said. "I just want to be fair."

Miriam nodded. "We should be. It's very possible she doesn't know."

"Would Emma just do this out of the blue? There has to be some connection somewhere."

"Now you're doubting Rebecca."

"Maybe, yet we have no reason to."

"No, we don't," Miriam agreed. "She has always behaved herself above suspicion."

"Should we tell John?"

"Maybe." Miriam sounded noncommitted. "You think he can handle it?"

"He's better at those things since the accident."

"It matured him," Miriam agreed.

Isaac walked over to the stair door and opened it. "John," he called, "come down here for a minute."

He waited until John's door opened, the light from the room flooding the hallway. Isaac, now that he knew John would come, walked back to his rocking chair and sat down.

"Yes," John said, sticking his head through the doorway, "you called."

"Sit down," Isaac said. "You need to read this."

John raised his eyebrows. He wondered what could be in *The Budget* that required such urgent reading. If someone had died, his parents would simply tell him. If other reasons existed, they were beyond him. *The Budget* normally didn't contain any great secrets begging for special attention or that required reading in the presence of parents.

Isaac pointed with his finger toward the heading of Milroy, Indiana. "It concerns Rebecca," he said simply. He now had John's full attention.

John read quickly, yet he hardly believed what he read. "There must be some mistake," he said, the paper drooping in his hands.

"Probably not," Isaac told him. "There might be a reason, though. Rebecca might not know."

"Why is it in here then?" John asked. "It doesn't make any sense."

"I don't know," Isaac told him.

"Maybe John ought to look into it," Miriam suggested.

Isaac shook his head. "Don't push him. This is hard enough. There may be a simple explanation."

"There may not be," Miriam said. John stood and stared out the window and into the darkness.

"I'd better go over," he said, a great weariness filling his voice.

"Surely it can wait," Miriam stated. "You'll see her at the youth gathering. There is one this week, isn't there?"

John nodded. "There is. This thing will be all over the place by then. I'd better know first. Aden might even ask."

"You shouldn't doubt her," Isaac said, as John went to get his coat and shoes.

"I don't," John said. "We just need to talk."

"Poor boy," Miriam said, as he went out the door.

"Poor girl too," Isaac added. "Seems like they've been through enough."

"Maybe it's not a big deal."

"Perhaps," Isaac said but didn't sound too convinced.

Rachel sat at the living room desk, her hands busy with another letter. Reuben saw her when he glanced up from his section of *The Budget*, the part he had left to read. He then scanned the room, searching for the rest of the paper. On the other end of the couch, he caught sight of it. When he went to pick it up, he thought to ask Rachel what she had written but changed his mind.

When she finished the letter, Reuben saw her sign her name, seal the envelope, put a stamp on it, and set the letter on the desk. He dared to catch a look at the address as he went to bed. The letter was addressed to West Union, Ohio. The recipient's name was covered by a book.

CHAPTER TWELVE

As he hitched up his driving horse, John felt a great sorrow sweep over him. Perhaps, he thought, it was the lateness of the evening. Perhaps his body rebelled against the drive after a hard day's work. He knew, though, it wasn't either of those reasons. The memories of another drive he had made at night haunted him. Then too he had left in haste. Would this one also end in tragedy?

John told himself it wouldn't. This time he wouldn't drive to Rebecca's place in fear with doubts running through his mind, causing his whole body to hurt. He would go because he loved and trusted her and needed to stop this before it got any worse. That it could get worse, he was sure of. He only had to remember his parents' faces to know the answer.

He got in the buggy and urged his horse on. They drove down the long slope of Wheat Ridge toward the town of Unity. When he passed his place on the right, he gave it only a quick glance—not quick because little could be seen of the house in the dark, but quick because he thought the fear could rush in. The fear might come in like a lion if he even thought of what all might be at stake.

The noise from the clattering of his horse's hooves crossing the Harshville covered bridge disturbed him for some reason. The peeping of the frogs and songs of the night birds suddenly became silent. Although the racket was amplified in the still night air, it was not unusual nor any louder than normal, heard a hundred times before when he drove across the bridge. Yet the occurrence seemed ominous, threatening, a foreboding of danger to come.

John shook his head and slapped the reins. The horse jerked forward, then slowed back to its steady pace. *We'll make it,* he told himself. *We have been through so much already. God will not forget us. There is a reason for all of this.*

He felt a calm come over him and found the Keim driveway easily. The pull of the reins came too quickly, and the buggy bounced, as it hit the side of the culvert. John pulled left sharply and missed the bump with his back wheel. He shook his head again. At the barn he found his usual place to tie the horse. Since he had no plans to stay long, he didn't unhitch the buggy.

A light burned brightly in the living room, two of them he was sure because he heard the loud hissing sound of the lamps. He knocked on the door. There was a pause in which he felt a moment of hesitation and the possibility of a returning fear, but he gathered himself together.

Mattie opened the door, her eyes hesitant as they adjusted to the darkness.

"Good evening," John said, so she would hear his voice.

"John…well…come in." Mattie opened the door wide, her smile genuine. "What a surprise."

"Hope he's not bringing trouble," Lester said, seated on his recliner, a farm magazine in his hand.

"What a thing to say," Mattie scolded. "He never brings trouble."

Lester chuckled. "Have a seat. Rebecca's upstairs."

Mattie was already at the steps, calling to her daughter, "Rebecca, John's here."

There was a general bang of doors and a few thumps, about which Lester chuckled again. "The children are all there. Guess they thought you were going up."

"Do you want to?" Mattie asked hesitating, her hand still on the door.

John thought for a moment, then decided he didn't. This matter needed to be discussed in front of Lester and Mattie. Rebecca had nothing to hide, he was certain. Any conversation with Rebecca would have to be repeated to her parents, and the second time around might be no easier than the first.

"No." He shook his head and took a seat on the couch.

Lester looked ready to say something but paused at the sound of soft steps coming down the stairs. Rebecca appeared, her smile—genuine as John had expected—was unable to disguise her surprise. His eyes found hers. He felt pleasure rise in his chest, even though he knew what his mission was.

"I wasn't expecting you," Rebecca said and took the seat beside him.

"I wasn't expecting to come over either," he told her. "Something came up unexpectedly."

For a moment a shadow crossed her face, but then the smile returned.

"Mighty urgent like," Lester offered. He bent to set the magazine on the floor.

For the first time, John noticed *The Budget* beside the couch. The irony of it struck him. He offered a smile, sure his lips were tense and contorting his face. "It's about something in what's on the floor there," he offered.

"*The Budget*?" Lester asked. He laughed heartily. "You came all the way over to talk about *The Budget*?"

John nodded solemnly. "It's in the Milroy section."

"My…we are mysterious," Lester said. He stood, walked over to the couch, and picked up *The Budget*. Lester sat back down and turned to the correct page.

"Milroy?" Rebecca asked John from beside him.

"Yes," John said. He searched her eyes for any indication she knew but saw nothing, only puzzlement.

"I just came from there. Emma's funeral. Has something terrible happened?"

"You would think so," John said nodding.

"Your parents were there too," Rebecca offered.

"I know," John said and glanced at Lester, who seemed intent on what he had in front of him. Apparently he had found the page.

"I don't believe this," he said a little louder than John expected. "You know anything about this, Rebecca?"

"About what?" Rebecca answered, turning in his direction.

"Mattie, come look at this." Lester motioned toward his wife, ignoring Rebecca's startled look.

Mattie went over and read silently. "That's mighty strange. Did you know this was coming?" she asked glancing toward Rebecca.

"Would someone tell me what's going on?" Rebecca's alarm was evident in her voice.

"It's not your fault," John said. "We just need to talk about it," John continued but wasn't sure she heard him.

Rebecca got up, took the section her father held out to her, and read the article. The page dropped to the floor. John saw her face register stunned disbelief as she turned in his direction.

"It's okay," he said and got up. "Really, it is. I just thought we should talk about it."

"Is it true?" Rebecca asked. "Is someone playing a joke?"

"I'm afraid not." Lester's face was stern. "Not if it's in here. Do you want to tell us about this?"

"There is nothing to tell." Rebecca sat back on the couch, and John followed.

"You didn't know anything about this?" Lester's voice was tense, his expression puzzled.

Rebecca shook her head.

"You did see Emma when you went to Milroy to help Leona with the baby, right?"

"Yes." John could see Rebecca meet her father's eyes.

"Did Emma say anything about leaving you money? About marrying Amish?"

Rebecca shook her head. Quickly, John thought, which confirmed his confidence in her.

"Did you talk about John? About Atlee?"

"Yes," Rebecca said, letting her gaze drop to the floor, "I asked her advice. She told me some good things."

"Nothing about money? For…" Lester said, almost choking on the words, "marrying someone?"

"No," Rebecca replied, her voice angry now. "You surely don't think I would?" She looked around the room.

"Of course not," Mattie said quickly. "I'm sure you didn't."

"I already said it's not your fault," John added.

Lester seemed to ponder the question. "Mighty strange," he finally said. "Embarrassing too. That's the worse, I guess. Even if it was true."

"It's not true," Rebecca said, her voice sharp, "that I would marry for money or know I'm getting any."

"I believe you," Lester said, his voice calm now. "Just asking. Better that way than wondering. It could still be true you are named in the will."

Rebecca turned to John and seemed to see him again. "Do you believe it? That I would marry you for money?"

"No," he said. "I came over to warn you. Thought we should talk about it."

"Really?" Her eyes searched his face.

"Really," he said, and she seemed satisfied.

Silence descended on the room. The only sound heard was a thump or two from upstairs.

"You think Rebecca is getting money?" Mattie asked.

"If she marries John." Lester let a grin cross his face. "From the sounds of it."

"Now isn't that a surprise. Emma left you something," Mattie said, "even if you didn't expect it."

"I don't like it," Rebecca said. "Just don't. Something's wrong about the whole thing. Something is really wrong."

"Now don't turn down good money—not when it lands on your

doorstep," Lester told her. "It might come in handy. A few thousand doesn't go far, but it might help a young couple just starting up."

Rebecca shook her head.

"It sounds like more than a little," Mattie offered.

Lester found the paper again and scanned the article. "I guess it does. What do you think, John?"

"Rebecca has nothing to do with it. Of that I'm sure," he said. "Beyond that I don't care. I hope to provide for my own family. Hopefully she'll be satisfied with that."

Lester's chuckle told John he took the joke well. Rebecca rolled her eyes at him but managed to smile a little.

"It'll all blow over," Lester said confidently. "People will forget all about this next week. More troubles. More houses burned down. More people got married. It'll all be over. I wouldn't worry."

"I'm glad someone feels so," Rebecca said sighing. "There's something fishy going on. That's all I can say."

"Your father knows what he's talking about," Mattie assured her.

"I suppose he does," Rebecca allowed.

"Are you going to go to Milroy for the money?" Mattie asked Rebecca.

Before Rebecca could answer, Lester said, "No. If she's got money coming, they will find her. The English are probably involved—with a will and all that. Just let it go."

"I will, Dad," Rebecca said. "I'm not going anywhere."

"I have to be leaving," John said and got up. "Really. I have work tomorrow."

"Don't we all. Good you came over," Lester said from his recliner. "Right smart young man, there."

John felt warm inside and nodded his acknowledgment in Lester's direction. He hoped Rebecca would follow him outside, and she did. Together they walked to his buggy.

"It was nice of you to come," she told him. "Like Dad said, it was wise too."

"Maybe I've learned," he allowed. "I'm trying."

"You didn't doubt me, did you?" she asked still questioning.

"Dear," he said and let his voice carry the emotion he felt. His hands found hers in the dark. "You would never marry me for money. I never doubted that."

"That's nice of you." Her fingers tightened around his. "Did you think I knew anything of the will?"

"No," he said, speaking without hesitation, "you didn't know."

"That deserves something," she whispered and pulled him close. She lifted her face to his. He yielded and kissed her gently, their fingers entwined.

The horse sneezed violently behind them and broke the moment. John said chuckling, "My horse is trying to help us."

"I know," she said. Rebecca let go of his hands and slipped away from him. He watched her go, her form highlighted in the glow of the gas lantern from the living room window. When the front door closed, he untied his horse, held the reins tight, and got into the buggy.

When he unhitched at home, Miriam and Isaac were still up. They had obviously waited for him.

"Problem solved?" Isaac asked, not looking up from what he was reading.

"She didn't know anything," John said.

"Talk to her? By yourself?" Isaac asked.

"A little. After talking to her with Mattie and Lester."

"That's good. There's a better chance for a straight answer with Mom and Dad around," Isaac told him.

"You don't expect trouble?" John asked.

"Of course not," Miriam said, while Isaac only shrugged.

"Guess not. Just with what's in there," he said and pointed toward a page of *The Budget* on the floor.

"She didn't do anything wrong," John told them. "If Emma left her money, that would have been Emma's idea for who knows what reasons. Old maids are strange sometimes. Maybe she hated men. Maybe someone broke her heart. Maybe she didn't like Mennonites."

"That's a mouthful," Isaac replied.

"I'm sorry," John said. "Rebecca isn't to blame."

"Will Rebecca get the money?" Isaac asked.

"I don't know. She doesn't care."

"That's good." Isaac nodded. "Real good. Hope this thing will just blow over."

"It will," John said. He walked toward the upstairs door and opened it.

"One would hope so," Isaac said, as John shut the door behind him.

"You shouldn't be so hard on him," Miriam said when the sound of footsteps on the hardwood steps had stopped.

"It's not me that will be hard on them," Isaac said sighing. "There's many a tongue will wag over this."

"But they did nothing wrong," Mattie said, the concern obvious in her voice.

"No," Isaac said, "I guess they didn't."

CHAPTER THIRTEEN

Manny Troyer looked out of his plane window, his large frame cramped in his seat. The Columbus International airport had just been announced on the intercom. They were twenty minutes out. He reached for his seat belt and wearily tried to fastened it. The first two tries failed, but the clip caught on the third.

A stewardess gave him a professional smile as she walked by. She saw his fastened seat belt and raised seat and moved on. Her face reminded Manny of someone he thought he had forgotten.

Yet he knew he would never forget her. There were times when her face, dimmed by time and distance, no longer could be seen clearly. The years had done things to him, to his memories, and to his body. He groaned and shifted in his seat, but when it came to Emma, he still remembered.

Strange that I've never married, he thought. *Yet, is it so strange?* He didn't know sometimes. The strangest thing was how well he had been accepted in his church world as an unmarried man. Men in Mennonite and Amish worlds were expected to marry. Manny had been the exception. Things had just kind of happened—or rather not happened.

He was an old man now, in more ways than one. He was weary in body and soul. Life had been good to him, though, he often told himself. Not everyone got to do the kind of work he did and enjoyed. His work had begun as a missionary at the Mennonite mission in Haiti. Later he became its director, and now he was the executive director of all mission activity on the island. He sat on a half dozen American church and university boards, a respected and sought out voice when it came to missions.

There were days when he wondered whether life would have turned out like this if things between him and Emma would have been different. Would his passions have been directed toward a more earthly goal—wife, family, children, and now grandchildren?

Outside the plane window, low banks of clouds hung on the horizon. The sun was about to set, and its last rays lit up the sky above and the clouds beneath with multiple layers of color. Gold, red, and orange set that side of the universe on fire. Manny took the sight in, the display soothing his spirits.

He saw others in front of him react too. A woman brought her child up to the glass. A man nudged his wife and nodded his head to direct her vision outside. God had once again displayed His glory, Manny thought. In unexpected and startling places, He reminded humans of who He was. They were all drawn to the vision almost by reflex, whether they worshipped Him or not.

"We are now descending," the calm voice of the pilot said over the intercom. The plane creaked and groaned as if it heard his voice. Manny felt his ears sting and then pop. He rubbed them with his index fingers and felt better. *Old man,* he said to himself. But he knew his ears always popped on flights just as he knew his love for Emma had always been there.

Few knew of their long-ago relationship—at least that's what Manny believed. He certainly never spoke of it. Others would, no doubt, consider the story a tragedy, a thing to shake their heads over and pity him for. Manny wanted no pity, and he didn't want to think of the past at all.

Manny believed thinking of the past was an unhealthy exercise. It was always best to leave things alone, and that was how Manny had left them—very alone. The letter in his briefcase, addressed to him from a law firm he had never heard of, had brought the past home to him.

That summer, now so many years ago, he had attended an Amish social of some sort. Manny couldn't remember exactly what sort because normally Mennonite youth didn't go to such events. But this time his Amish cousin had persuaded Manny to accompany him. The cousin had been visiting from Pennsylvania and needed the company for courage, he said.

Manny didn't believe in love at first sight even though he had been thoroughly smitten that night by the tall Amish girl dressed in a dark blue outfit. Her white apron only added to the charm. He caught her eye when she walked past him. He knew there were things in his eyes he wished weren't there, and he knew they showed. He also knew she knew.

Apparently things were obvious enough to cause his cousin to whisper in his ear, "Don't make a scene. Quit looking at her. You're not Amish. I'll ask her afterward."

Later that night—late even for Manny, the Mennonite boy—after the social ended, the cousin discretely talked to the tall Amish girl and made arrangements.

She had planned to walk home, the cousin said, because she didn't live far away. The cousin found a way home with someone else.

"Behave yourself," Manny remembered his cousin whispering and made a face at the tease. "You're a stinker," the cousin told him. "By the way, her name is Emma. I already told her what yours is."

Manny hung on to his wildly bucking emotions and wondered what in the world he was about to do. He knew enough about Amish ways to know that one didn't pick up an Amish girl unaccompanied by family members, even if she walked home alone. It was highly forbidden.

At the social the girl had paid him no more attention, apparently lost in her own world, as she chatted with both boys and girls around him. When the social ended, she got her coat and walked out the back door without a backward glance. Manny waited a few minutes and went out with a group of boys, who split with him in the yard. They went to the barn for their horses, and he to the yard where his car was parked.

He kept the lights off, started the car, and eased forward. Two buggies came from the barnyard and made him reconsider the lights, so he compromised by turning on his fog lights. By their dim light, he waited until the boys drove the buggies to the house, picked up the girls, and drove away. Thankfully they all turned east at the road, their horses trotting into the night.

Manny had moved as quickly as he dared and before more buggies came along. At the blacktop he had turned west. Just over the crest of the hill, his headlights caught her blue dress. The white apron stood out in darkness like a shiny beacon of light. He slowed to a crawl and stuck his head out the window. She looked at him, and he expected the adventure to end right there, with a motion from her hand that he continue, a scowl on her face at his boldness.

Instead she said, "Good evening, stranger," walked around the car when he stopped, and got in.

"I'm Manny," he said. The darkness hid everything but the dim outline of her face.

"That's what your cousin said. He's visiting from Pennsylvania."

"Yes." Manny accelerated, afraid a buggy would appear behind them, and the driver raise the questions he didn't want asked.

"My place is just up the road," she said.

"Why do you walk?"

"I'm the youngest and have no brothers to drive," she said. "I drive when it's too far."

"What will your parents say about this? Can I drop you off at the end of the lane?"

"You're just giving me a ride home," she said and laughed, the sound rippling through the car. "Isn't that what you're doing?"

Manny swallowed hard. The words wanted to stick in his throat, and he felt the precipice beneath him. "I had hoped it was more than that," he said.

"Really," she said and laughed again.

He didn't think she was mocking him with her laugh. He thought she also hoped there was more. "Maybe I can see more of you. I know it's kind of sudden. I've never seen you before tonight. But…"

"Maybe you ought to come around more often."

"To see you? At your house?" Manny couldn't keep the surprise out of his voice.

She laughed again, and he knew it was more beautiful each time he heard the sound. "Silly. The socials."

"Oh…but I can't really do that. I'm Mennonite."

"I guess you are," she said, as if she had actually forgotten for a moment. "That wouldn't work too well. Oh, my driveway! Stop right here."

Manny had brought the car to a stop, and she reached for the car latch to get out. The moment was here. It was now or never. Plunging off the precipice, he asked, "Can I see you again?"

"Well," she said, and Manny couldn't tell what that meant, but the car door was still not open.

"I would love to," he said and found he meant it from the bottom of his heart.

"Really," she said, and again Manny wasn't certain of the tone.

Behind them the sound of horses hooves could be heard clearly, carried on the silence of the night. Something would have to be decided, he knew, and quickly.

"On Tuesday night I will go out for a walk." Her words came out in a rush, tumbled over each other. "Just before dark. If you wait till then, no one will see us."

The car door closed, and she was gone. He almost risked staying to watch her until she disappeared into the darkness, but the buggy behind him was too close.

He had followed her instructions and found her on Tuesday night. She was where she said she would be, on foot just a little below the house—her brother's house she told him that night. Her parents had died recently.

They settled into the routine of meeting on Tuesday nights and then expanded their time together when he asked for more time, but always at her discretion. Moments they were, only snatches of time, caught when she would be alone or when her brother and family were away on a visit somewhere. On those nights he spent all evening with her, multiple evenings in a row, and left late. He hid his car, as best he could, down the road in a little dirt lane, and hoped no one would make the connection.

All that summer they continued until her brother discovered them. Perhaps they became too bold, were convinced of their own invincibility, and believed their relationship actually could work.

He had pulled his car up to the driveway on a Tuesday to drop her off but didn't quite get it done. It turned out to be more of a take off than a drop off. Her brother waited there.

Mullet Miller was his name, or "M-Jay" as they called him in the Amish community, although she had never mentioned either. He had many things to say that night, after he had extracted his sister from the car and sent her into the house—things about duty and loyalty to one's faith and Mennonites who messed with Amish girls. Manny hardly heard M-Jay's words because his own agonizing thoughts talked too loudly.

They told him this was over, that she would never come back. He heard M-Jay's voice in the distance, but he saw and remembered only her face. The next week he drove out on Tuesday night, the air still warm though fall was obviously on the way. She didn't appear.

He checked again the week after that and then a week later. She was nowhere. He thought of a visit to her brother's house, tried that twice, and then gave up when no one would answer the door. There was no bridge to provide a crossing between their lives. That much was obvious. With the years that passed, the sorrow and ache in his heart had lessened.

Manny heard the clunk in the belly of the plane as the wheels extended, the whine as the engines slowed, and the noise of the wheels touching the ground. He was pressed forward in his seat as the pilots brought the metal bird back to earth.

"We will be at gate eight in five minutes," the crisp voice of the pilot said. "Please remain seated until then. Welcome to Columbus, Ohio, and Rickenbacker International. The temperature outside is forty-five degrees, and the sky is clear. Enjoy your stay and fly again with Continental."

Manny unbuckled his seat belt and leaned back to wait. He wondered why Emma had never married. Was it for the same reason he hadn't? Was there an explanation? Despite the letter he carried in his briefcase, it still made no sense.

He planned to stay two months in the States, but it could be extended as needed. The itinerary so far included two board meetings at the Eastern Mennonite University in Harrisonburg, a string of Sunday morning speaking engagements, and a meeting with a girl in southern Ohio. He wondered where that would all lead. Atlee had filled him in on some of the details, but even he seemed to know little.

CHAPTER FOURTEEN

Bishop Martin called the Sunday morning ministers' council to order. Isaac sat beside the bishop on a straight-back chair. They were upstairs in the larger of the three bedrooms. Babies slept in each of the other bedrooms to either side of them. The bishop knew of this and kept his voice low.

Not that he was wont to raise it. Such a thing would be highly inappropriate—and not just for babies who might hear and object. The whole congregation sat downstairs, their songbooks in their laps, their singing loud enough to be heard even in the bedroom.

"Communion is next month," the bishop said. "We all know that. Pre-communion church is two Sundays before that. It's not too soon to start preparations."

There were chuckles all around. The deacon ventured his opinion saying, "You must think things have gone badly."

"Maybe he thinks you weren't doing your job," one of the ministers offered as an explanation. The chuckles deepened.

"If you'd preach better, maybe the people would behave," the deacon retorted, in defense of his reputation.

"Now...now. We mustn't squabble amongst ourselves. The world is hard enough on us," Bishop Martin said and brought things back under control.

"That it is," Isaac said. They all agreed with nods.

"Maybe we could start with our own problems—perhaps with Eli Mast's tractor driving," the bishop said. They all knew what he referred to. No matter how many trips the deacon made to Eli's place on Saturday afternoon, Eli just didn't seem to be able to help himself. Winters weren't much of a problem, but each spring the reports came in again. Summers were even worse. Eli would be seen pulling a hay wagon back to the fields. Eli was out on the blacktop with his tractor. Eli even pulled his hay rake with the tractor in one summer's report.

"We have given a lot of mercy to him," Isaac ventured. "Maybe some more is in order?"

"That's what I thought you'd say," Bishop Martin said nodding. "Anyone else have any ideas? We can't just continue ignoring this problem."

"Maybe a new confession would help. That might wake him up," the deacon offered. "Maybe one on his knees and in front of the church."

"Eli?" Bishop Martin allowed himself another chuckle, which turned into a laugh by the time he was done. Several of the others joined him. "Excommunication wouldn't wake him up."

"You think it's that serious?" Isaac asked.

"Maybe you ought to try it," the deacon offered again.

"What? Excommunication?" Bishop Martin turned in his direction.

"It might help," the deacon said, apparently uncertain where his thoughts would lead him.

"Never heard of anyone being excommunicated for tractor driving," Bishop Martin snorted in exasperation. "Something must be done with the man, though. His oldest son was in town without a hat last week. One of the girls saw him. Did you hear about that, Deacon?"

The deacon shook his head.

"Spreading his laxness around, I would say, to his children," Bishop Martin said. "That's what comes of these things if they are left alone. Apparently Eli thinks your little talking-tos are pretty harmless."

"Maybe you should go," the deacon said but didn't meet the bishop's eyes.

"So what are you here for?" the bishop said staring at him.

The deacon squirmed and obviously felt the heat. "I'll try again," he managed to say.

"Tell Eli how serious this is," Bishop Martin instructed. "His son is involved now. Maybe that will make an impact. Thank God we don't have a Mennonite church around here yet."

"Yet," Isaac said. "We can be thankful we're just a young community."

"Let's keep it that way," Bishop Martin said. His voice contained both instruction and hope.

"We can't be too hard on people," Isaac said, warning in his voice. "That's what gives Mennonites their chance."

"Or being too lax," Bishop Martin told him. "That gives them a chance too. We have to be careful both ways."

They all nodded, Isaac included, because they all knew this to be true.

"That brings us to something else." Bishop Martin cleared his throat. "I'm afraid you won't be too happy, Isaac. I have bad news."

"Really," Isaac said, giving the bishop his full attention.

"I received a letter." With a rustle of paper, Bishop Martin produced the object from his suit-coat pocket. "I thought it important enough to bring along. I wanted all of you to see it."

"It must be important," the deacon offered.

Bishop Martin silenced him with a look. "It's quite a serious matter—one that I have no idea how to handle. It's quite beyond me, and yet we have to deal with it. *Da Hah* will have to give us *gnawdi* on this one."

"Maybe you should read the letter," Isaac said, knowing he obviously was involved in this startling news.

"That would be best," Bishop Martin said and glanced in Isaac's direction. "You sure, though? If you would prefer, I could let you read it first."

"No," Isaac said, "let's just hear it. I don't think I have anything to hide."

"I suppose you don't," the bishop said shaking his head, "but some-one seems to."

Isaac couldn't keep the puzzled look off his face. What this could be was beyond him, even though he searched his mind completely. John and Rebecca's situation didn't quite merit treatment in a Sunday morning ministers' council—at least not from the information he had read in *The Budget*.

Bishop Martin opened the letter and began to read the words.

> *As you have likely read by now, an incident from our commu-nity has been reported in* The Budget. *My aunt Emma left her inheritance, which is considerable, to one of your members, Rebecca Keim, of whom she was close to. She did this on the condition that Rebecca marry Amish.*

Bishop Martin glanced at Isaac, then continued.

> *I am writing to inform you of things you perhaps don't know. There is much background that goes with this news. Rebecca apparently has a history in this community with someone by the name of Atlee Troyer, a Mennonite boy. There are even reports that he gave her a ring, which she might still have.*

> *While I don't know many details, of course, it is possible that Emma made her decision in an attempt to keep Rebecca, who was her former student, from disgracing herself by marrying outside the faith. Because this matter has already been spoken abroad by* The Budget *article, I decided it best not to keep the rest of this information private. It might be better for all concerned if you knew first.*

"Signed, Rachel Byler." The bishop folded the letter. The crinkle of paper sounded loud in the silence of the bedroom.

"Does she mean Lester's Rebecca?" the deacon asked, his voice full of surprise. "Reuben's a deacon in Milroy."

"Did you know of this?" Bishop Martin asked Isaac.

"Of *The Budget* article, yes. The rest, no."

"You think John knows?"

"I don't know," Isaac answered, his mind riddled with hurried thoughts. "We talked at length, after we read the article. John even went over to speak with Lester and Miriam that night. He has never mentioned anything like this."

"He might not know," the deacon offered.

"I suppose not," Bishop Martin ventured.

"This is serious," the deacon continued. "We have to do something—at least find out if it's true."

"What if it's true?" Isaac asked.

The deacon wasn't at a loss for words. "If she has the ring still in her possession, then the rest must be true. We can't let that stand." His eyes were wide.

"That's what I thought," the bishop said nodding. "It's not easy, though. You are dealing with matters of the heart. It's Isaac's son too. You know how this might make him look."

"I wouldn't worry about that," Isaac said. "This might not be true at all. They have been through a lot, with John's accident and all. They seem to be quite close. I've never seen any signs that Rebecca would marry for money. That would surprise me greatly."

"The ring, though," the deacon said, "that's the problem beyond the money and how this all looks. What's going to happen when the news gets out? If it's in *The Budget*, it's just a matter of time."

"I know that," the bishop told him, then turned back to Isaac. "Do you trust your son? Do you think he would have picked up on the ring if Rebecca has one?"

Isaac pondered the question. "I don't know. He likes her a lot."

"There you go," the deacon said. "How can you expect the boy to know. It could slip by any of us. In my days, I would never have thought it either. Never once did such a thing cross my mind. Who was this boy anyway—the one who gave Rebecca this ring?"

"The letter doesn't say," the bishop told him, "other than he's Mennonite."

"He probably went to school with her," Isaac ventured. The information came from somewhere in the recesses of his mind. His head felt like it was underwater.

"So do you know that?" the bishop asked.

Isaac shook his head. "Well…yes, I heard that somewhere, but I think they straightened the matter out. Miriam mentioned it after John's accident. John told her a little bit, but I didn't pay much attention."

"Did he mention the ring?" the deacon asked.

"No," Isaac said shaking his head, "she only talked about her school days and that same boy. John seemed satisfied with the situation."

"Maybe he knows about the money—what she is to receive," the deacon said.

"I don't think so," Isaac told him.

"We must be careful here," Bishop Martin said. "We can't just go throwing things around. Someone must look further into it, though. That is for sure. It's simply too serious to ignore."

The deacon opened his mouth but didn't say anything.

"Not you," Bishop Martin told him. "Isaac had better handle this."

"But the ring," the deacon got out.

"Yes," Bishop Martin said looking at Isaac, "make sure you ask about it. Find out if she still has it."

"If she does?" The deacon apparently couldn't let the subject go.

"We'll deal with that when the time comes," Bishop Martin said firmly. "First, let Isaac talk with them both. Isaac, don't try to get information only through John."

Isaac nodded.

"Communion's coming up," the deacon said.

"I know that," Bishop Martin said, glancing around the room.

"We can't go to communion if she has a ring in her possession. That's worse than the Mennonites moving in," the deacon gasped.

"Not quite that bad," Bishop Martin replied and chuckled, apparently in an attempt to lighten the heavy mood in the room. "We really need to get back downstairs."

The deacon fumbled in his pants pocket and produced his pocket watch. "Yes, we'd better," he said. "It's a quarter after ten already."

"You read the Scriptures, as usual," Bishop Martin said in the deacon's direction. "Henry will have the opening, and I'll preach the main sermon."

Isaac was deeply grateful for the reprieve. He knew that in accordance with their unspoken schedule, it would have been his turn to preach the sermon the bishop had just taken. Isaac nodded his thanks, as the others took notice of the bishop's action.

They rose and followed Bishop Martin downstairs. Their Sunday shoes sounded loud on the hardwood stairs, made even worse since the singing had halted. Isaac felt the burden on his shoulders, the weight almost more than he could bear. His earlier gratitude had already worn off. The knowledge of what lay ahead stared him in the face.

Bishop Martin must have had this in mind when his turn came to preach. The bishop said God gives grace for the task at hand. That no matter how dark things seem, there is always light ahead in the tunnel. Isaac listened and was grateful, even though the words failed to remove the feeling of dread.

It was not that Isaac doubted. When the time came for testimonies, he pronounced the bishop's sermon to be in accordance with God's Word. Thinking about John and Rebecca and their obvious love for each other, Isaac desperately wondered what this could mean for their future.

Chapter Fifteen

John brought the buggy around to the front walk, remembering his father's request, spoken to him after church. What could Isaac want to speak about this afternoon? He made it clear that he needed to speak with both Rebecca and him. Surely, he thought, the matter could wait and didn't need to interrupt his time with Rebecca. Isaac had been insistent, though.

Delight filled him when he saw Rebecca coming down the walk, her shawl wrapped around her shoulders, her bonnet firmly on. Next spring seemed like an awful long time to wait to marry this girl, to call her his wife.

"Hi," he said, as Rebecca deftly stepped in. She settled herself on the seat and let her shawl drop behind her. The bonnet came off too as he drove out the lane.

He drank in the emotion he felt as she turned her eyes to his face.

"We have to go to our place," he said. "Dad wants to talk with us."

"Serious?" she asked still facing him.

"I don't know."

"Did we do something wrong?"

"I don't know," he said and didn't really want to know at the moment. It was enough that he was with her, wherever that was.

"I have to tell Mom," she said. "She'll be wondering."

He nodded. "We can stop in as we go by."

"They're not home yet," she said. This was information John hadn't known. His attention had been elsewhere.

"Maybe we should leave a note."

"Is it that important?" Her face was puzzled.

John shrugged and replied, "Dad seemed to think so."

"Then we'd better. I was going to show you paint chips and my choices. They're at my place. Remember? I took them home."

"You can bring them along," he said. He made no attempt to hide his eagerness.

"At your place," she said, and made a face, "maybe your parents don't want us talking about paint on a Sunday or fixing up the house."

"It's not really work," he assured her. "They won't mind."

"Okay," she said, settling back into the seat.

He slapped the reins and urged his horse onward. At the Harshville junction, he turned west toward the covered bridge. His horse didn't object, even though it was away from home. These were familiar roads.

At the Keim house, John waited in the buggy while Rebecca rushed inside. She soon came back out, her hands full, and her face flushed.

"I left the note," she said, "but couldn't find a bag for these. Are you sure your parents don't mind? They'll see these because I'll be carrying them in."

"They like you," he assured her. "We can look at the chips in my room."

He was certain she blushed, but he kept his eyes on the lane. At the blacktop he turned back the way they had come. At the river they rattled across the bridge again and drove up Wheat Ridge Road toward Unity.

Isaac and Miriam were already seated in the living room when they walked in. John figured the conversation with his father could wait, so he led Rebecca toward the stairs door.

"We have some things to look at," he said as explanation. He knew a silly grin played on his face, and he made no attempt to hide it.

"You can put your things in there," Miriam said to Rebecca. John was surprised at the sober look on her face.

"We'd better talk first," Isaac said. He rose from his chair, then must have thought better of it and sat down again.

"Really. This can wait," Rebecca told John and went toward the sewing room. She came back out with her hands empty. John waited until Rebecca was seated before joining her on the couch.

"Bishop Martin received a letter yesterday from a Rachel Byler. Do you know her, Rebecca?" Isaac asked, his voice gentle but firm.

"Well...yes," Rebecca said. John thought her voice sounded hesitant, uncertain.

"How much does she know about your life? Your past life?"

"Dad," John interrupted.

Isaac held up his hand. "Son, this is a serious matter. Hard as this may seem, the whole world apparently will soon hear this. We might as well be ahead of the news."

"But...Rachel," Rebecca began, then must have changed her mind. "I don't know. What would she say about me?"

"She's one of the family. Emma's will," Isaac said.

"I have nothing to do with the will," Rebecca told him.

"So you said," Isaac paused, apparently in thought. John knew the conversation wasn't over.

"What I said was true," Rebecca told him.

"We don't doubt you," Miriam assured her.

"It's what you might not have said," Isaac continued.

"This is really painful," Miriam interrupted. "We all wish this wouldn't be happening."

"What is happening?" Rebecca sat up straight on the couch, her back pulled away from the back cushion.

"You told John about Atlee, correct?" Isaac asked.

"Yes," Rebecca said nodding.

"Dad," John said again.

"Have you told him everything?" Isaac continued.

"As far as I know."

"There's something about a ring—the one Atlee gave you?" Isaac asked, leaning forward in his rocking chair.

"Oh..." was all Rebecca said.

"You didn't tell John that?" Isaac asked.

She shook her head.

"Maybe you had better tell us now."

"We had nothing to do with this," Miriam interrupted. "It was in the letter—the one Bishop Martin received."

"How would Rachel know about that?" Rebecca seemed to ask the question to no one in particular, her face drawn in pain.

"It doesn't matter how she knew," Isaac said. "It matters only if it's true."

"It's true," Rebecca said, her gaze looked blank, fixed on the living room wall. "Atlee gave me one when we were in school."

"But Rebecca," John said, finally finding his voice, "you didn't mention that in the hospital."

"I know," she said. Her eyes focused on his face. They looked frightened, John thought, and his heart reached out to her. "I didn't think it was important. I did tell you everything else."

"She did. I still remember even though my brain was fogged up," John said but didn't feel like he ought to add anything else. Their conversation had been private, almost sacred to him, not to be spoken of in the presence of his parents.

"Do you still have the ring?" Isaac asked.

Rebecca shook her head.

"When did you have it last?"

"Before Christmas."

"Last year?"

Rebecca nodded.

"You were a church member then, not just a schoolgirl. You know that."

Rebecca nodded again.

"I'll have to pass this on," Isaac said. "I hope Bishop Martin will understand."

"You know he won't," John spoke up.

"I still have to tell him," Isaac said. "Someone will let you know what is decided then."

John glanced at Rebecca's face, now that his father was done. It was all the time he needed to decide. "Get your things," he said. "I'll take you home."

Back in the buggy, he saw her eyes fill with tears. He drove slowly. Where they went, here or there, made no difference at the moment, and he assumed Rebecca felt the same. Above them the sky was still clear, the weather even warmer than earlier. Yet he knew they had just experienced the first cloudburst of a hurricane. He needed no words from Rebecca to know she also knew.

"You should have told him," he said, as they drove through Unity, "about needing the ring to meet Atlee."

"That was not for their ears," Rebecca told him.

"It just made the situation worse."

"Don't tell anyone."

"I won't if you don't want me to."

"I don't," she said, her lips tightly pressed together.

"I'll try to talk to Dad when I get back."

"Don't do that either. The problem's not him."

"Then who is it?" he said almost shouting. "Who is pushing this stuff? Who's behind these rumors, the letters to me and to the bishop? What about the money coming to you if you marry Amish—if you don't marry English?"

"Or Mennonite," she added. "You're not leaving me, are you?"

"No. Why would I?"

"For lots of reasons," she said. Her voice trembled, the tears close again.

John held her hand, which didn't seem to help much.

"It's the whole world," she said. "I feel as if it's out to get me, to get us, to destroy what we have. First the accident and now this—is God against us, John? Do you think He is?"

"No," he said shaking his head, "He's for us. I've known this since the accident."

"Then why is He allowing this? Do you know what this could mean? Communion is coming up next month. This ring thing could make the other seem believable. You know people will object."

"About the money?"

She nodded.

"It'll be okay."

"No, it won't, John. You know it won't. Things like this don't blow over. They have to be solved. The deacon will get involved—you know he will. With the deacon nothing is easy. I had a ring in my possession, and they know that now. They'll have me do a knee confession, and that would be let off easy."

"No, they won't," John said, horror in his voice.

"How are you going to stop them? It's not enough to be a minister's son."

"I guess you have a point," John acknowledged, a frown creasing his forehead. "There must be something I can do."

"Will you still love me?" she asked, tears spilling down her cheeks.

"You know I will."

"Even if I can't go along to communion?"

John nodded. "I won't go either."

Rebecca shook her head. "That won't help anything. Go anyway. Will you?"

"First we have to know what they will do. We shouldn't borrow trouble."

Rebecca looked at him. "You know Deacon as well as I do."

"Maybe Bishop Martin will overrule him."

"With the will hanging over my head?"

John made a face. "Maybe you have to do the confession."

"It won't do any good, John." She bit her lip. "Can't you see that?

The ring proves my motives—at least to them it does. I am guilty not just of the ring, but for wanting to marry you for money. They can't allow that."

"They will have to," John insisted.

She gripped his arm, "You won't leave me, will you, John? They won't marry us. Can't you see that? I'd give the money away—give it to anyone—but I can't now, not without marrying first. That's the only way to access the money, to prove my innocence. And they won't allow us—not now—not with the ring to prove I'm guilty."

"There has to be some way," he said, more distraught over her state of mind than with what she had told him.

"A miracle," she told him, "that's what it would take. Do you believe in miracles?"

"I believe in you," he said.

John expected Rebecca's face to light up, but it didn't. Instead she sighed and replied, "I'm afraid it's going to take more than that. A whole lot of other people will have to believe in me too."

"They will," he said. "You're a wonderful person."

She smiled this time, but the smile fled quickly from her face. John brought the buggy up the Keim driveway and then unhitched by the barn while she waited. There was a youth hymn singing tonight, but he doubted whether either of them should go. Once inside Rebecca shooed her brothers and sisters upstairs and told Lester and Mattie the story.

"You should have told someone sooner," Lester said, after Rebecca was done.

"It was a detail I didn't think worth mentioning," Rebecca replied. "I threw the thing into the river. What was there to say?"

"Apparently plenty," Mattie said. "What is she going to do, Lester."

"I'll see if I can talk to the bishop," Lester replied.

"I don't want anyone else in trouble, including John and certainly not you," Rebecca said firmly.

"It won't get me into trouble. John maybe, but not me." Lester shook his head, as if he couldn't believe the turn of events.

Rebecca yelled up the stairs to let the children know they were free to roam the house again. The rest of the evening was spent in the living room with Lester and Miriam. Only after supper did the two venture up to her room.

The room was dimly lit by a kerosene lamp, its pale light splashing off the walls. Rebecca threw herself on the bed and allowed the tears to spill again, hard and heavy this time.

John felt quite helpless but sat beside her until the emotion receded.

"We should be talking about our plans," she said. "Instead I'm crying."

"It's okay," he whispered.

"No, it's not," she said, then sat up on the bed. "It won't be for a long time either—I just know it."

John couldn't think what to say, so he said nothing. They let the silence linger, till it brought its own healing of a sort.

"I really should go," John said. He saw by her alarm clock that ten o'clock approached.

"You won't doubt me?" she whispered.

"Never," he said, then left. In the living room, he said goodnight to Lester and Miriam. At the barn he hitched the horse alone and drove slowly down the driveway.

CHAPTER SIXTEEN

Rachel Byler tried hard to control her impatience. If someone had been around at the moment, she would have vented. Last night Luke had caught the worst of her fury. Reuben had already gone to bed, but she was up, unable to sleep. She met Luke when he came home from his date with Susie.

"Haven't you any sense?" she said, confronting him just inside the front door. "There's still time to change things, Luke. You can dump the girl."

"I'm not going to." At the moment Luke had the same look as his father. Perhaps that was what drove her to say what she did.

"I'm taking care of the money," she told him. "It's coming our way."

"I want nothing to do with your plans or your ways," he said, his face stern. "You leave Susie and me out of it."

"You used to help. Remember?" Rachel tried another tack. "You took Emma's letter."

"Go tell the world, then," he said and went past her. "I don't care. If Emma were still here, I'd apologize."

She watched Luke go upstairs and shut the door behind him. The sound snapped in the night. He was shutting her out from the life he now lived and the control she once had over him. The pain came first, cutting deep into her heart, and then she covered it with anger again.

Rachel had allowed the emotion to rise. She welcomed its strength, embraced its razor edge, because it removed the pain of his rejection. Then she remembered he was her son, her only son, and she redirected the tide against what stood beside Luke—Susie. Rachel definitely didn't like the girl.

This morning the anger was still there. She intended to remove the problem—Rebecca—the one who stood in the way. The letter would do its good work. Reuben might be lost along the way but not Luke. He was her flesh and blood, carried in her body. Luke was hers and Reuben wasn't.

She could wait, if waiting was required, but this—the loss of Luke—this road seemed too hard. Luke didn't understand and was obviously beyond the ability to help himself. She must help him, save him from himself, but how?

A moment later Reuben came into the house to ask for help. He asked her to come with him because a goat needed to be moved. One was sick, he said. *They all are,* she almost said but decided not to.

"You'd better put something else on," he said, glancing down at her dress. "It's muddy in the barnyard."

She went to change her clothes and then followed him across the yard.

"I'd do it myself, but the vet is coming," he said, "and I don't want to drag the goat. Who knows what damage that would do."

"I'm with child," she said.

"You look okay," he said.

"I shouldn't be lifting anything too heavy," she told him because he obviously didn't understand.

"You won't," he assured her.

When they arrived, Reuben held the door open for her, then shut it carefully behind him. She compared the action with the knowledge that he usually cared little about closed barn doors. In times past cattle often got into places they weren't supposed to be because Reuben had forgotten to shut gates. Obviously his goats meant a lot to him.

The animal in question lay half in and half out of the mud.

"I can't do this," she told him. "It's too much."

"But we have to," he said. "It might get hurt if I drag it, and it's one of my best animals."

"What about me?" she asked.

"You?" he asked. "Oh…the baby. It'll be okay."

If he didn't care, she didn't either Rachel decided. She took the head of the animal and prepared to lift.

"Careful," Reuben said, as they lifted together.

The smell of the animal hit her hard. Perhaps the move had stirred its filth, Rachel thought. She gagged, which produced a chuckle from Reuben.

"It's the smell of money," he said, as they set the animal down on dry soil.

"Not my money," she retorted, anger flashing in her eyes.

Reuben nodded wisely. "Honest smell this is. Don't think I don't know what you're doing."

A momentary fear flashed through her, but she knew she was on solid ground. Even if Reuben found out about the letter she sent to Bishop Martin, there was nothing he could do. Or was there?

"I wrote Bishop Martin a letter," she said. Reuben might as well know. If he planned on some action, perhaps she could head him off. "I told him what I knew."

Reuben snorted. "I told you it smells rotten. I didn't know exactly what you were doing, but I knew something was up."

"We need the money," she said. "It doesn't belong to Rebecca."

"It belongs to whomever Emma gave it to. That's what I say."

"That's why you have no say to it," she retorted. "It's between me and Ezra and Abe and Jonas."

Reuben turned his attention back to his animal. He seemed to have forgotten her.

"I'm going back to the house," she said, with the sudden urge to get out of her dress, which now smelled like goat.

"You're not getting any of the money," Reuben said. His words stopped her cold.

The smell of goat rose thick around her, but at this moment Rachel didn't notice. "You're talking to Bishop Mose?" she asked. Wild scenarios of what Reuben might plan ran through her head.

"No," he said, his attention on his sick goat.

She sighed in relief. If he wasn't going to Mose, what worse thing could Reuben be doing? Was not the bishop the power she feared the most? Things seemed to rise and fall on his approval—certainly not on Reuben's.

"We're not taking it," he said, a quick glance in her direction.

She caught something unusual in his eye but spoke up anyway. "Say's who?"

"I do."

"Why?"

"Because I have the first check coming next week for the goats I will sell tomorrow. If this one gets well, which it will, the money will continue. For once in my life, Rachel, can't you see it? I'm making money."

"You can't keep my father's inheritance from me." She knew her eyes showed her anger but didn't care.

Reuben rose to his feet and faced her, "I'm the one who will supply for my family. Not your father. Not Emma. Not someone else. I will. Do you understand that?"

"No," she said meeting his eyes, "I don't. The executor will come with the money. Rebecca can't marry Amish now. The harder she tries, the worse it will be. It will expose her as the conniver she is. They won't let her marry, and you can't stop me."

His eyes now blazed with an inner fire, surprising her. "I should have stopped you a long time ago, Rachel. I mean to now. It is you who is the conniver—the money hungry woman who meddles with things she shouldn't. It has to stop."

She kept his gaze. Obviously he wasn't done yet.

"You will never touch that money. Not if they bring it here in wheel-barrows. I won't allow it. Ezra can have it. Abe and Jonas can have it. I don't care, but you won't. I am supplying for my family. I am successful for once. You always despised me for not being as rich as your father and called me *shiftless* behind my back. Don't deny it. I know it's true. Now I've had enough of the wicked things you are doing. *Da Hah* only knows what they all are."

"Leave *Da Hah* out of it," she told him.

"He's in it whether you like it or not. On my side too. Don't forget that."

"Because you're a deacon." She spat the words out, the taste bitter in her mouth.

"Because I'm your husband," he said. "It's a wonder *Da Hah* didn't smite me a long time ago for being so lax with you. You leave Luke alone too. If you even so much as speak a word against Susie—don't look at me like that. I know what you can do. She's off limits. Do you understand?"

"No," she said, "I don't."

He ignored her. "I will have another child soon. *Da Hah* be praised. He has seen fit to make me fruitful in my old age and has restored my youth like an eagle's. I am to have children again. It's an honor beyond what I am worthy of."

Rachel saw the tears in his eyes and hated Reuben for it. She hated him right then because those tears pulled at her heart—pulled her toward him. They made her think she might have been wrong about the man. Maybe there was more to life than what she had always seen, but then she remembered the money. She remembered that he was a deacon and was supposed to say things like this. He only pretended with his tears—hoped to make her like him. Her heart turned cold. It froze inside till her chest hurt, and the hatred turned to scorn.

"You're beyond hope," she said. "Blind as a bat, you are."

"Don't say such things," he said. "No one is beyond hope."

"I wouldn't bear this child if I had a choice," she said. "This baby has turned you into a monster."

"*Da Hah* forgive you."

"So I'm beyond hope?" She relished the look of pain on his face.

"No," he said shaking his head, "no one is."

"Then I will wait for the money."

"No," he said and shook his head again, "it is time this stopped. Isn't this what you've always wanted? Me working? Making money?"

She turned and left him. The veterinarian drove in as she crossed the yard. Inside the house she became dizzy with fear. A great emptiness clutched at her heart, a feeling beyond pain, a numbness that was indefinable. As if in midair, she clutched for something—anything—to give her strength, to stop the flight her soul was on.

Her hands found their grip, her will its purpose. Reuben had taken leave of his senses. It was now up to her to help him. She must be kind and understanding, but Reuben could not be allowed to succeed.

For Reuben to succeed would be their ruin. Luke might no longer support her and think her out of line, but he could use the money when it came. Luke wouldn't refuse even if Reuben did. Perhaps through him she could still get something done.

That Reuben was serious, she no longer doubted. Reuben hadn't mentioned Bishop Mose. He tried to reassure her he didn't need him, but to Rachel that was a move no one would fail to make. If she made trouble for Reuben, he would go to the bishop for help.

Bishop Mose would support Reuben. He would say what Reuben always said, that love of money and love of God couldn't go together, that money corrupts, and that in the end no one could take it with them. No, Reuben was serious, but so was she. There must be a way. *Da Hah* would help her. He was not on Reuben's side.

She began supper, as good a supper as she ever cooked. Reuben seemed cautious when he came in from the barn but mellowed out when she acted normal. Luke had surprised her with the announcement that he was going to move into Emma's house, but even that didn't bother her.

"That's fine," she said. "Someone needs to take care of Emma's place. Maybe I can bring food over sometimes. Someone has to if you're all alone. You're not such a good cook."

Luke let a smile cross his face. "We hope to get married next year. Maybe I can rent the place then."

"You and Susie," she said, as if she really meant it.

When Reuben went to bed, she followed him in and let him draw her close.

"I'm glad you're taking this well," he said. He touched her face, his fingers tender on her skin.

She kissed him until he settled into an astonished silence.

CHAPTER SEVENTEEN

Bishop Martin wasted no time two Sundays later. They were gathered upstairs in the bedroom again. There were no visiting ministers present. Isaac thought the bishop looked troubled, burdened with his task, as he himself was.

"You have talked with Rebecca and John?" he asked, after they had settled on the chairs.

The deacon's chair scraped on the hardwood floor.

"I talked with them," Isaac said.

"Well..." Martin drew in a deep breath. "Maybe Isaac should tell us what he found out. Perhaps it was just a false alarm."

"I doubt it," the deacon said, his chair scraping on the hardwood floor again. "It sounded like serious charges to me."

"It's all true," Isaac said. He knew the words came out heavy. "Rebecca does have a history with a boy in Milroy, and Atlee was his name. Amish then, but his parents joined the Mennonites. He did give her a ring, but she doesn't have it anymore."

"That's what she claims," the deacon said.

"I think she's telling the truth," Isaac said.

"So..." Martin cleared his throat. "Where do we go from here? Like always these things happen just before communion time."

"It brings out the worse in people," the deacon said. He sounded grim.

"That's just because you spend too much time on the road," Martin said attempting a chuckle. "Perhaps you should have your wife make an extra pie. Maybe a shoofly pie about now."

Even Isaac joined in the laughter. He forgot for just a moment the trouble his son might be in.

"Wouldn't help," the deacon grunted but couldn't keep back the smile that crept across his face.

"So what are we going to do?" Bishop Martin asked.

"Can we just ignore it?" Henry asked.

"A ring? Ignore that?" The deacon sounded horrified.

"No, we can't ignore it," Martin said. "Maybe she could make a confession."

"She did have it while she was a member, right, Isaac?" Henry asked.

Isaac nodded. "So I understood."

"That's assuming she still doesn't have it," the deacon said.

"We will assume the best," Martin told him.

"That doesn't always work for the best," the deacon replied. "Why would a girl throw away a ring—especially if she kept it all this time? It must mean a lot to her, don't you think? Maybe Emma tried to stop a bad thing, tried to pull her back from danger. Perhaps Emma even made her throw away the ring. Did Rebecca say why she threw it away?"

Isaac shook his head.

"You do spend too much time on the road," Martin told him, but no one laughed this time.

"We do have to consider these...well...possibilities," Henry said, his brow wrinkled. "It was printed in *The Budget.*"

"Yes, it was," the bishop said sighing. "I would suggest we at least get past this communion time. We can then see how things play out. Maybe more information will come in."

"But we can't," the deacon said. "There is no way."

"This can't be ignored. It's too serious," Henry said, adding his opinion. "The ring is bad enough, and perhaps a confession would be sufficient there, but we can't have a member receiving an inheritance from another Amish community just so she will marry Amish."

"I don't think Rebecca is," Isaac spoke up.

"You are too close to know," the deacon said. "What if it turns out to be true, and people learn we knew? What a ruckus that would make."

Bishop Martin seemed to be in deep thought.

"Do you know what would happen afterward?" Henry asked, his tone indicating he already knew the answer.

The deacon answered for him. "She would leave—and take John with her."

Isaac felt the weight of their arguments heavy on his shoulders, not because he was convinced but because they were serious. These were matters not brushed aside easily.

"It is serious," he acknowledged. "I just don't think Rebecca is up to anything. This could all be just by chance."

The deacon snorted at that.

"So…" Martin said haltingly, "what if we asked Rebecca to voluntarily abstain from communion? That would give us some time to see where this goes and let the people know we are taking it seriously."

"It would be something, at least," Henry said. "My wife already got a letter from her sister in Pennsylvania. She wanted to know what this was all about—*The Budget* article, I guess."

"See?" The deacon's eyes were big. "I said so."

"We really must not be too harsh," Isaac said. In his mind he saw John and Rebecca's faces. "They are speaking the truth."

"That may be as it is," Martin said, "but we have to deal with how things look until we have evidence otherwise."

"True," the deacon grunted. "We ought to require Rebecca to give the inheritance up."

"Yes." Henry's face brightened at the thought.

"I already thought of that," Martin told him. "Doesn't work. From what I understand of the rules—wills and all—this one states she has to marry before she gets the money. Rebecca can't give away the money until she has it."

"I'm sure she'd be willing to promise that," Isaac said.

"I don't know," Henry said.

"I don't either," the deacon agreed. "Perhaps we could take the chance. But what about the ring? If Rebecca can break the rules like that, she could break this promise too."

"Money can make people do strange things," Henry said, making his opinion clear.

"Then it's decided," Bishop Martin said. "Rebecca will be asked to abstain. That will keep things in place until we know more, okay?"

Everyone nodded except Isaac, but they didn't check with him.

"Who will tell her?" the deacon asked.

"Isaac," Martin said.

The deacon nodded his assent.

The bishop pulled his watch out of his trouser pocket, checked the time, and rushed through the rest of the proceedings. They trouped downstairs, all in a straight line. Isaac was in second place because he had the main sermon.

Henry had the first sermon, and the deacon read the Scriptures during the break. Isaac got up without any idea about what he was going to say. Usually preaching came easily for him. The words flowed from his heart.

People whispered to one another about how easy it was to stay awake while Isaac preached. Isaac didn't harbor those words in his heart or ever speak about them, even to Miriam, lest pride rear its ugly head.

Isaac clasped his hands on his chest, his white beard brushing his fingers. He was an old man, he thought, too old and tired for this. Slowly he turned to face first the living room where the men were seated, then the dining room and kitchen where the women sat.

He said nothing. He just let his gaze flow over the congregation, and no one thought it strange. A few eyes met his. Others focused on the floor. Some were definitely distracted. This was the start of the second sermon with at least an hour yet to go.

"We must comfort ourselves in this hour," he said, as he found his voice. "King David said in his psalm, 'The LORD is gracious, and full of compassion; slow to anger, and of great mercy.'"

Isaac cleared his throat and allowed the thoughts to come. "Our Lord, when He came down from heaven to walk on this earth, how great must have been the sorrow He felt at our condition. Here we are, so full of sin and evil. He had come from heaven where all is only joy and perfection."

Isaac's hand's were now by his side. "Jesus came with the heart of His Father beating in His chest. He told us a story about a man who had two sons. One left with his father's inheritance. When all the money was spent, the son found himself in the pigpen. In sorrow he repented and returned, expected simply to be a servant in his father's house.

"Instead the father welcomes the son home, gets him a new change of clothing, cleans him up, and makes a great supper. That is how much God loves His children who have gone astray."

Isaac paused. He had caught sight of Rebecca in the kitchen. It threw his concentration off. Surely she wouldn't think he was preaching at her. He didn't think of her as a prodigal, one who had to repent from the pigpen and come home to a great feast.

It flustered him, and he wished Rebecca and John didn't know their fates had been discussed that morning, but they did. It wasn't something he had gone out of his way to say. John had asked the simple question, and the rest had come from a knowledge of how Amish things worked.

Isaac's mind found another story. He cleared his throat. "Our Lord also spoke of a shepherd who had a hundred sheep and lost one. The shepherd didn't stay at home that night tending to his own needs or warming himself by the fire. No, he got out of his house, maybe even left his supper, and went to look for the sheep he had lost.

"Out on the mountains, he found the sheep. The shepherd carried it back, wrapped its wounds, and placed it once again amongst the others."

The thought flashed through Isaac's mind that perhaps this was a good lesson for the deacon, who now sat with his head bowed. Instantly he rebuked himself for such unholy imaginations. He told himself the deacon had a good heart and was just trying to do his job.

Somehow he got through the sermon, his usual ease lost, and asked for testimonies. He didn't really listen when those were given. There was hardly anything to find wrong, he figured because he hadn't really said anything worth saying.

His spirits were low as he closed the service. Even at the meal afterward, the lively conversation did little to cheer him up.

Miriam asked him on the way home, "Why are you in the dumps?"

"I have to talk with John and Rebecca again," he told her.

"Not good news," she concluded.

"No, it isn't."

John must have known too because he brought Rebecca home with him after the service. Isaac thought Rebecca's eyes looked red, as if she had been crying. John led the way to the couch, and they both sat down.

Isaac got right to the point, thinking that would be the least painful way. "There was a decision made. It's being asked that Rebecca abstain from communion."

"From communion," John half rose off the couch. "She's not doing anything wrong."

"There was quite an uproar. It couldn't be ignored," Isaac said.

"You didn't agree with this," John stated, hoping it was a true statement.

Isaac shook his head. "It was the ring story. If not for that..."

"The ring," Rebecca spoke up, "I don't have it anymore."

"You had it, though, while being a member," Isaac said, his voice gentle. "It's as I said. It was decided. I hope you can find it in your hearts to submit. In the end it may all work out for the good. *Da Hah* is like that."

"But communion," John said, "that's serious."

"I know." Isaac nodded. "There is no other way, though. Maybe things will calm down later if nothing else comes up."

"Then I'm not taking communion either," John said, his jaw taut.

"But you must," Rebecca said, grabbing his arm, her fingers digging in.

"It will only make things worse," Isaac agreed. "It will make you look stubborn."

"I'm not," John said, "whether it looks stubborn or not."

Isaac saw the tears begin and then run in streams down Rebecca's face. Miriam jumped up and rushed out to the kitchen for something. He wasn't sure what, wasn't sure if she knew what.

Miriam came back with two handkerchiefs, using one to dab her own eyes and giving the other one to Rebecca to do the same. How she found two in the kitchen, Isaac had no idea.

"It will work out for the best," he said, but his words didn't stop the tears or ease the painful look on his son's face.

CHAPTER EIGHTEEN

Rebecca knew her parents needed to be told she must abstain from communion. She had stayed at John's place for the afternoon and later attended the hymn singing with him. Lester and Mattie were in bed by the time John brought her home. In a way Rebecca was glad. It gave her a chance to have a good cry, unhindered by anyone sympathizing with her.

The morning, warm enough to open her window before she went downstairs, held the hope of a pleasant day. Rebecca had heard Matthew's footsteps earlier and had decided to join him in the barn for chores. He could handle things well enough himself but never complained when she showed up to help.

Mattie hollered from the kitchen as Rebecca went past the door, "I could use some help in here."

"Yes," Rebecca told her. She knew what her mother meant. Apparently Mattie was planning to serve a large breakfast this morning. The routine varied, based on her mother's mood.

Outside the morning air felt fresh on her skin. The sun was not up yet, but the eastern sky showed the first streaks of color. *So new,* she thought, *so filled with new beginnings. How unlike my life.*

The tears stung her eyes. Last night was enough, she figured, but the fresh emotion caught her by surprise. Apparently the emotion wouldn't be over for a while yet.

John, how precious he had been yesterday. He stood with me, she thought, *and will at communion time too. What a sacrifice. But is it to no avail?* The thought chilled her, and the tears dried up. *What if this is all for nothing. Skipping communion for me would leave a mark on John's record. People will remember. Is there any way around this problem?*

John had spoken at length about it last night. She had said little because she didn't know what to say. One of John's solutions had been to move the wedding date up. Right out of the blue, he had suggested it, which warmed her heart and scared her at the same time. It all seemed a little desperate to her and not likely to work.

Bishop Martin would see right through the maneuver as an attempt to beat the fall communion date. Marrying John that soon could allow things to go fairly smoothly for a while, but after that even Isaac would be hard pressed to protect them if another communion was missed.

"We can't," she had told John and managed to smile in spite of the pain in their discussion. "You're a dear to be willing. Of course I'd marry you," she had told him, "but don't you see? It wouldn't work."

"Why not?" John had demanded, obviously determined his plan would work.

"First of all there is the planning of the wedding. You can't just do it suddenly. We would have to start now. Even that's a little too late, really. I can't do that to Mother. In fact she mentioned something about that the other day."

"So you have thought about moving the date up?" John asked.

"Not for this reason," she had told him. "I didn't know this was going to happen."

"All the better," he said. "It all works in the plans."

"It won't," she had told him. "Bishop will know why we're doing it, and it makes it look even more suspicious—like maybe you are involved too."

"Sure. I want all that money," he had said.

"Maybe you do," she told him and had to smile at the look on his face, even while her heart hurt.

John had gone into pretend mode. He tried to cheer her up by prancing around the room, looking like a high-rolling *Englisha*—whatever that looked like—but she knew what John aimed at.

"Money!" he had said, his head in the air. "I want servants—one for the upstairs, two for the barn, one for each buggy, and three for the kitchen. Come, is it not dinnertime, my dear? And is the ship ready to sail? Have we not a long voyage to make? The club will just have to wait."

She had laughed heartily for their one moment of levity that evening. Anyone who saw them then would never have imagined what lay beneath the surface.

"There's just one little problem," she had teased. "I have to marry Amish. For all this to come my way."

"Of course," John said and walked the floor. "Let us be married then."

"No," she said shaking her head, "I will not be married under such a cloud. This has to clear up first."

The alarm showed on his face. "But that may never happen. We can just be glad if they let us marry. You are out of this communion. I'm out of this communion. Have you forgotten? Do you know what that means?"

"I do," she said nodding. "How well I do."

"Then we must marry in the fall."

"I can't. John, I can't." She had felt the tears come again. "It's too much to ask even if it could work."

He had taken her hand and held it until she could smile again. "I will do what is necessary," he said. "We'll make it together."

John had left then not just because it was time to go, but because Rebecca knew she needed to be alone and assumed John did too. These were not things they could fully share yet. The gulf, to be bridged only by the sacred vows of matrimony, still existed between them. The way across such a chasm had not been discovered. She felt like a deer that had come to the edge of a cliff, the hounds close behind, the hunters' approach sure, and the other side too far away to leap across.

Matthew grinned when she walked into the barn. "Sleepyhead, wake up," he commented.

The reasons were plenty for why she should look so, but she just grinned at him. She didn't want Matthew to know any of this yet. At twelve years of age, he would find out soon enough. When she and John didn't go along for communion, he would learn that something was wrong. Before that she didn't want him burdened with the matter.

She knew this was a defense tactic, not totally justified, and about as effective as the deer that stomped its hooves at the hounds. It felt good, as if she had some control.

"You shouldn't stay up so late," Matthew said, his tone admonishing her. "Children who can't get up should be in bed by ten."

She made a face at him, not able to help it, which just encouraged Matthew.

"I can make you some soup, but I don't think it will cure love sickness. When are you and that songbird going to tie the knot?"

"His name is John," she said, as if Matthew didn't know.

"John…John," he sang in a singsong voice, holding a milker on one arm and using the other to push against a cow to bring it into position. "My sweet John, my darling lovey-love, why don't you marry me?"

"You are despicable," she said, knowing she shouldn't let him get under her skin.

"In the morning I see your face," he crooned. "In the evening I hear your name. Won't you be my lovey-love, my darling teddy bear?"

"You are worse than despicable," she said. His teasing finally got to her. The urge to laugh at him came in spite of her mood.

Matthew laughed with her good naturedly. At the moment he seemed to be much older than his twelve years.

"Where did you hear that song?" she asked, suspicion in her voice.

"I just made it up," he said with a straight face.

She glared at him.

"Well…" He turned a little red in the face. "I heard it playing on the radio in town the other day when Dad took me in. It sounded something like that. I can't remember, really. I made most of it up. Seeing your face made me do it."

"I don't look that bad, surely."

"Not really—just sad."

This caught Rebecca off balance because it came from Matthew. The stinging tears returned.

"I'm sorry," he said, "for whatever it is." He then went back to placing the milker on the cow.

"I have to help with breakfast," she said a moment later. Already she had taken longer in the barn than planned. Mattie might well be ready for her help in the kitchen.

Matthew seemed to understand. He nodded his head, as she slipped out the barn door. In the kitchen Mattie didn't take long before she asked Rebecca to tell her about yesterday. Rebecca knew there was no time for a long quiet conversation, so she let her troubles slip out while mixing pancake batter and warming the pan.

Mattie listened quietly, busying herself with the bacon and eggs. When Rebecca finished she simply said, "Your father needs to be told, the sooner the better."

"I know, but he can't do anything anyway."

"Sounds like you need all the help you can get. Who would have ever thought, you—of all people—could get this deep in trouble."

"It's not my fault," Rebecca wailed.

"You haven't done much to help," Mattie said kindly enough. "That much I know. Why did you hide that ring for all these years—in the house, to boot, and right under our noses? What were you thinking? That no one would find out?"

"I hid it well. You never did find it."

Mattie glanced at her. "See? That's what I mean. You have a record. Can't you see for yourself? You can blame the bishop or the deacon. I know how he is. He doubts everyone. In this case I have sympathies."

"I didn't lie," Rebecca insisted.

"I believe you on that. But now you have a mess to deal with. Go get the girls up for breakfast."

Rebecca went upstairs and made certain her sisters were awake and actually dressing themselves before she returned to the kitchen. She set the last plate on the table, as they came in sleepy eyed.

"It's time you started helping me in the mornings too," Mattie told the oldest, Katie. "Rebecca's not going to be around forever."

"Where's she going?" Katie wanted to know, as she slid along the back bench. "Is Leona having another baby?"

"She's growing up, just as you are," Mattie said. "Next spring the wedding will happen."

"Oh that." Katie made a face. "I suppose so."

Rebecca's heart skipped a beat. She hung onto her mother's words. Next spring. So her mother did believe there would still be a wedding in spite of all this. The hope soothed her soul.

After breakfast Lester announced he needed to drive into town right away. One of the plow blades loosened yesterday, and he had broken the bolt trying to tighten it. Matthew would have to get the horse ready for school on his own.

Rebecca thought her mother would protest, but she didn't. For the rest of the day, Rebecca had no chance to tell her father about the troubling news. After dinner it appeared as if Rebecca was going to have a chance, but she must have decided not to broach the subject with Matthew around. Not till after eight, when the children were in bed and Matthew was upstairs, did the chance come.

Lester listened soberly.

When Rebecca had finished, he wanted to know what Isaac thought about this.

"I don't know," Rebecca told him. "I don't think he likes it."

"Likes what?" Lester asked.

"That I have to stay back from communion."

"I see." Her father seemed to think long and hard.

"We don't like it either," Mattie said.

"I hope it doesn't come to something else," Lester finally said.

"To what?" Rebecca wanted to know, a dread creeping over her.

"You may have to call off the wedding," Lester said.

"You really mean that?" Mattie asked before Rebecca could respond. "Their wedding is planned for the spring."

"Let's just hope for the best. Sorry," Lester said, glancing at Rebecca.

Rebecca couldn't believe what she had just heard. Her father thought she might have to tell John their courtship was called off. The fact that she was twenty-one wouldn't help in this case, she knew. Her father's word would still carry, if he were to demand such an action.

"Surely I won't have to!" she said, knowing her voice trembled.

"We hope not," Mattie said. "You're father is just saying the worst thing that could happen. It doesn't mean that it will."

"That's right," Lester said. "We'll hope for the best." He reached for the latest copy of *The Budget* and opened it, the sound of rustling paper ending any further conversation. Rebecca slipped quietly upstairs and found relief in tears again.

Chapter Nineteen

Rebecca knew that the strange glances had started. The youth gathering, held tonight at the Miller's place on the hill, already was in high gear. She had caught a glimpse of John earlier, while he was propping up one of the buggy wheels to raise a volleyball net higher for the game that was soon to start. His gaze wandered in her direction, and they exchanged brief smiles—their only exchange all evening.

John's tender look was most certainly more pleasant than the other looks she received that evening. Rebecca doubted whether anyone knew about the upcoming communion debacle. Pre-communion church would be this weekend. Likely the news of *The Budget* article had made its way around, though. Such things couldn't be kept secret even from the youth, but that didn't dull the pain now that the sting had come.

Wilma just blurted out the question on the way over. She and Will had picked her up tonight. Rebecca had considered driving on her own but decided to face the music instead.

It hadn't taken long. Will had just turned onto the blacktop from Rebecca's driveway when Wilma asked, "Is it true you are really going to get it—all that money? I can't believe it!"

Seated in the tight buggy, Rebecca chuckled, surprising herself when she considered what this involved.

"Then it's not true," Wilma said. "You never can trust that *Budget*. I've told Mom many a time. You hear that, Will?"

"She hasn't said anything yet," Will said, his voice calm and not too interested. Rebecca knew he had taken one of the Wengerd girls home a month or so ago. She came from one of the west church districts.

"It's true," Rebecca said. "All of it."

Wilma's hand went over her mouth. "I can't believe this."

"So you're rich?" Will asked, curious now.

"You want to marry me?" Rebecca asked. She figured she might as well play along with the story.

"Sure. Tomorrow," he said, with a straight face, "if Bishop Martin will do it. You have to marry Amish I understand."

Rebecca made a face at him, to which he burst out laughing.

Wilma wasn't so amused. "Would you two quit joking about this? It's serious."

"Martin seems to think so. I'm not to go along with communion," Rebecca told them. They might as well know. The news would get around with a better spin if it came from her own mouth. A sympathy factor in her favor, she figured.

Will whistled, the sound drifting into the evening air.

"Would you quit that?" Wilma told him.

He answered with another whistle—a longer one this time.

"I agree," Rebecca said. Will hadn't said any words, but his whistle was exactly how she felt.

Wilma made some more exclamations, dug a little bit deeper, but Rebecca offered no more information—nothing about the ring at least. If it had to come out at all, this, she figured, would have to come out of someone else's mouth.

The crowd of girls around her chattered away. Over by the buggies, the boys were ready to start the game. They had two playing fields set up, outlined with white flour from the Miller's bakery, which was just across the road.

Four captains were appointed. They pulled away from each other and began to choose teams. The process wasn't done with a lot of care. Winning wasn't the big thing—playing was more important. An approximate equal number of boys and girls needed to be on each team. With this they were careful.

Couples were usually left intact, the favor both granted and expected in return. When no matches were known, the hapless pair might be anyone, the decision sprung at the discretion of the captain. No magical endings were expected from these pairings. Plenty of other times existed for that.

Rebecca stood beside John. She relished the moments in public with him. He seemed to stand taller when they were being watched. He didn't appear to be ashamed to be beside her, at least that's what Rebecca thought. She wondered if this would change after communion and decided it wouldn't. John would not participate either. He would share in her misfortune. Her smile in his direction showed her gratitude, the warmth of her feelings, her love for him.

"Let's get going," some boy said. "These love birds make me nervous."

"Get yourself one," someone said in response. Chuckles sounded around them.

The ball flew overhead, and all eyes followed, love forgotten for the moment. Rebecca saw the ball come her way and knew it would land in her territory. She felt terror. It would not go well for her if she missed. Groans would sound around her, and cheers would erupt on the other side of the net.

She lifted both hands skyward, concentrated, and brought her fingers lightly in contact with the ball. It bounced back skyward, straight up above the net. John obviously knew the routine. As she stepped back, he moved over and jumped as high as he could. He slammed the ball through two outstretched arms on the other side, smashing it to the ground.

"Now that was a play!" a boy said from across the net, admiration in his voice.

Rebecca felt warm inside. Red crept up her neck, but she figured the moment was worth it. John and she had played together as a team. They were meant for each other. The assurance might come in handy in the weeks ahead, especially if her father talked further about her and John's breakup. That was a horror she had tried to block out of her mind.

As the score climbed higher, each team became more and more excited. Boys tried to stay in their assigned spaces, so the girls beside them could play. Sometimes the temptation was too much, and sometimes the boys simply forgot, caught up the fervor of the moment. Couples usually didn't tangle—those boys were on their best behavior.

Rebecca set the ball for John again and again, when they were in the front row near the net. She knew her face glowed with happiness. John grinned sheepishly at the wry comments. They needed it, she thought, thankful for what this evening gave them.

After the game ended, they switched sides and played again. When the darkness made it difficult to play, two lanterns were set on top of the buggies, and the action continued. Somewhere around nine o'clock, card tables were set up, and ice cream and homemade rolls were served. Rebecca stayed with John as they went through the line and sat with him on blankets spread on the grass. There weren't enough chairs to go around.

Rebecca thought about telling John what her father had said, just as a warning, so he might know it wasn't her idea. With so many people around, she changed her mind. It was for the best, she figured. She might just not say anything at all. Surely her father just had a bad moment the other night.

"Some game," John said.

"Sure was," she said and chuckled, still warm inside despite the ice cream.

"I'm glad spring has come, but the nights are still a little chilly."

"Yes, they are," she said, suddenly aware she needed her coat. It was over in Will's buggy, but she really didn't feel like leaving John to retrieve it. Each moment with him seemed short enough the way it was.

"Ice cream doesn't help," John shivered glancing around. "Did you come with Will?"

"Yes. Wilma came too."

"I know," he said.

"You wouldn't be jealous, would you?" she whispered.

"A little." He grinned. "I get jealous of any boy who gets to drive you."

"Not so loud," she whispered again.

"No one is paying attention," he said, waiving his ice-cream bowl around to demonstrate.

A few looked up from their conversation, at which Rebecca made a face.

"See," she said.

"I guess you're right." His mood seemed to change, becoming heavier, as if he just remembered something.

"You don't have to stay back Sunday from communion," she told him, her voice low. "Really you don't."

"But I want to," he whispered.

"I know. Knowing you would do that for me makes me feel good, and that's good enough. You don't have to hurt yourself."

As if weighing the thought, he replied, "Are you sure?"

"Sure," she said and smiled, though her heart hurt. It had been such a comfort to think John would stand with her. It really wasn't necessary, though, she told herself. This would only hurt John when she might need him later.

"I don't know," he said, his face sober.

"Think about it," she told him, as Wilma came in their direction. No doubt it was time to go.

His face revealed the pain he felt as he thought about what lay ahead.

"Really...I have to go," she told him and got up.

"Sunday then," he said. They both knew they would not see each other again until after the fateful decision would be made. Their world would then know that Rebecca had been left out of communion—a most grievous and severe complication for any Amish church member.

"We have to go," Wilma said from beside her.

Rebecca turned to follow and hoped the burning in her eyes wouldn't produce tears. This was not how she had desired the evening to end but supposed it couldn't be helped. She felt no ulterior motive for the offer she had just made to John—no test to see if he would or wouldn't take it. The only thing she felt was the pain in her heart, and she hoped to spare him of the same.

Will had brought the buggy around already. Rebecca put her coat on before climbing in.

"Nice game," he said. "There should be more of them now that the weather is warmer."

"I didn't see you with the Wengerd girl," Rebecca said. She wanted to distract herself from her troubles, and Will just happened to be handy at the moment.

"They didn't put her beside me. That Johnny Byler doesn't know I go with her."

"Poor, poor dears," Wilma crooned. "Love missed its song tonight."

"Don't tease him," Rebecca said. "His heart hurts."

"I'm going to hurt both of you," Will snapped and slapped the reins for emphasis.

"Oh!" Wilma pretended to be horrified. "The wolf stalks the earth, looking for his mate."

"For love," Rebecca added for good measure. "His hackles raised to the moon."

"You two are gone," Will pronounced. "Gone crazy—completely."

Rebecca and Wilma erupted with peals of laughter.

"Now look who's howling at the moon," Will said.

"There is no moon out," Wilma told him and made a face in the darkness. Rebecca caught a glimpse, made possible by the headlights of a car coming toward them.

"You are the ones who said there was," Will retorted. He tightened up the reins as the car approached.

"He's love sick," Wilma concluded.

"It does happen," Rebecca said. Thinking of John, the laugher died in her throat.

"I suppose so," Wilma allowed. "Why doesn't it happen to me?"

"It will soon enough," Will said, surprising Rebecca and apparently Wilma with his sudden change of attitude. "You're a nice enough girl."

"Thanks," Wilma said.

"When you're sleeping," Will added and burst out in laughter.

"That wasn't nice at all," Wilma told him. "You could break my heart."

"At least you don't have anyone who could really break it," Will said, as if he knew something he wasn't telling.

They drove on in silence, each lost in thought. Rebecca feared her heart might break come Sunday—and wondered if she could endure it.

Chapter Twenty

M anny Troyer looked at the box, which sat beside the desk in his Ohio office. Outside on 39 the spring tourist traffic had already begun. At four o'clock the line of cars was stacked up, stopped by the lights downtown, and stretched past the office buildings of the Haiti Mennonite Outreach. They called it the *HMO* for short. Although some thought the abbreviation amusing, he thought it fit.

Little ripples of dust lay on the top of the box, apparently missed by the cleaner yesterday. She must have thought the object too unimportant or lowly to be worthy of attention. He knew it wasn't and also knew the reason the box had remained unopened. He didn't quite have the courage to open it yet.

By next week the scheduled trip to Virginia would be here, and Manny knew he needed to open the box before then. No way could he concentrate on the scheduled board meetings if the box stayed as it was, its contents unknown.

The mission rented an upstairs apartment in Berlin. Why the board hadn't bought it, Manny never understood. He stayed in the apartment while in the states. Others who stopped by on mission business did as well.

He decided he would take the box there. Privacy was uppermost on his mind. Not that the office wasn't private, but something in the recesses of his mind told him opening the box at the apartment would be a wise course of action.

Manny had no definite routine, and he was finished with all his appointments for the day. He might as well leave, he figured. That would make time to see what Emma had sent, before going out for supper to a local restaurant. For the last few nights, he had dinner with the church people who had given him supper invitations, but tonight his calendar was open.

He dusted the box off, placed it under his arm, and went out the door.

"Leaving?" Fannie Esh, the young girl who filled in three days a week at the front desk, asked.

"Out for the night," he said and didn't slow his step.

"Have a good evening."

"You too." He let the door swing shut behind him.

He walked briskly up the sidewalk. Berlin lay on a knoll. The early settlers apparently liked the view and built their town on the highest hill around. Mostly he passed tourists. With his box sticking out from under his arm, he hoped no one he knew would ask him about the box and require an explanation of him.

He reached the apartment without having to stop anywhere and breathed a sigh of relief. He wondered what it contained and why Emma would ship something to him, now that she was gone.

Manny found a sharp knife in the kitchen, slit the wrap on the box, and opened it. He quickly removed the paper covering the contents. The first dozen papers were drawings, and they were good. He had no problem recognizing the 1956 cream-colored Chevrolet Corvette. It was his own, he was certain. He searched for and found the missing piece of hubcap, which saved him ten dollars off the purchase price. Even then the car had been out of his budget, but he had splurged. He loved that car.

Why would she send him the pictures? At the bottom of the drawing, he made out a name in faint letters—*Emma*. So she knew how to draw or had learned. This he had not known. The next drawing was of two people. He recognized himself, but the girl had her back turned. It was dusk, and the sun colored the horizon. The tan Corvette could be seen in the background. He turned to the next page, and there they were holding hands, close together and deep in conversation.

The others pictured more of the same—always at dusk and always showing the girl turned away. He had easily recognized his own face in the first drawing, shed of fifty years, but by the last page, he was no longer certain. At the bottom by the signed name, words had been added. Written in much smaller letters were the words, *no longer can remember.*

A date was also written on the left-hand corner. He calculated that some of the drawings had been created twenty years after he had seen her last. Why send these now—after she was gone? Was there a purpose to this? He didn't feel tormented, just empty on the subject. He had made peace with this a long time ago.

Was Emma trying to make a point? If so, what? Did she think this would hurt him? Did she know he had never married? Did she think it was because of her? Nothing really made sense to him.

He dug deeper and came up with letters. He recognized the return address as his own. Three of them had been written soon after the door had been closed by her brother. In the chance they might reach her, he had sent them. So Emma had received them, but why did she keep them and never respond? Did her brother really have such a hold on her?

It didn't matter now, he told himself. The pain had been intense back then. He had sold the Corvette for more than he paid and made a nice profit, but that had not lessened the hurt. It was only when he made peace with the God who could create such love in the heart of a man and then allow it to be denied that peace had come.

He had dedicated his life to the service of his fellow man. There had been other chances, but he hadn't taken them. He could have married, but he chose not to, not out of bitterness but because he didn't want to.

The envelopes were already open, so he sat down and pulled the first letter out.

"My dearest Emma," he said aloud, reading his own words.

You know of my love for you, yet I feel like saying it again and again. I am left with the memory of your face, but already it is being crowded out by the memory of how our last visit ended—you were climbing the hill to the house, your brother at your side.

I hope and pray with all that is within me that our love will not be lost. You need not tell me of the wide gulf that exists between us, erected by religion. There is but one religion, our love for God and our love for our fellow man. Can you not see that, Emma? My heart aches that you might.

Surely your brother cannot believe me so evil that we must be parted. I cannot even know if this letter will reach you, and yet I could never rest if I did not try. You know how much I care for you. Have I not told you a hundred times? Were the moments we spent together not precious though few?

Can you really think, Emma, that being apart and never seeing each other again is the will of God? Surely that is not something that even crosses your mind. Yet when I have driven out to our place, at dusk as always, you have never been there.

The sun set as it always did, but I felt only the emptiness that was left beside me and in my heart. On some of the evenings that I wait, I believe the sunset puts on a grand display for my sake. I take courage in this thought and search for the hope that it's true.

Yours truly, with all my love,

Manny Troyer

He set the letter down, lost in thought. So she had received this—his heart's cry, his agony—yet he had heard nothing back. Why would she keep the letter? It puzzled him. Perhaps the answer was yet to be discovered, as there seemed to be more letters. On the verge of digging deeper, he felt drawn to the two remaining letters—his letters.

He felt strangely stirred, as he heard his own voice from across the years. The passion moved him. How long had it been since he had felt such emotion? He knew the answer. A very long time. Not even in his service—in his best service—he felt such passion. He hadn't planned it this way. He had just left the emotion behind as a thing that did not belong to him, a subject that had passed him by.

Yet here it was again. He unfolded the second letter.

My dearest, dearest Emma,

My heart is full tonight—full of sorrow—like the ocean is full of water and salt at the same time. I went out to our place under the tree again. The sun made no effort to say anything. It set like a stone without ripples, the clouds the color of clay.

Have you received my other letter? Surely your brother would not block such a thing. I can't imagine him as such a mean creature, even though he is Amish. You are Amish, and yet I hardly think God ever made a lovelier creature than you, Emma.

The light of your eyes makes me weak inside. The touch of your hand always felt like the dawning of a brand new day. When I met you on those evenings, Emma, it was as if I came alive again for the first time. I thought the feeling would go away, but it never did. Perhaps that is why God is taking you from me. Is it because I have loved too much?

I have never loved like this before, Emma. I really haven't. There were other girls, as I suppose there were boys for you. I was a little interested, but when I first saw you, a flame leaped up in my heart.

I told myself it was impossible, that I should never have come, but how is one to turn off the stars or keep the moon from shining, Emma? I could no more stay away from you than I could keep from breathing.

This must be why God has taken you from me. I am angry with Him. Perhaps I shouldn't tell you this, but I figure you won't read this anyway, not after I failed to get a response from the first letter. Yet I must tell someone and why not you, even if you never read it.

There is no use saying that I love you, Emma. The whole world is saying it for me, and surely you can hear.

Manny Troyer

"Well…" Manny said, "what a rascal I was." The trace of a smile crossed his face. He opened the third letter.

My dear Emma,

This will be my last letter to you. Today I went to the house. I knew someone was home because there were buggies in the yard—two of them. I don't know Amish people that well, but in my world, two cars in the yard indicates someone is at home.

The ache in my heart has gotten no better. I suppose it never will, but then I expect many before me have thought the same. My calamity is not that strange, I have decided. I have loved, and loved with all my heart, but then so have others before me.

I will join them, bitterly and unwillingly, but I will do it. Of this I am determined. I made peace with God last night at our church. It was there I imagined you would stand one day. The pulpit was removed as they do when the special day has arrived. The people had gathered. There you would be, my Emma, my beloved one, to claim, to love, and to promise sacred vows with.

I now know it will never be. I am sure you didn't come to the door. The courage it took to come there was great. Perhaps you will never understand that. I tried to bridge the gap between us with the only tool I had, myself, but the door didn't open.

Goodbye, Emma. I sold the Corvette today. The sale brought quite a good price but no joy to my heart. That was lost the last time I saw your eyes light up with love for me. You will forgive me for giving up. Surely you will understand.

I wish to thank you, Emma. Perhaps that will surprise you too, if you do read this. As I said in the last letter, I was bitter against God. Yet I am thankful to you and to Him, that He made love like this, and that you allowed me to feel it. For this I am in your debt. I now know what it is to love.

In this I may have sinned—I did not love God the same way, but I now know how, and I will try.

Goodbye, Emma. I never got to kiss you. Wish I would have.

Manny Troyer

"Well…" he said again. "So…who would have thought it."

He glanced at the clock. The time was well past his suppertime, but he dug deeper into the box.

Chapter Twenty-one

Sunday morning couldn't have dawned more cheerful. The sun rose without a color in the sky, its light bright and piercing. Already the trees were green, buds bursting from their long winter-imposed sleep. Rebecca went out to help Matthew hitch up for the drive to church. He insisted on driving the single buggy lately, even though he wasn't with the young people yet.

"It's too tight in the surrey!" he declared vehemently earlier that morning at the breakfast table.

"He's growing up," Lester replied, speaking over his head.

"A little too fast!" Mattie said.

"Please," Matthew had begged, trying that angle. "Rebecca shouldn't be driving in the surrey anyway. She's almost married."

Lester grinned at the logic but allowed the request with a nod of his head.

"He's not getting too big for his head?" Mattie asked.

"Just growing up," Lester replied.

Rebecca paused outside the living room door to watch the pair of robins build their nest. They were busy in the tree near her upstairs bedroom window. One of them landed next to the half-built nest and wrestled with the piece of twig in its mouth, while the other flew off, apparently in search of fresh material.

"Would you hurry?" Matthew hollered from beside the buggy. Rebecca knew he could easily get the horse under the shafts himself, so she lingered. So rhythmic were the lives of birds, dictated by forces outside themselves, sprung by the change of seasons—summer, fall,

winter, then spring. Love for them seemed nothing more than a bio-
logical timing, over which they had no control.

Humans, she thought, *they mess it up because they have control.* The
day in front of her made the case. Before this, choice had always
seemed attractive, but it now lay down a path strewn with obstacles
and implications all tangled up in a frightful mess.

Last night, after the younger children were in bed, Lester had
called her back down to the living room. Mattie sat on the couch, her
hands in knots in front of her. As Rebecca could tell, her mother had
been deep in thought.

"We need to go over this," Lester said, motioning to Rebecca to sit
on the couch beside Mattie.

Rebecca had no objections to the talk they were about to have.
In a way she felt relief. Perhaps her father knew of a way around the
problem or could find a way.

"You are about to make a big decision," Lester said. "Seems to me,
we should be certain."

"He means to ask whether or not there really is a problem," Mattie
added.

"Are you sure this is true?" Lester asked.

"You mean Emma's will?" Rebecca asked.

"Yes." Lester nodded.

Rebecca threw her hands in the air. "I only know what I've been
told and read from *The Budget* and all."

"So we're basing this whole thing on *The Budget,*" Lester said sound-
ing exasperated. "Shouldn't we have asked someone and verified this
thing? Maybe Leona knows something."

"How would she?" Mattie asked. "They only tell family."

"I suppose so," Lester allowed. "I don't like it. I just don't. Seems
like a lot is being made of something when all this time no one has
talked with a lawyer or someone who really knows."

"You wouldn't get a lawyer, would you?" Mattie asked. "Surely
not."

Lester shook his head. "No, not like that. We could talk to the one Emma used."

"I wouldn't know how to do that," Rebecca told him.

"She can't," Mattie added. "I won't have her asking questions or running out to Milroy as if she's after the money. You know how that would look."

"I suppose so," Lester agreed. "I still don't like it."

"The bishop has made up his mind," Mattie said, as if that proved everything. "He doesn't want Rebecca going along with communion. Do you think he would decide such a thing on a rumor?"

Rebecca could see that her father had doubts, and she grabbed eagerly at the slender thread. "Do you suppose it's all a rumor?" she had asked.

"It's not," Mattie said. "Such things just aren't."

"It still seems a little wild, this accusation. Why would Emma leave her money to Rebecca—and for such a reason?" Lester glanced at Rebecca. "Did you ever give her reason to think you were leaving the Amish? Dropped a hint? Is that why? Did she try to persuade you?"

"No," Rebecca said shaking her head. "I talked with her about Atlee but said nothing about leaving."

"You sure?" Mattie asked.

"Sure," Rebecca said. "She asked me whether or not I was thinking of leaving. I said no."

"Still strange," Lester said. "This whole thing is strange. It makes no sense at all—not a bit of sense. Leaving money for such a reason is so out of the blue."

"Maybe the girl said more than she knows," Mattie suggested. "Sometimes people think they hear things and believe they are true when they are not."

"Still makes no sense," Lester said. "Anyway, we have pre-communion church tomorrow. Do you really plan on going through with this?"

"It's not me," Rebecca said, raising her hands in the air. "I have nothing to do with it. Isaac said I can't. The ministers decided it. They want to wait it out and see if something else might show up to clear the matter."

"I guess that's reasonable," Lester allowed. "I hope something shows up. Maybe this is all based on a rumor."

"You're grasping at straws," Mattie informed him.

"Might be," Lester agreed. "Is John really not going along with communion?"

"He said he wouldn't," Rebecca told him.

"Did you try to persuade him?" Mattie asked.

"No." Rebecca shook her head.

"Then I'll talk to him," Lester concluded. "He shouldn't stay back. It'll just make things worse."

Rebecca knew it would, and perhaps her father would have a chance this morning to talk with John and persuade him otherwise. Inside, though, she hoped John would stay back. It was a selfish thought, she figured, but it felt good. It would be lonely to go through this by herself.

"I'm leaving by myself," Matthew hollered, this time from inside the buggy. His hands gripped the lines, ready to release them.

Rebecca knew he wouldn't dare leave without her. If he did it would be the end of his privileges with the single buggy. She smiled at him as she climbed in, and he made a face. As Matthew let the lines out and the horse shot forward, their father came out of the house to get his own horse.

"You'd better take it easy," Rebecca warned him. "Maybe I should drive."

That Matthew wouldn't let her was a forgone conclusion. The very idea was a joke in itself. To drive into church with his sister at the lines might well destroy his masculinity beyond repair.

Matthew confirmed her conclusions with a snort through his nose.

"I'm your sweet sister," she told him.

"All the more reason for me to drive," he said.

"You are making no sense."

"Perfect sense," he said. "I drive."

After Matthew dropped her off at the end of the walk, Rebecca went in to wait in the wash room, a line of women ahead of her. She left her bonnet and shawl on the corner of the table. Slowly she moved with the line, time seeming to hang still in the air.

She figured most of them knew about her and Emma by now, the news received when they read *The Budget*. What they didn't know, they were to find out before this day was over. She, Rebecca Keim, had to stay back from communion. It would be the beginning of many uncomfortable days.

Rebecca saw Wilma with several other younger girls. She was certain Wilma would not turn away from her. Drawn by the hope, she walked over and stood beside Wilma, though there were still other women she had not shaken hands with. This morning the matter would have to slide.

"We heard from Milroy," Wilma whispered.

Rebecca leaned toward her, their shoulders together.

"It's true. Mom heard from her sister. She talked with Ezra's wife, Elizabeth, and Emma did leave you almost everything if you marry John." Wilma's eyes were big.

"I'm not marrying for money," Rebecca whispered back.

"I know," Wilma said, and the line moved toward the living room.

So it is true, Rebecca thought, as she followed Wilma. Her father's hope that some new information would surface lay on the hardwood floor, stepped on, squashed flat. Her head hurt already, and the day was young.

They were early Rebecca noticed when the line of girls walked in front of the seated women. Usually the boys were already at their benches. She sat beside Wilma and waited. The house was still and silent, broken only by the soft shuffle of feet on the hardwood floor and the squeak of hard benches as bodies settled down on them.

Rebecca searched for John's face in the line of boys. They came in, one after the other, almost shoulder to shoulder. They took rapid steps forward, their faces turned to the ground. Rebecca found John's face and wondered, *Did Father speak with him? Will he stand with me today—in this hour of trouble?*

She felt shame in her hope yet yearned for his support. *Is he not to be my husband? Am I within my rights to expect this much of him?* She imagined this might soften the blow. Perhaps it would make it harder for the ministers to leave her dangling in the wind. With John, a minister's son, by her side and abstaining too, the ministers might have more of a chance of changing their minds.

They would change their decision, she was certain. She had done no wrong. She didn't regret the past. She felt as if she would do the same thing again, and yet she knew things might not look so to others. Others might misunderstand. *Surely,* she thought, *the tide will soon turn and the matter will clear up.*

She found and held John's gaze, the warmth of his look filling her and almost causing her to gasp. Wilma glanced sideways at her in astonishment. John dropped his eyes, but in the moment of their contact, she knew. She was certain John would stand with her. He would risk all to show them her innocence. He would demonstrate his belief in her. Today they would be together in heart and mind.

With the song announced, the songs began, and they heard the familiar sounds of the ministers' feet moving upstairs. What they said this morning, Rebecca really didn't care. The delight of the prior moments still filled her. John would stand with her. With that love she felt impenetrable, like a fortress that couldn't be breached.

She wondered if it would always be so. Was this what it felt like to be wrapped up in John's arms and held? Was this how God created love to feel like—so safe and secure, so like Himself? The voices rose all around her in song, and she joined in, her heart full. This surprised her because she knew what would come afterward.

As the ministers returned, the singing stopped. Isaac got up first, and then Bishop Martin completed the last sermon, his voice rose and fell with a rhythmic sound. He closed the service and asked the members to stay seated. The younger children stood up and filed out.

In the silence that followed, Martin got to his feet again and began. The list of items he had to go over was long, which wasn't unusual. A few old rules needed refreshment, and some new rules needed consideration. Rebecca listened, but her heart wasn't in it. It didn't matter anyway. Women would get to express their views when the deacon or one of the ministers came around, but few did. On rule changes, the word of the men carried.

Although she wanted the end of this to come, she dreaded it at the same time. She would soon have to whisper the dreaded words, *Ich kann nett mitt gay*—I can't go along. She would wish them God's blessing both because she did wish them a blessing and because it was expected.

Then with his round completed, the deacon would give his report. There was a sister, he would say, who stayed back. She wished them all God's blessing and hoped by God's grace to be able to go with them to the sacred table next time.

That it would be so, she knew, just not when. The voice of Bishop Martin went on and on. Then the time came. She spoke, and the report was given. Only one report was given. No brother stayed back and wished them God's blessing.

CHAPTER TWENTY-TWO

Rebecca felt frozen to the backless bench. The women stood up and moved toward the kitchen. Wilma turned to look at her.

"So you did it?" she whispered.

Rebecca nodded, the answer obvious. "I had to."

"I know," Wilma said.

Wilma would think something was wrong if she didn't move soon. Rebecca forced herself to her feet, her legs still weak. John had not stayed back. *Is Father to blame?* His arguments surely made sense, but sense did not console her heart. Her heart was gripped in the horror of what lay ahead. Communion was in two weeks, and she would stay back alone.

Rebecca told herself John's decision was understandable, but the pain wouldn't go away. Her heart ached as she joined in with lunch preparations. She carried peanut butter bowls, refilled the pickle jars, smiled when spoken to, and finally got to eat, the food tasteless in her mouth.

John would soon pick her up at the end of the walk, and she knew her face would show the hurt. She could make an effort to hide the fact, but things were beyond that. The attempt might not work either. Since the accident John was different, more sensitive, and would know anyway. *Why then did he not join me?*

Wilma must have sensed her distress and seated herself beside Rebecca, even though she had eaten at an earlier table.

"I'm so sorry," Wilma said, meaning one thing, while Rebecca really hurt over another.

"Thanks," Rebecca whispered. She was thankful for what Wilma could give, knowing that her troubles with John were things she couldn't share.

"This is all just so ridiculous," Wilma said. "It's not like it's your fault at all."

"Some of it is," Rebecca said.

"Like what? Did you ask for the money?"

"No."

"Did Emma offer it to you?"

"No."

"Then tell me how you are to blame?"

"I broke some church rules." Rebecca followed her urge to say it aloud. Chances were good that word would leak out. Not that she suspected the ministry, they wouldn't spread confidential matters, but it happened anyway. Better that Wilma know now than hear it some other way. Their friendship might be saved, and she needed friends at the moment.

Wilma made a skeptical face.

"See I used to like a boy in school. His name was Atlee."

Wilma nodded. "Don't know him. I never lived in Milroy."

Rebecca continued. "Anyway, his parents went Mennonite and moved away. Before he left he gave me a ring."

"A ring?" Wilma's eyes got big.

"Yes. I kept it until just recently, and then I threw it away."

"You kept it." Wilma spoke a little too loudly for Rebecca's comfort, but she could do little about it. Several women glanced their way.

"Yes," she said softer this time, in the hopes Wilma took the hint.

"All this time?" Wilma said whispering.

Rebecca nodded.

"Even when you were dating John?"

Rebecca let the look on her face answer.

"How could you?"

"I sort of forgot about it."

Now Wilma's face gave away her answer. She wasn't swallowing the story.

"Really. That's what happened."

"So you strung two boys along at the same time?"

"I didn't," Rebecca retorted, causing heads to turn again. *This is really stupid,* she thought. *If I argue with Wilma until the day I stay back from communion, everyone will start putting two and two together—if they haven't already.*

"You kept his ring. Did Emma know about this?"

Rebecca hesitated and lost her advantage. "I told her later and asked for counsel."

"No wonder the ministers are upset," Wilma said.

"It makes sense," Rebecca said, "from my point of view."

"Maybe to you," Wilma said, "but not to the rest of us. You really need to make things right both with God and the church. It's awful. Emma has to give you money to make you marry John. Really, Rebecca."

Rebecca shook her head.

The look of horror was already on Wilma's face. "So that explains it."

"Explains what?" Rebecca wasn't sure she wanted to know.

"The accident. That's why you were so sure of yourself. You stayed with John even when it looked like he was a cripple. Here I thought you were so wonderful and blamed myself for thinking I'd leave if my boyfriend was a cripple for life. You were doing it for money."

"No," Rebecca said trying again.

Wilma had moved away. Only a few inches, but the gulf was fixed. It stretched across two hearts, and the gap could not be mended.

The heavy silence settled over them, and Rebecca knew more words were useless. What she had intended as an extended hand, a heart shared, had turned bitter in a moment.

"You really need to make things right," Wilma whispered.

"How can I?"

"You must," Wilma said. "Your soul is in danger. Selling your love for money. What will John say when he finds out? You'll be excommunicated. He's a minister's son."

That he was, Rebecca well knew. Earlier this morning she would have whispered back, "He understands." Now she said nothing.

"I'll try to help you when I can," Wilma said, obviously trying to salvage what once was, but the gulf stood between them.

"You can't do anything."

"I know." Wilma nodded, then stood to leave. "I have to go. Will just left to get his horse."

Too distracted by the conversation to have noticed, Rebecca wondered whether John had already left for his horse. She tried to control her emotions while searching the room of men and boys. Some were still in the house, others out in the yard. Frantically her mind flew to the fact that John might already be outside with his horse in line, frustrated and ready to go but held back by the lines. What was she to do?

She dreaded the moment ahead. John had not stayed back. She would have to face him and hear his apology, given for whatever the reason. None of which would heal the hurt, now made even more painful by the severing of a deep friendship. Her world lay unraveled before her eyes.

Had the very heavens forsaken her? Had judgment come for sins she was unaware of? The possibility seemed real. She continued to search for John's face, driven by force of habit. Regardless of her own pain, it wasn't necessary to add to his by embarrassing him in public.

She needed to find her bonnet and shawl and go outside. If John wasn't in line, the mistake would be understood better than the alternative. At the very least, the boys would laugh at John's girlfriend, at her eagerness to be with him. That was better than to have her present reluctance known.

She stepped outside, women ahead and behind her. Women who knew where they were, where their husbands or boyfriends were. She searched the line of buggies but didn't see John. Four buggies down, her father's surrey came into focus. Matthew, alone now, was evidently overjoyed to be in his own buggy.

For a brief moment, she considered joining Matthew. Let John come find her if he wanted to. He deserved it, didn't he? Regardless of what her father had told him, John should have stood with her. Let Wilma imagine what she wanted, think what she would. If this was for money, how would they explain the risk she took?

The moment passed, though, and she gathered herself. *John has an explanation. Surely he does.* If not, then she would have to understand anyway. Her heart might struggle, but they would see each other through this. John had said he would, and she would not forsake him.

Resolved, she searched the line again and still found nothing. The line of buggies lurched forward. Another woman got in, and again the action was repeated. Rebecca's gaze was drawn to the constant movement of men out by the barn. It was John. He came out of the barn leading his horse.

"A little ahead of myself," she said to the woman behind her and stepped out of line. The attempted smile must have looked as queasy as her stomach felt, but Sarah, the bishop's wife, seemed not to notice. Her smile was genuine.

At least they don't hate me, Rebecca thought. She moved back toward the house, her smile still weak.

She considered walking across the lawn and offering to help John get the horse hitched. If her heart hadn't hurt so much, she would have despite the custom. Instead she waited.

Rebecca rejoined the line once John did. The pain around her heart increased the closer she got to the buggy. She knew her smile was tight, her face contorting with the effort.

"Hi," she said. Her step up carried her into the seat beside him. His closeness pressed in on her, and his smile lit up his entire face. Her heart refused to respond.

"Good to see you," he said, "after such a day." John let the reins out, and the horse pulled forward.

She wanted to scream, *Sure, you're still okay. What about me? Why didn't you stand with me?*

He glanced at her face, seeming to come to some conclusion. "I understand," he said. "It was a hard day."

"For me," she said. The words came out quickly.

"I understand," he nodded and turned the horse left at the blacktop. "Dad thinks things will clear up after a while. Handling it this way will be for the best."

"Really?" The question was bitter in her voice.

"Yes." He nodded, his face solemn. "I think so too. We talked for a long time last night. Dad, Mom, and myself. It makes perfect sense this way. We can be thankful Dad was willing to help us out."

"He was?"

"Yes. I assume the plan worked. Dad would likely have said something to me after church if it hadn't."

"Did my dad talk to you?"

"Yes. I didn't change my mind."

"So you have a good reason for this?"

"I think so." John had a puzzled look on his face. "You don't like it, I know. I wanted to."

"You wanted what?" Rebecca felt her breath come short, the expectation heavy in the air.

"To stand with you," he said.

"But you didn't."

He looked at her strangely. Then the smile came, broad and wide. He chuckled. "Oh, you don't know."

"Would you explain yourself? I was the only one who stayed back."

"No," he said. He placed his arm around her shoulder and pulled her toward him. "I stayed back too."

"How?" she asked.

"Dad arranged it somehow. He took it to the ministers' meeting.

That way it didn't have to be announced in public. It makes it easier for you—less attention and all. But they know where I stand."

She felt her body give in. She laid her head against his shoulder and let the tears flow. "I'm sorry," she whispered, "that I doubted you."

"I understand. It's just hard."

They drove in silence, but the tears didn't stop. Rebecca was tired—too tired to stop crying. "I'm so sorry," she said. "I don't mean to be a *bruts bobli*."

"You're not," he said, his arm tightening around her shoulders. "You're anything but a crybaby. You're a wonderful girl."

"Now I'm really going to cry."

He only smiled, as he watched the road and clutched the reins in his free hand.

CHAPTER TWENTY-THREE

Rachel's days were burdened, clouded by visions of what she hated. Ever present in the daytime, they haunted her dreams at night. The goats, the object of her scorn, now stood between herself and the inheritance. She never would have expected Reuben to bring home a herd of goats nor succeed in anything. It was beyond her imagination but true. Each week Reuben succeeded, and the critters multiplied themselves.

Even with the frequent veterinary bills, the income Reuben declared outgrew any expenses. She knew this because she secretly checked the accounts and carefully reviewed his books. The numbers were what Reuben said they were. He made money—and a reasonable amount of it.

She gathered hope each time a new problem afflicted the flock and lost it when Reuben found a fix. Rachel hid her determination to stop the progress behind an attitude of helpfulness and waited for the opportunity to spoil his efforts.

Daily her unborn child grew. Although her thought processes seemed to have slowed down and her attentions had been diverted, she was comforted by that fact that there was still time. Even after the baby's birth, there would be time left. Rebecca could do nothing quickly. From the reports she received Sunday, overheard from the deacon's wife, Rebecca had to stay back from communion.

So the girl's way was blocked. It would just be a matter of time before Rebecca would bolt—run right back to that Mennonite boyfriend of hers and give up on her plan to claim what wasn't hers anyway. Amish ways might be hard, but they did serve their purposes at times. This was one of those times. Rebecca wouldn't be allowed to marry Amish, she was sure, not under these conditions.

In the meantime she would do what she could when and if the opportunity presented itself. Rachel was not bothered by her devious actions. Instead her motivation was fueled by the conviction Reuben needed help.

Reuben's present success only drove her further. If Reuben thought money was so evil, why then did the creation of it cause him such joy? He was misguided. Money was important. Reuben's goals were just too low.

For now the cover must be maintained. If Reuben suspected she meant the herd harm, he would take necessary measures. As it was he often asked her help, which gave her access to see how the operation was run and discover weaknesses to exploit it.

Goats were hardy creatures, she quickly decided. Once she added salt to their feed bucket, a weak attempt at sabotage. One got sick, but she couldn't be certain from what.

Reuben said the vet thought it was acidosis and wanted the feed schedule evened out. This only produced more work and more trips to the barn in her condition. When she mentioned this to Reuben, he made a genuine effort to reduce her workload, which only limited her access to the goat barn.

When Reuben went to visit the bank in Rushville, Rachel decided to make another move. She was certain Reuben had gone to deliver the loan payment by hand. The man's delight in his success was phenomenal.

She walked back to the woods to search for strange looking plants. Faint memories of eighth-grade biology class returned, but she couldn't be certain of what she was searching for. The area carried few naturally poisonous plants. A half an hour's search produced some specimens but nothing too dangerous, from what she recollected. She fed them to two goats in the yard.

The goats developed a strong case of diarrhea. The vet found scraps of the offending plants in the yard and raised the point that such items were usually only found in woods. She readily admitted to finding the plants and feeding them to the goats. She counted on Reuben attributing the effort to her love for his prize animals. In this she was correct.

"Better leave the wood plants alone," the vet grinned, apparently amused at this Amish couple's intense care for their animals. "Not many people make such an effort."

"It's cheaper than feed," Rachel said, which wasn't a lie.

"That it is," the vet said chuckling, "before my bill, that is."

"We'll stick with store bought food," Reuben assured him.

Rachel smiled at them. This had been an easy effort—the first try, so to speak. It would have been great had it worked, but it hadn't been that hard to find a cover for her actions. Next time she would do better.

The first details of her final plan came to her one night, while she dreamed of goats. The goats were everywhere all the time. But instead of alive and well, now they lay dead, spread at her feet, and she was the architect of their demise.

The Rushville Library was close enough and large enough to contain what she wanted and possibly confirm her impressions from the dream. With one trip to the library, she learned the plan could be made to work. On the way home, she stopped at a plant nursery, hopeful she wouldn't be recognized and remembered. She ordered the seeds and paid for them with her own stashed cash. Reuben would never know.

Feelings of guilt assaulted her, intense in their claims against her. She had sinned against God and man, they said. Surprised as much as convicted, she rode them out, allowing the emotions to swirl around her. It was too late to turn back now.

Luke might be the only loose end, and this concerned her enough to invite him home for Sunday supper. When she took food over to Emma's old place and he made a face at her invitation, she knew what the problem was. He didn't want to miss time spent with Susie.

"Bring her too," she said with a smile.

"Mom, you don't like her."

"Perhaps it's time to start. People will begin talking soon."

"So that's why," he said more than asked, a sigh on his lips.

She let him think so because she needed a reason he could believe. *It is partly so,* she told herself on the way home. When Luke still made no effort to bring Susie home for supper, she enlisted Reuben's help.

"We need to get to know Susie and invite her here to our home," she told him. "Would you ask Luke to bring her over sometime?"

"I suppose he knows you don't like her."

"Yes," she admitted readily, "but it is time to deal with that."

Reuben must have agreed because the next time she saw Luke, he told her they would come.

"This Sunday night before the singing," he said, a glint in his eye. "You'd better be nice to her."

"Of course," she said and smiled her best mother's smile.

"You're not planning something, like breaking us up?"

"No," she said, which was true. "You're marrying the girl, right?"

"I hope so," he said.

She caught a glimpse of his face, soft with his thoughts of Susie, but was unmoved. Resigned, Rachel was saddened by his choice.

What's to be will be, I suppose, she told herself when Luke left. *No sense in losing the money too.*

The packages of seeds arrived on Saturday morning. Reuben left for his afternoon church rounds a little after two. He didn't tell her how long he would be gone, but leaving this early indicated his visits would take a while. Apparently Bishop Mose had given him a long list.

With the sound of his buggy wheels rattling down the driveway, she dressed in an old dress and walked toward the woods. She surveyed the swamp on the neighbor's property and the fence line nearby. It would be an easy matter to loosen some wires when the time came—perhaps late summer when the plants were full grown. Reuben would think the goats had forced the wire, left loose by his own carelessness.

She planted for two hours, careful to follow instructions. Although the swamp looked disturbed when she left, she didn't think the bent weeds would be considered unusual. Reuben arrived well after she had changed her clothes and had supper prepared. His face seemed saddened, weary over something.

"You had problems today?" she asked, as she set the table.

Reuben nodded. "The Yost Mullet family is suffering, and I had to talk with them at length. His wife's in poor enough health. Now the vet thinks his cattle have picked up some strange disease. Milk production is way down, and I suppose the church will have to help."

"Nine children," Rachel said, with sympathy in her voice.

Her statement seemed to lift Reuben's load. She wondered why but didn't have to wait long before he answered, "I already left them money."

"You did?" She could tell now he had expected her opposition. "From your goat money?"

"Yes," he said nodding, "this was one of the first times I had money to give someone like that."

"It's good you could help," she told him, her hands busy with the food.

He seemed surprised, and that bothered her. She wondered when he would stop reacting as such. Surely she had been nice before.

That night, in the stillness of their room with Reuben asleep beside her, the horror of her actions nearly overwhelmed her. Her mind raced. Why did she do this? Was she evil beyond even her own imagination?

The money, she told herself, *that's why.* Yet her thoughts refused to quit. Her rationalizations didn't hold their ground. Fear swept over her like the ocean waves she had seen as a child during a family vacation. As if she still stood on that beach, sand between her bare toes, fear overwhelmed her heart just like those great mountains of water crashed onto the shore.

Her mother's arms comforted her then, feeling tender around her shoulders. There was no mother now, just the voice thundering inside her and the blame burning like a fire.

"It's the child," she whispered. "It's his fault."

Her mind sought sanity. She got out of bed, not caring if her movements disturbed Reuben. He stirred and turned in her direction. She knew the moonlight was bright enough to reveal her swollen body, and she groaned to let him know she suffered.

"Baby troubling you?" he asked.

"I think so," she said. "I can't sleep."

"It's *Da Hah's* way," he said. Reverence filled his voice even at this hour of the night.

So unchanged, she thought, *he thinks he's still holy. I absolutely know he loves money. He has become like me—only not enough yet.*

"He has made us fruitful in our old age," Reuben said into the stillness of the night. "Can I get you something?"

"I'll be okay soon," she said and sat down on the edge of the bed.

When he had fallen back to sleep, she slipped under the covers. Something about the sound of his voice had cleared her brain and chased the tormenting demons away. She chose to think it was her own power, the strength of her own will, and resolved to triumph over the obstacles life placed in her way.

The same thing happened when Reuben read the Scripture the next morning in church. At the sight of Reuben's face and the sound of his voice wrapping around the sacred words, her feelings of fear and shame cleared. Rachel dismissed her improved emotions as imagined.

That evening when Luke brought Susie home for supper, she watched Luke's face as he gazed at Susie. He loved her. Goodness seemed to wash over his whole being. She watched in astonishment. Luke had become a man. Yet they didn't have money, she reminded herself. She could never forget that.

As Luke and Susie prepared to leave, Rachel smiled and said, "You have to come back again."

"We will, Mom," Luke said, but the look in his eye was the look of a skeptic. He would not be won over easily. Rachel knew she must do nothing to raise his suspicions, at least till after late summer.

Chapter Twenty-four

The weeks after communion passed slowly for Rebecca. John had taken her to the west district for services that Sunday. Although a few raised their eyebrows, John and Rebecca experienced less discomfort there than they would have at their home district. There they would have had to remain seated, exposed before all, while the other members partook of bread and wine.

Rebecca's time with John had taken on a dismal feel. They talked of everything except what bothered them most. On that subject the door was shut.

"There's all summer," John had said, when he left on Sunday night.

"It seems like plenty of time," Rebecca had replied.

"Surely something will come up."

She held the door open for him. "At least you love me."

"You know I always will."

"Little use if we can't get married."

"Don't say that," he had said, his foot on the step. "There will be a way."

"I hope so," she had replied, and then he was gone. She hadn't followed him out to the buggy but had stayed on the steps in the soft warmth of the night. The light of the kerosene lamp behind her, she had waved at the black shape of his buggy as it left and stood there till the sound faded in the distance, the music of horses' hooves on blacktop.

This afternoon the weather was balmy, the first fluffy clouds of summer in the sky with their promise of more to come. The morning sunrise had been bright red, with great streaks of orange spread skyward. Mattie had taken one look and moved up wash day. Behind the house their hurried work now hung, the wash not yet dry.

Rebecca felt the urge to visit the covered bridge again, and Mattie agreed when Rebecca suggested the outing. As long as Rebecca came back in time to help finish the wash. After some calculations between them, she set out.

Late last fall was the last time she had made the walk to the bridge. With winter and all that had transpired, there had been neither the time nor the inclination for walks. Today the memories of past excursions urged her on.

She had often come to the bridge to get away from the constant work that needed to be done at home, to pause, to hold life at arm's length, to hear water run over rocks, to think of things greater than herself.

At the first curve, a smaller bridge spanned a little creek. Rebecca paused but quickly moved on. She wanted to reach the larger river, which the Harshville covered bridge spanned. A little burg lay beyond, its quaint charm contained by the bridge on one side and a swell of low hills on the other.

The last sweep of road revealed the bridge, which sat low over the river, a noisy contraption when driven across, wrapped in white clapboard, its roof a rusty red. Here John had asked her to be his wife. The memory held its delights, but she sought other delights today.

She desired a release from earthly attachments, to think of God, to notice the marks of His fingers in the land around her, to feel, to reach out to the One who could not be seen. Rebecca stepped off the road and navigated carefully down to the water's edge. The density of the underbrush increased with its nearness to the gurgling current, the path from last fall still there, overhung with the budding life around it but kept back by wild visitors who used this shortcut to the waters below.

A car rattled across the bridge, disturbing the silence but not her enjoyment. Across the water, two children, about preschool age from their size and mannerisms, came down from the houses nearby. They waved to her but soon retreated when they heard the distant sound of their mother's voice.

Rebecca was alone, her spirit still, and her thoughts lifted skyward. *Where is God in this life I am living?* She knew the answer, yet she wondered, *Why don't I see Him?*

Is He so beyond comprehension that He leaves only His will as the path home to His dwelling? Home—she thought—*heaven, a place of comfort.*

She found the thought of death flowing together alongside that of life in this place. The waters came from somewhere beyond her knowledge and flowed eventually to the ocean. There it became a part of that vastness but never ceased to exist. Yet here, the part she could see, was steady, sure, calm.

Like us, she thought, *when we are in His will. He will care and protect us, because we are His creation.*

Her thoughts came back to the present. She hoped to have a home soon with John just beyond those hills on Wheat Ridge—to live, to do what was right, and to die some day when it was His will.

From behind she heard a car approach and waited for the rattle of the bridge. When there was none, it broke her concentration and made her turn her head. The driver had parked on the shoulder, away from the bridge, just around the last bend. Already he had climbed out, the car door closing behind him.

The distance between them was not great. She could see his outline but not the features of his face. He looked older. His car was a dark blue, expensive from what she knew of automobiles. With a glance behind him, he came toward her, his step quick, certain. His arms swung briskly at his side.

If he had been younger, she would have felt fear. He stopped above the bank and made no effort to come down.

"Rebecca Keim?" he asked. His voice reached her clearly.

Surprised she answered, "Yes," but made no move to join him.

"May I come down?" he asked.

"Who are you?" She still felt no fear.

His laugh was low, bubbly, she thought, a sweet note in it, and she felt no guilt at the observation.

"Manny Troyer. I asked at the house. Your mother said you were down here."

She nodded her head, and he slowly made his way down. His age showed more than she had noticed at first.

"Good thing I still know how to climb mountains," he said and laughed again. "I suppose you are surprised that I should be looking for you."

"Yes. I don't know you."

"You know Mary, the van driver. You've met her...a few times," he said smiling again, "and Atlee?"

She knew her face showed the answer, and he nodded again.

"You know them. But who am I? I'm Atlee's uncle. But I'm also something else."

When she said nothing, he continued.

"I'm the executor of Emma's will."

"Emma," she said. The world by the river crashed down, and the other returned with force. "So it is true?"

"You don't know?"

"Yes. Well...they said," she laughed, the sound hollow in her ears. "I've been paying for it already. I guess it had better be real."

"Paying for it? I thought I was supposed to pay you?"

"That's not the way it's working out."

"I see." He paused, watching the flow of water and then continued, "Do you mind if I ask you some questions?"

"You really are the executor?"

"Yes." He paused, then produced his wallet. "I have the lawyer's papers in the car. But for now...I am Manny Troyer." He handed her a plastic card with his picture on it. "And this is my Haiti driver's license."

She studied the picture briefly. He looked younger, his smile broad, head alert, happy too, she thought.

"I see," she said and handed the card back. "You have questions?"

"May I sit down?" He pointed toward the river bank.

"Sure," she shrugged. "Must be long questions."

"Maybe. It's a long story. You don't look like I expected—not at all."

"Really?" she said raising her eyebrows.

"No. Beautiful though. Like Emma."

"Oh…" She felt the red creep up her neck.

"I'm sorry," he said and settled on the ground and shifted to make himself comfortable. "You have to excuse me. That sounded crude. I've been through a lot during the last few weeks." He waved his hand at her when she glanced at him. "I know. You don't understand. I wish you wouldn't have to understand all this, but there seems to be no other way."

She could not have been more puzzled, and she knew her face showed it.

"The questions. Yes." His eyes had found the water again, and he watched it flow downstream.

"So you knew Emma?" she asked, before he could continue.

"Yes." His smile was grim, his eyes still on the water. "I thought I knew her. Long ago. Turns out I didn't, after all. Are you like her?" He turned sharply toward her.

"I don't know. Emma? I doubt. She was much better than me. She was a schoolteacher, a very good one."

"That's what it sounds like." His eyes stared at the ripples now. "Emma was beautiful too. I had myself convinced there couldn't be two of you. That's why I said what I did. I guess I was wrong. You are beautiful. I guess you're like Emma. Not quite but in a way. Does something else mean more to you than love?"

"You don't think I would," she replied, hearing the shock in her own voice mingled with horror.

"Isn't that what you are doing now? This Amish boy, does he know?"

"Know what?"

"Well…about the money, of course. But before that, about Atlee— that you loved him? That you will marry him only because he's Amish?"

She felt anger rise, and the shock subside. "I have no secrets with John. You are welcome to tell him what you wish. He already knows. I want to marry him because I love him. Of course he has to be Amish. It's the money that causes us the trouble. Do you know we couldn't go along with communion this spring?" She knew her voice rose, but she didn't care. "John didn't have to stay back. He stayed back to stand with me. Why don't you just take this money and give it to the family it belongs to. I don't want any of it."

"Emma seemed to think you might be tempted to marry for money," he said, his eyes gazing on the water again.

She knew he waited for her answer. "Then Emma was wrong. I'll give the money back as soon as I can."

"Noble," he said.

She glared at him.

He smiled. "You do look like Emma. Be that as it may, neither of us can do much about the money one way or the other. That's not really why I came to see you."

"Really? You have more nice things to say?"

"Not really. Do you trust Emma?"

"Of course," she said, turning to face him.

"I see."

"Thought for a minute maybe I shouldn't go through with it."

"Would you stop talking in riddles."

He sighed and settled back. "It's like this. Emma wants me to give you some letters—letters she wrote to me but never sent. I was her boyfriend way back when."

She looked sharply at him.

He laughed at her look. "Nothing like that. Just love, not even a kiss, but love."

"Emma?"

"Yes, Emma." His tone carried sorrow. "Seems she wants to be noble now. Noble to the end. After it's too late. Seems a little...well, strange to me, but you knew her better than I did. I mean...in her later life. You sure you trust her?"

Rebecca stood up straight. Emma's face flashed in her memory. "With all my heart."

"I...well, I can just leave, and you'd never know. Maybe that would be best. You sure?"

"Of Emma? Yes," she said.

"I suppose so. Imagine Atlee wants to know too," he sighed and slowly got to his feet. "I have them in the car. Come."

CHAPTER TWENTY-FIVE

W hat did you say about Atlee?" she said, standing beside the car, as he reached inside. What he brought out was a small brown package that bulged in the middle. Behind them they heard the sound of a buggy crossing the bridge. She tensed as the sound ended, the clip of hoofs on pavement approached.

"Someone you know?" he asked, when it had passed.

She nodded. That it was the deacon's wife, she didn't inform him.

"Oh, Atlee," he said, as if the thought had just returned.

"Yes," she said, her mind distracted. "Why would Atlee be interested in Emma and in what she left?"

"Only because it involves you."

"Me? He's engaged."

"Was." He raised his eyebrows at the look on her face. "Don't blame me. I didn't do so well myself."

"But he knows I'm getting married. He wouldn't...think I would change that?"

"They had problems anyway. Atlee didn't know about this then. He thinks it might work in now—at least he wants to know."

"Wants to know what?" She didn't try to keep the anger off her face.

"Sorry," he said. "I really am. As I said, perhaps it was a mistake, but you said you trusted Emma. You want to see what she wrote?" He held out the package.

Rebecca hesitated, then took it, her mind a whirl of conflicted thoughts. Yet the thought of Emma brought sanity to the moment. Emma, her solid rock through her school years, her source of wisdom.

"When you have read them, write me. There's an address in the front. It's mine. Either way, please write. I'll wait, okay?" He made as if to leave.

"Letters?" she asked, the package held at a distance.

"Emma's," he replied nodding. "Mine aren't in there. Not necessary. She wanted you to read hers."

Rebecca stepped back as he closed the car door, and then he abruptly swung it open again.

"I'm sorry," he said, his smile apologetic. "I forget my manners. Let me drive you home."

She thought to protest but knew the time to bring in the wash had already passed. Her mother would no doubt have the first hamper inside and be glancing out the window in the direction of the bridge, ever more frantic with each moment that passed.

He opened the car door on her side, and she slid in. With a soft thump, he shut the door, the sound causing a lump to form in her throat. Why she wasn't sure. It seemed to transport her from one life to another. From a horse and buggy to a car, shut in and caught, yet she had driven in automobiles before.

Perhaps it's this, she thought, glancing toward the package on her lap.

He turned the key, looked behind, and eased the car forward. "Getting old," he said and groaned. "Oh, to be young again."

She had to chuckle in spite of herself. "You're not that old. You said you worked in Haiti. Where Mary goes?"

He nodded. "I'm the director there."

"Not too old for that?"

"Keeps me young," he said. "Helps at least. Good mission down there. You ever think of visiting?"

"I'm Amish."

"Amish come," he said smiling, "from Holmes County, some-times."

"That's what Mary said."

He slowed down for the Keim driveway, then accelerated up the driveway. Used to the slow climb in a buggy, it seemed just seconds before he stopped beside the kitchen door. Mattie came around the corner of the house, a hamper full of wash in her hands.

"There we are." He smiled again, then nodded in Mattie's direction. "Tell your mother not to work too hard. Let me know."

She thanked him and got out. The car door shut with a soft thump. Mattie nodded her head as he took off, but her smile disappeared the moment the car was out of sight.

"I'm sorry I'm late," Rebecca said. "He's the executor of Emma's will."

Mattie sighed, the cloth hamper clutched in her hands. "That does explain it. I hope you got everything straightened out."

"Not really. He gave me letters from Emma. I have no idea what's in them. Let me take that." Rebecca took the hamper from her mother's hands.

"I hope it's not more trouble," Mattie said, as they walked toward the house. "You really don't need it."

"I'm sure anything Emma wrote…won't cause more trouble."

"She left you the money," Mattie told her. "Don't be too sure. Did anyone see you while you talked to him? What was his name? He told me but I forgot."

"Manny Troyer. And the deacon's wife went by."

"Oh, well… It's explainable, I should think. Though I'm getting tired of all the explaining. Troyer? He wouldn't be related to Atlee, would he?"

"He's Atlee's uncle."

Mattie held the front door open. "I don't like this Rebecca. I really don't. This is all disturbing, much too disturbing for our lives. For you and John too. Nothing good can come out of all this. First there's money, lots of it. Then *The Budget* article about you. This is just too much. Now you get a visit from a Mennonite man. At least he's older. He seemed nice enough. Don't get me wrong."

"Maybe this will explain things." Rebecca motioned with her eyes toward the package that lay on top of the wash.

"One would hope so," Mattie said sighing. "I have to start supper. Can you handle the rest of the wash?"

"Sure," Rebecca said, setting the hamper down, "I'll just put the envelope upstairs." Her mother had already disappeared into the kitchen.

Rebecca left the package on her dresser, resisting the temptation of see what was inside. That would have to wait until she had more time. Anything from Emma needed to be opened with care, with reverence.

Outside Matthew rattled into the driveway with his four sisters, home from school. The rush of the evening had begun. Downstairs her sisters had their lunch buckets all lined up on the kitchen table and had disappeared themselves, no doubt under orders from Mattie to change. She quickly unpacked and placed the lunch buckets in the pantry and then grabbed the hamper again.

When Rebecca came back inside with another hamper of wash, Katie, the oldest of the school girls, was busy at work, piles of folded wash around her.

"Where's your sister?" Rebecca said, meaning the next oldest. "She should be helping."

"She's out here," Mattie said from the kitchen. "I'll need Viola's help with supper. Martha can put things away. Just tell her how."

Eight-year-old Martha didn't look too happy but followed the instructions Rebecca gave her. A trip upstairs with her arms full of folded wash was made without mishap.

"You listen to Katie while I get more," Rebecca instructed and left for what she hoped would be the last hamper of wash. Not everything fit in, though, and another trip outside to the wash line was needed.

Matthew passed her, on the way to the barn for chores. She stayed until the pile of wash was manageable for her sisters, then joined Matthew in the barn. He was already on the second round of milking, surrounded by the swish of the two milkers and the sound of chewing cows.

Her younger brother would soon be a man, and she was not sure she liked the thought. She felt old herself, filled with the need to slow time down.

"The boys talked about you and John today," Matthew informed her, his moments free as he waited for a milker to finish. "The older ones."

"Really," she said, not that interested.

"They seem to think there's something to it—you marrying John for money."

"How did you find out about this?"

"Not from around here," he said making a face. "If you stay back from communion, then John does too. Doesn't take too smart a fellow. Even he'll figure out something's going on."

"Emma left me money in her will. We're not taking it," she informed him, since he already seemed to know.

"Meaning you and John?"

"Yes."

"You have to get married first. Right?"

"Yes."

"Deacon says he's not allowing it. Staying Amish ought to be from the heart. That's what his boy said he said. It should never be for money."

"I had nothing to do with it. Really I didn't."

"You didn't know Emma would do this?"

"No, of course not," she snapped. "Sorry. You don't deserve that."

Matthew shrugged. He bent over to unfasten the milker. The other one quit at the same time, and she went toward it. "I believe you."

"Thanks." She felt relief even if he was just her younger brother.

He lifted the milker toward the next cow and used his shoulder to keep its tail away from the machine. The snap struck him across his middle, but he ignored it.

"I've seen you and John. I think you love him."

"I would hope so," she said, moving to the next cow.

"I mean…not for money. I told the boys that."

"Thanks," she said again. A comfortable silence settled between them.

With the third round of cows done, she left Matthew to finish up and returned to the kitchen. Martha and Katie had the wash completed and the supper table set. Her mother motioned toward the oven and said, "The casserole is almost done. Can you see to it?"

Rebecca lifted the steaming pan and carefully placed it on hot pads in the center of the kitchen table. She knew the rest of the routine. She sliced the bread, the thick slabs falling over one by one as she cut. Butter came from the pantry, store bought because her mother claimed it was cheaper than homemade.

The pecan pie came out of the pantry, made two days ago and still fresh. Mattie already had a fresh salad tossed and pulled a pan of just-set Jell-O from the refrigerator. Rebecca found the strawberry and raspberry jam, which joined the bread and butter on the table.

With supper out, Rebecca sat down, while her sisters slid in on the bench seat against the wall. Mattie still bustled about, apparently up to plans for later meals. Rebecca hoped her father and Matthew would be in soon. She couldn't wait to get upstairs and read Emma's letters.

"Call Dad," Mattie said in Katie's direction.

"I already did," she said.

"Try again. Things are getting cold," Rebecca told her.

Katie slid out of her seat, went to the door, and hollered her loudest, "Supper."

There was no response from the barn, but a door slammed in the distance.

"They're coming," Mattie said. She sat down with a sigh. "My, it's been a long day."

"It's report card time next week," Katie informed her.

"I hope all your grades are good," Rebecca told them.

"We try," Viola informed her. "We have a good teacher."

"You all do," Mattie told them. "We can be thankful for that. Good teachers are hard to come by. All of you did well last report card time. I'm sure you'll be okay this time."

"We work hard," Katie said.

"I like my little girls," Mattie told them. Her eyes found each of their faces. "All of you. The big one too. How fast you are growing up."

Rebecca smiled at her sisters, as they brightened up under their mother's praise. She was surprised to find she liked it herself, even if she was the big one.

Outside the sound of Lester and Matthew's entry came with a shuffle of feet. They took turns at the wash bowl, then came straight to the kitchen table.

"My...my, what a feast," Lester boomed. "We are blessed with a good cook."

"Just sit down and eat," Mattie informed him, but the edges of her face showed a smile. Apparently she liked praise too, Rebecca thought.

"I'm going to have a wife, one who cooks like this all the time," Matthew informed them, as he took his chair.

"I thought you weren't getting into such troubles." Rebecca teased him.

He made a face at her.

"Now...now. We all grow up. Let's just be thankful for that," Lester said. He bowed his head in prayer, and they all followed.

CHAPTER TWENTY-SIX

Rebecca excused herself as soon as the supper dishes were done. Her mother seemed to understand her haste to get upstairs. "Let me know what they say," Mattie whispered because the others were in the living room.

"I need to talk to you later," her father said, as she walked to the upstairs door. *The Budget* lay open on his lap.

"Surely not," she said, her eyes searching what he had read.

"No," he said chuckling and then sobered. His eyes made a motion around the room. Rebecca knew what that meant—when the others are in bed. She wished he didn't want to talk tonight, obviously about something serious. It didn't take much for her to venture a guess.

From the size of the envelope, the letters would occupy her time all evening. Yet her father's talk would have to take priority.

"Yes," she said and opened the stair's door.

Apparently Mattie overheard and stuck her head in from the kitchen. "You should do it now, Lester," she said. "Rebecca has some reading to do."

"The children." His gaze went around the room again.

"I know," Mattie responded. "Can it wait?"

"I suppose so," he said smiling. "It's trouble that doesn't seem to go away."

Rebecca felt relief, thankful for the allowance of time this evening to spend with her beloved Emma's letters. Perhaps she would find courage, even hope, from them to face the subject her father wished to address.

"Thanks," she said, "maybe tomorrow night."

Her father nodded, focusing on his *Budget*.

She took the first two steps of the stairs and shut the door behind her. In her room, she gently opened the package and a multitude of letters tumbled out. Twelve, she counted slowly, and a cover letter, apparently written in a man's hand.

She lit her kerosene lamp, opened the window shade to let in what daylight remained, and sat on the bed.

> *Dear Rebecca,*
>
> *I haven't met you yet, but will have by the time you read this letter. I have already cried my tears over what is contained in these letters. I don't know what your response will be. I hope it all turns out well. If it were up to me, I would not pass this on to you, and perhaps I won't once I meet you. Obviously if you are reading this, I already have.*
>
> *These are letters I had no idea existed. Emma sent them to me, at my office in Berlin, Ohio, just the other week. All of them were stamped but unopened, till I opened them. They are the record of a part of her life no one knew about. I wish she had not kept it secret, especially from me, but regrets are too late now.*
>
> *She will refer back to letters I wrote her. I think it's self-explanatory, so I have not included them. And just so we are clear with each other, Atlee doesn't know what is contained in these letters. He knows only that he wishes things had turned out differently between the two of you.*
>
> *I told him he ought to speak with you, and he said he would. That was when I told him to wait until I received your response. I hope with all my heart the two of you will not make the same mistake Emma and I made.*

The letters are dated, and let me assure you, Emma wants you to read them. The explanation comes at the end.

The best,

Manny Troyer

Rebecca found the first letter, its date written on the outside, written in what she recognized as Emma's handwriting. Many times she had seen that neat handwriting during school years, the letters written in large expressive curves. She opened the letter and turned the kerosene lamp up as high as it would go. Just before the moment the flame turned into smoke, she stopped.

"Manny," it began.

I just got your letter today. I won't call you "dear" or some such thing. Not because I don't want to, but because it hurts too much. I know you know as well as I do, this must go no further. My brother spoke to me at length, and I think sense has entered my head. You surely know he meant no harm. He does what he thinks is God's will about this matter.

My intense feelings are evident. I have only to pause to feel the pain or look into my heart to see how much I care about you. Remember when you dropped me off the last time and Mullet, "M-Jay" as we call him, was there? At first I was angry that he would interfere. I now see this was the kindest thing he could have done. He sees his move as the rescue of his sister, and I have to agree, Manny, no matter how much it hurts.

The world is what it is, Manny. Surely you can see that. Our worlds are so far apart. Our people think so completely differently. In some ways it would be easier had you been from the Englisha. At least then I could think of leaving it all behind, running off into the night perhaps because that is what it would seem like to me. Surely you understand.

Why my heart doesn't agree with me, I don't understand, but as M-Jay says, we must not be led around by our hearts. It is already given to another, to God, who has called us to a higher purpose. Sunday at preaching, you were all I could think about. I felt so unclean, so wrong in bringing my fleshly desires into the very temple of God. That is how it seemed to me.

When I listened to what the preacher said, I was even more ashamed. It seemed as if he were speaking to me, Manny. Maybe you don't understand. I think and hope you do. Can you not see what forsaking the world means to me? It means you. I heard the message so clearly.

I suppose you suspected the preacher knew about us, but I know he didn't. Only M-Jay knows, and he is too loyal to me to spread such things around. His heart is like gold, Manny. I wish you would believe that.

Just writing this, I know I will never mail this letter. I'm sorry, Manny. If I did I know where the path would lead— right back to you. I would not be able to resist if I knew that you knew. It is better this way, to walk in the will of God in silence, to live a life of holiness.

It is holy, Manny. It is. I tell myself that when my pillow is wet with tears. I whisper your name when I can no longer stand the pain. Surely God will understand, since I did not seek out this love for you. The preacher said it was lust, lust for the world. I heard him as plain as day, though he could not have known about us.

How could he know how much I want to see you? How could he know how much my heart yearns, aches with feeling? Did God do this? I cannot believe He did. It must be right. How could it be otherwise. We must have fallen, Manny, fallen with the rest of the world. This must be what Eve felt when she saw the apple in the garden. If it is, then I am not surprised that she ate it.

Manny, I know you never dared kiss me. You didn't because you thought you'd preserve what was sacred to you. Perhaps you thought that in your touch I would feel we were unclean and turn away from you. You cannot know, I suppose, but if you had tried I might not have been able to resist.

I can only imagine what your kiss would have been like. The burning, the flame it would have ignited in me. Yet in my imagination I can resist, but in reality I'm afraid I couldn't. So, Manny, your holiness was your undoing, if you want to look at it like that.

For this I have you to thank. I hope God will reward you for your effort. There are other girls in your world much better suited for you than I am. Surely you know that.

Emma Miller

Rebecca let her breath out. The sound came slowly, as if she hadn't breathed for a long time. So Emma had loved a man. Her hand paused, then reached for the next letter. The single page came out easily.

Manny,

I will not say "dearest" or "I love you" even at the end because this is the end, Manny. I received your second letter, then your third. I write now to keep my heart from breaking. That is the only reason. I will never mail this letter. It cannot be.

The pain is almost more than I can bear. I know now that you feel the same. I also see that you have come to the same conclusion I did. What we feel cannot go further. I did see you at the door when you came. It took all the control I had to keep from opening that door and running into your arms.

I know the gulf into which I would have fallen would have been my damnation. I told myself so again and again all the time you stood there. It seemed like hours, though it couldn't have been. I watched you go, saw your broad shoulders and your firm step even in your rejection.

I cannot believe God made a man more wonderful than you, Manny. I just can't understand why He would have to make him a Mennonite, but then perhaps that is our fallen state. I place my mind on spiritual things, as the preacher said the other Sunday. It is the only way I save myself from insanity—that and putting these thoughts on paper.

I never would have imagined my heart to be capable of what it feels. The preacher said that too. How wicked our hearts can be. How they betray us. How their depths are past finding out. Only God can find them out and judge them properly. I hope He is judging mine.

So it is goodbye. I suppose I knew that when I didn't go to the door, but your letter made it official. My writing the words down makes it even more so. I hope God is watching as we part ways. I hope He finds pleasure in the cost. His altar is hard, His requirements seem too much at times, yet we must forsake everything. I just never knew what everything was.

Goodbye, Manny. I have no tears left to cry. I hope you find our love again in the eyes of another girl, in her arms. I say that, but I'm screaming a silent "no" so loud it must be heard throughout the house. This is silly, I know, but it seems real.

It feels as if I'm dead inside, as if the sun will never come up again, yet of course it will, just as life will go on. I kiss this page because I know it will not lead me astray as your lips would have.

Emma Miller

Rebecca folded the page carefully, her emotions in shock at what she had read, in unbelief that Emma could have written them. Yet there it was, all clearly in Emma's handwriting. Otherwise, she knew, she would not have believed this possible.

Outside in the hall, she heard Matthew's footsteps on the stairs, heard him pass her room, and then the door shut with a soft click.

CHAPTER TWENTY-SEVEN

She reached for the next letter. The date was a year later.

Manny,

I say "dearest" now because I know you will not read this and because the words just come up out of my heart. I have confessed my sin before God, and yet it's still there. Surely I have forgiveness. God must know what I feel anyway, so why keep it a secret from Him, as if that were possible. It does more to help the pain than anything.

Emery Yoder's David asked me home on Sunday. I haven't told anyone, nor will I. Yet I am telling you because you won't read this letter. How strange the world is. I said "no." Why, you ask? Was he ugly or clumsy or not handsome? No. He's one of the best looking young Amish men we have.

I know several girls who have been waiting with high hopes. I suppose one of them will get the question next. That's the way things go around here. They call it love, but I know better, Manny. I know it because of you.

David will make a fine husband and would have made me a fine husband. Before you, Manny, I would have said "yes" in a heartbeat. I would have thought my ideas of him to be more than enough. He's got a farm in the family and should have possession of it before he marries. I don't think that means anything to me. I suppose that's your fault too.

I must have changed, Manny. I don't know how. Some have commented, said I look sad lately. I suppose it shows on my face even when I try to hide it, and I do try. M-Jay said the strangest thing the other day. He told me that if I forget about you, he'll pass his inheritance on to me instead of his children.

I don't suppose that's much because he just bought his first farm, and his children are still young. I know he thought the delight on my face was due to the money, but it wasn't. His kindness is what moved me. He does give me a place to stay, as he has since our parents passed away. I try to help him out by doing what I can around the house and staying out of his wife's way. She's nice enough, but two women in the house at the same time is never good.

I stay in the room attached to their house—a dawdy haus *from the previous Amish owners, only I'm not a* dawdy *or a* mommy. *Instead I, young Emma, volunteered to teach this year. It's still summertime, and so it seems a long time away. Yet it will come, as all things do.*

I never thought of myself as a teacher. The thought just came to me last week. Why don't you teach, Emma? Just out of the blue like that. It must have been God bringing me comfort, as poor M-Jay's solution surely didn't. As if I would have let you go for money. The thought is too awful to even think about.

For the first time, I felt joy spring up in my heart again. I thought it was dead, Manny. I really did. I thought it would never live again, and yet the thought of teaching brought a little jump back. I felt a little of what you used to bring me. No, not even close, just the slightest, tiniest, smallest, little bit of the same thing. Yet it was enough to live for again.

You will never know, Manny, how thankful I am.

Emma Miller

Beside her the kerosene lamp flickered. Smoke puffed upward and darkened the upper glass. Rebecca reached over and turned the wick down, a slight turn, done with practiced experience. The next letter slid out of the envelope, and she held it in the other hand.

Manny,

Greetings. It's strange writing to a person whom I once knew, one who will never read this. Perhaps you've changed now, but you don't seem changed to me. You will ever be the man I loved.

Another boy asked me home Sunday night. The fifth one now since David. I said "no" again. Maybe I should have said "yes," but I didn't. I suppose it will be my last chance. It's been five years now, and I'm already known as the old maid. Three years ago, the unmarried boys my age were gone. The question on Sunday came from a widower. He was visiting from somewhere. He looked okay, and I wavered but turned him down.

This time I was found out and soundly chewed out by M-Jay. He thinks I've lost my mind. Rather he thinks it's the money, the inheritance he's promised me. I think he regrets it now. He thinks I'm turning away marriageable men because I know I don't need support.

I'm certain I'm not, but then how do I trust my heart? Perhaps it is deceiving me again. The awful thought came to me the other day. What if it is the money that's making me do what I'm doing? I think it's my convictions, my devotion to God, my love for the truth. But horrors, what if it's not?

To make matters worse, M-Jay is prospering. I don't know how he makes all his money, but he makes plenty. I'm sure this farm is already paid off. Even with the expenses of supporting his growing family, it is.

I put these thoughts away and think of you. I wonder if you've ever married. Is there someone else in your arms? Someone who loves you? You deserve it. Yet I want you to be as lonely as I am. I want you to still hurt like I hurt. I thought it might get better, and at times it does, then something reminds me of you.

I will admit something here that I wouldn't admit to anyone else. Do you know the reason I almost said "yes" on Sunday? It was because he reminded me of you. They said his wife had died of cancer. They didn't have any children, from what I understood, and were only married a few years. Long enough to have children, I would think, but they must have been childless for some reason out of their control.

He had a kind face, just as yours always was. It's been a while now—years or so it seems since I saw you. I don't know how you look now, but I can imagine. They said his name was Mose, a baby sort of name, but it gave me a start.

The other women were all so helpful to him. Not that I'm a woman—just a girl. Levi Troyer's wife became his message bearer. I think he stayed with them.

She said he wanted to speak to me. All flustered she was, more red than I became. I stepped outside and walked toward the barn. There was no sense in hiding the thing. It's not like I'm young anymore.

He met me beside the remaining buggies—people were already leaving. I felt sorry for him. Poor fellow, he really was dear. His accent was Pennsylvanian, but that could be lived with. He said his wife had passed away, which I already knew, the women having made certain I did. I think a lot of people were in on this one.

He said he thought it was Da Hah's villa, *as if any of us*

*knows that. Quite a mouthful to say right from the get-go,
but that's what he said. He felt we were led together and said
something about how the trip had gone from Pennsylvania.
He said his heart had been heavy, burdened greatly since his
wife's passing, that today was the first day since then any girl
had brought hope to his mind.*

*I saw our children in his eyes, Manny—a dozen of them.
It was the strangest thing, yet it was as if he already knew
what would be, that I would say "no." His eyes were so sad.
He said he understood, that he didn't have much to offer. I
told him that was not the reason, but he didn't believe me. I
could tell.*

*How could he know what M-Jay promised me? No one knows
but me and M-Jay, and I know the money means nothing.
I turned him down because I loved you, Manny. It was too
much to ask. It would have hurt too much to allow my heart
to care again.*

*I'm afraid I would have cared for him, Manny. Love, I do
know I would have loved his children. I would have loved
them, but I thought of you. I told him "no," Manny, and you
will never even know.*

*We start school again tomorrow. This will be my fourth term.
I think the parents like me. The pupils perhaps do. I love
teaching. It still warms my heart. I think I will start wearing black every Sunday. Perhaps then the marriageable men
won't bother me, but I don't think they will anyway.*

*The ones my age are married, and word has gotten around
to the others, the few there are. It must be something to love
another person, to keep a home, have a family, children around
you, to look forward to growing old. I think sometimes I am*

growing older on the inside faster than I'm aging on the outside.

Goodnight, Manny, wherever you are.

Emma Miller

Rebecca closed the letter. She noticed the flicker of the lamp's flames dancing on the wall. The window was dark, and she got up to draw the blind. Carefully she opened her door. Downstairs the light was still on, its beam shone on the bottom step. Her parents must still be up.

Both Matthew and her sisters' rooms were dark under the doorways. She wondered if anyone would notice that she was up late. Hardly she decided. Her parents wouldn't come up unless there was a reason. Rebecca returned to the bed and slid out the next letter.

Manny,

I do declare I am using this as therapy, as the Englisha *would say. I read about those in one of our school books. Hopefully no one ever finds this. I suppose it would be more damaging to my reputation than anything else. Not that anyone would hold it against me. Amish, after all, go by what one does, not by what one feels.*

To have loved a Mennonite has happened before—I suppose often enough to be understood. It's the staying single part that might not be excused. I have the feeling my being such a beloved schoolteacher is cutting me the slack I need. This allows me a place in peoples' minds where I can dwell safely.

Isn't that strange? Emma's being wasted. That's what they'd say otherwise and hold it against me. It must be the mercy of the Lord extended to me. There can be no other reason, at least in my mind.

If I were ugly or deformed, they would understand. Passed

over for a reason, but not how I am now. You always thought I was beautiful, Manny. Didn't you? I think so. If you did, then I will always believe I am.

By the way, there is no mental illness in our family. M-Jay is well respected, and so are his children. No signs point in such a direction as explanation for the life his sister has chosen—a life that's barren, unfruitful, without offspring to build the Lord's kingdom in the generations to come.

But I am a schoolteacher. I laugh out loud with joy, Manny, because I love being a teacher. I became one because it made me feel a little like being with you, and teaching has become my salvation. Is that not how it should be? Is that not what one would expect? Anything to do with you is good for me.

Thinking about this, I had my first doubt. What if I was wrong way back all those years ago? What if I misunderstood? What if M-Jay misunderstood the will of God? What if this good that seems to come out of so little that is you would have been an even greater good if I had all of you?

I thought about it and then decided I was wrong. I saw a Mennonite drive by today. He drove slowly past the schoolhouse. I have no idea what he was up to. Perhaps he was looking for someone's house and had been given the schoolhouse as a bearing point.

Whatever the reason, I imagined me as a Mennonite driving a car, and I couldn't bear the thought. It was too much, Manny. One's faith comes first even before the love of a man. Surely you can understand that.

Then there is the inheritance. M-Jay has just purchased his second farm. He still needs to pay it off. How he does so well is hard to imagine. Others around here are not doing as well.

He told me again he plans on keeping his promise. I told him not to bother, but he thinks it's a bigger deal than I do. I almost think he believes it's the reason he's prospering. Do you think that could be true?

If it is, then things are really strange in this world—Da Hah blessing a man for helping keep his sister in the faith. I wonder.

Emma Miller

CHAPTER TWENTY-EIGHT

Rebecca opened the next letter. Her hands moved slowly as she slid the paper out. The house was silent around her.

> *Manny,*
>
> *It's been twenty years now. I just checked the date of the first letter. I am still teaching school. M-Jay's wife isn't in good health. It's the one thing that doesn't seem to prosper for him. His oldest boy has just married, quite well I thought, but then what do I know about such things.*
>
> *M-Jay has three other boys and one girl—a haughty child if I do say so myself. I wish her mother would bring her under control. I suppose she tries, and M-Jay too. She has just started dating. I think she's a bit young, but then what do I know. I have only you and me to judge by, and that didn't turn out too well.*
>
> *The girl, Rachel, is dating a boy from the community. He seems nice enough. He comes from the other district and never went to my school. M-Jay seems to dislike him. Why, I'm not sure.*

Rebecca paused, then read on about the family and Emma's schoolwork, the turning of time and pages in Rebecca's hands. The dying started—aunts, uncles, a few accidents, and then M-Jay's wife. She glanced at the clock once, saw it was near eleven, but kept going. The letter that especially held her attention was written during a time she was all too familiar with.

> *I am seeing it happen before my very eyes. I do declare, Manny, if it isn't the two of us all over again, a little younger than we were but the same.*

> *The girl's name is Rebecca, just out of the lower grades. I feel a special affection for some of my children, and she is one of them. The boy too, as far as that goes. That such love happens so young is amazing. They are in love just as you and I were. I watch and say nothing, but my heart burns.*

> *They have such decent manners, the two of them, as Amish children do and should. I doubt if being inappropriate will ever cross their minds. Rebecca's mom seems aware of her daughter's feelings but allows her to continue being around the boy. They see each other in school, of course, and some on weekends.*

> *I assume someone will soon intervene because they are getting to the age where their affections for each other will begin to raise eyebrows. How sweet, I think, watching them walk home from a day at school. What must it be like to fall in love so young and have it last throughout life? I will not be surprised to see them date as soon as they are old enough.*

Rebecca read on, then opened the next letter. Her interest was peaked when she read the second paragraph.

> *M-Jay died today. Not unexpectedly, but I still feel completely alone. I wasn't expecting it, Manny. I also wasn't expecting the fury that rose over the inheritance. No one knew, of course, but M-Jay kept his word. He was true to the end. It would have been easy for him to tell me "no," but he didn't.*

Rachel especially took it hard. I suppose I had some idea how much her mind was on the money. The problem is mine is also on the money. I've always told myself the money had nothing to do with my decisions. In my heart I still believe it, but when the time came, I wanted it, Manny. I wanted the money with an intensity that alarmed me and still does.

Here I am, though. The funeral's over. I'm living on the home place. Rachel's fuming is about over, I think. The spoiled child. It will do her good to live without her heart's desire for a few more years. Eventually I'll see to it that she gets it back.

In the meantime, I have the inheritance in my hand. It's strange how it affects me, even soothes my heart—the freshness of it, the numbers in the bank, the rolling fields that bear my name, the animals that live and die because I want them to.

It's delightful how men, young and old alike, look at me, that intent look of respect in their eyes. I never got such looks before when I was Emma-the-schoolteacher. Sure I still teach, but I am now the Emma who owns three farms and money besides. You would almost think I was in love, Manny. Isn't that crazy? But then the thought breaks my heart, and I cry. I'm left with an agony that doesn't go away.

The inheritance increases in value each day. I take comfort in it. I tell myself it is Da Hah's reward for my faithfulness to Him and the faith all these years. Does His Word not say, those who obey Him will prosper?

Rebecca glanced at the clock, its hands were approaching midnight, but she pulled another letter out.

Manny,

I am frightened tonight and sick of myself at the same time. Remember the boy and girl I told you about? His parents are leaving the Amish. I was expecting Rebecca to show up in shock at school, her face long, but she hasn't. She looks resigned, but not worried. Instead she is almost happy.

I wish I knew why. I thought at first she had not been told, but then I asked her, and she blushed. She knows, but she is not devastated. Does she know something I don't?

But that's not really why I'm frightened or sick of myself. I found out today that I'm dying. Yes, Manny, the end cannot be far away. Sure, the doctor comforted me with words. He said with the advances in medicine...all those things...and I do have money. It will be a while yet, he said. Years, in his words, but I know better.

My time on this earth is short. The preachers have always said that, but this is different, more different, more real, more shocking than I had ever imagined. What is it like over there? Do they really have streets of gold? Are there really rewards for all the sacrifices we have made here?

I think the unthinkable, the awful, and I come up with only doubts. I am sick of myself. The money, the farms, they now just make it worse. I know I came by them by no desire of my own, but I have enjoyed them willingly enough. I have even tried to use their pleasure to heal my heart.

Will I have children in heaven, Manny? I ask, and I tremble at what I have lost. Maybe I should have had my eyes opened years ago. I wonder if you ever had any. Is there a boy or a girl who carries your blood, the color of your eyes, your twinkle in their eyes, your ability to love. Are you childless, Manny?

Can God really make up for my mistakes? I shudder at my nerve in asking, yet I shall soon see Him, so I might as well ask now as later. He is not one who doesn't know what I feel anyway.

I should have loved the widower, Manny, all those years ago. I would have felt disloyal to you, to our love, but it would have been worth it. I tried to do the right thing, but it was the wrong thing. I see now an even worse thing. I should have loved you, Manny. I should have. I never thought the day would come when I would say that. Is it because I am dying?

I thought you were wrong then, but that wrong would be easier to make right than what my life has become. I know it, Manny. I know it with every ache and beat of my weary heart. I'm sure my heart is dying because I never allowed it to love. The doctor would tell me I'm crazy, but I just know. I know because I was there through all the pain.

Now I am left with numbness. The pain doesn't even come that often anymore. That is frightening too. I am dying, Manny, as sure as my heart has been dying for a long time.

Rebecca didn't look at the clock, as she removed the last letter. The pages rustled in her hand, the kerosene lamp flickered, and she reached over to turn up the flame without her eyes leaving the white paper.

Manny, Manny, dearest Manny,

At last I can say it. I now know what to do. The relief is immense. My joy returned for a while at least, and then the sorrow returns. Rebecca was here today. She told me the story of her and Atlee, and I told her what I was supposed to say.

Even in my dying, I could not but say what is right. I told her she must, of course, marry the Amish boy. The words came out of my mouth, but my heart was crying. I'm too old to change, Manny. I know it, and I accept it. I saw that today. I can never change, but I know I should have. I should have loved you.

In my dying I can still save Rebecca. Perhaps that is the atonement for my sins, the purging of my life. That in death I should save another and be rid of this accursed money in the process, I cannot but look at it so. It brought me a false joy, comfort for what should not have been comforted, peace where there should have been none.

Rebecca is young. She can do what I cannot do. She has the time I do not have. Today I mailed the first letter to my lawyer. In the letter were my instructions to draw up the proper papers. I will use you as the executor of the will. I don't know how I know you are still alive, but you are Manny. Even if you've married, your wife surely won't object because I'm no longer here. That is by the time you read this. Perhaps you have even told her about me, in which case she already understands.

I will mail you these letters, so Rebecca can read them. You can too, and I say I'm sorry again, but there is no longer time to make things right between you and me. Rebecca must not make the mistake I made. She must follow her heart. She must dare to love what is forbidden. She must.

I will write the will to say she doesn't receive the money if she marries outside the faith. What joy the thought of her choice brings me. She's a good girl in a way I never was. She has deep convictions. She will choose love. Let her spurn the money, as I never could. Let her take it under her feet as our Lord did the serpent.

I know she will. Rebecca will never let the love of the inheritance influence her, as I know it influenced me. I told myself it never did, but I doubt that now. My heart is quite wicked, Manny. I am sorry. It should have been yours, and you could have saved it. I know you could have. Left to myself, I only became a worse person than I already was.

This will open Rebecca's eyes. Perhaps my confession here will help. Let her see all of this, Manny. Let her see and reject what I did wrong. It is my hope that out of the dust of my broken life may grow another who is wiser than I am. She will return to her love for Atlee. I know she will.

Goodbye, Manny. It really is goodbye this time. I go to cross the river soon and before my time because my heart has failed me in more ways then one. Rachel can have her cursed money, the farms, the animals, the emptiness they all bring. I would take your kiss, Manny, any day—just one in place of them all.

Emma

P.S. Emma. I think that's what they will call me in heaven. The last name "Miller" doesn't belong. If they insist, I'll tell them it should have been "Troyer." Your name sounds so much better.

CHAPTER TWENTY-NINE

Rebecca got up from the bed, the letter clutched between numb fingers, walked over to her window, and let the shade up. Outside the stars twinkled, little flames of light in a dark sky. The tail end of the Milky Way's great wash dropped almost to the horizon. Behind her the kerosene lamp flickered, its light dimmed by the display of glory in the sky.

"I'm not Emma," Rebecca whispered. The letter slipped from her fingers and slid to the floor. The pages landed without a sound.

What am I going to do? she wondered. *What if someone finds out how Emma felt?* She could imagine the talk, the questions, and it would make things between her and John all the worse—almost impossible.

She realized the letter was no longer in her hand. Panic filled her, the night exaggerated the fears, and wild thoughts filled her mind. Was the letter already lost, swept away from the eyes of the world?

On the floor she saw the white pages and bent to pick them up. The letters would have to be hidden or destroyed just as the ring had been hidden. As the thought registered in her mind, she recoiled. That action had lead only to distress and finally revelation, which played its part in her present trouble. The letters would have to go.

Rebecca walked back to where the package lay on the bed. Several of the papers had slid to the floor, and she gathered them up carefully. A search confirmed that she had found all of them. Tomorrow they would be sent back. The conclusion came quickly. She would tell her mother, and Mattie would understand.

They were letters from Emma, she would say, which Emma wanted her to read. They contained private things, and Rebecca wanted them returned to the Mennonite man, since they really belonged to him. More than that, she wouldn't tell. She wouldn't need to tell.

Released of her urgent concern, she lay on the bed and let Emma's emotions sweep over her. Tears for the agony expressed stung her cheeks. Then she froze in shock, wondering if she truly was like Emma. Had she rejected Atlee for reasons her heart would regret?

The question took her breath away. The voice behind the question was Emma's, and she would have given it no credence, but the years of admiration, of respect, of submission demanded an answer. *Was Emma right?*

She clutched the edge of the blanket, fear gripping her heart. *Am I deceiving myself as Emma apparently had? Does devotion to my faith drive my decisions? Does it cloud my judgment, blind me to the happiness I could have? Will I grow old, only to regret this choice, this direction of my heart?*

Visions of Atlee returned, as if from the faint and distant past. She remembered his eyes, his face, the tone of his voice, the ring he handed her, the sound of water under the bridge. She wondered at the memory, whether she had extinguished the flame by force of will, by dedication to a higher cause.

She saw the answer, but her trust of Emma caused her to hesitate before reaching to open the door to her future. Then she trembled and crossed over the threshold. In honesty, she found the courage to step forward. In her sorrow, she left behind her youth, her faith in the absolute, which was Emma. She chose Rebecca. She wept because she was alone, fearful to sever the past. But then it was done, and she cried for joy, which sprang unbidden, unasked for, guilt its shadow, as if she had transgressed against the holy.

She felt a great love for John. It washed her being, burned like fire in her soul, and brought her upright in bed. She wondered in amazement. Was it the starlight, the twinkle of their bewitchment, the drape of the night, which so moved her? Perhaps Emma had stirred her passions and affected her emotions.

"If she did then so much the better," she whispered into the darkness. *She let me see. She opened my eyes even more to the love of a man, what it can do, what it feels like, and what it means to life itself.*

She didn't quite intend for me to take it that way, she thought and slowly reclined. Sleep seemed out of place at the moment, but she felt the weariness of her body. The hands of the clock showed two o'clock. *What is to happen now? I suppose Emma did offer a way out.* She smiled at the thought. *It would have been a way to solve the money problem. Now the problem is still there.*

Others would have to resolve the issue, she decided. It was beyond her. She would stand where she had to stand, and that was all she could do. Tomorrow she would return the letters and her answer to the Mennonite man. She wished there was more time but dared not keep the letters longer. The danger of their discovery was simply too great. Atlee might think her hasty and conclude she was like Emma, but it couldn't be helped.

Sleep came then, and the dreams followed. She was with John. The buggy door was open, and the night outside sped past, but then it was Atlee, his hands clutching the lines. He laughed when she asked him how he knew how to drive a buggy. He said he always had, had never forgotten, had been Amish once. He said he was coming back for her and knew how to stop her marriage to John, which wasn't to be.

He told her he would know how to talk to the bishop, what things would need to be said to convince him. He would tell them, he said, how she used to love him. He would tell the deacon things that would make his hair stand on end, how she cared for the ring he gave her, how she kept it. Hadn't she? He laughed again, a great swell of sound that echoed out into the night.

She begged him to stop, to be let off. It's the middle of nowhere, he told her, and drove faster. The horse had lathers of sweat on its harness, and the specks flew backward and covered the storm front. When she told him to stop before they had an accident, he said that was what he wanted.

Perhaps if he had one, he told her, she would love him, love him like she used to, when they were children and followed their hearts. There were car lights that passed them, from the front and the back. Then he turned out the lights of the buggy, and she knew the next one would hit them.

She reached to grab the reins, to pull into the ditch, but he held on. Her hand found the light switch and turned on the buggy's running lights and the dome light. Her eyes filled with terror, sought Atlee's face, but it was John's face she saw, hurt in his eyes. He asked why she wanted to drive, didn't she trust him, wasn't he good enough for her.

She woke upright in bed, her fingernails dug into the palms of her hand. Sweat soaked, she listened for sounds in the house, hoped she hadn't screamed and given notice to her family of her distress.

"It's just a dream," she whispered in the silence but found no comfort in the words. The world seemed to be out of control, wild, and careening faster than an *Englisha's* car around a curve on their blacktop road. Its end seemed almost as certain, a crash in the ditch, a decision by the deacon and Bishop Martin that she couldn't marry John.

She had seen the mangled results of an *Englisha's* car when it went astray and imagined her own life in the same condition. It could easily happen. Of this she had no doubt. Already the road seemed open, the conclusions almost foreknown. Because if she couldn't go along with communion until this problem was solved and because it couldn't be solved, she wouldn't be going. John would stand with her, of this she had no doubt. They would both be in the ditch and not married.

Rebecca got out of bed and sought comfort at the window. Now, though, the sight of the open heavens only jarred her further. They seemed so perfect, so in order, each twinkling spot in place, so unlike her life. Could heaven really help this chaos?

Was she to be cut adrift, separated from her people, not by choice but by necessity, because she stood by John, because she loved him? The irony didn't escape her.

The thought of an escape presented itself, and she considered it for a moment. Should she wait a while to mail back the letters and cut ties with Atlee? With her life ruined, why drag John down with her? Perhaps she should do what was best for him. Perhaps she should reconsider Atlee. Surely there would be worse things in life than being married to a Mennonite.

She rejected the idea and noticed the anger that rose inside of her. If she couldn't have John, if they took him from her, then she wouldn't settle for a lesser love, even if it meant a single life.

A life like Emma's, the thought came quick and poignant. *I am like her—stubborn and willful. If I can't get what I want, I take nothing.*

In her mind Rebecca heard the words from Emma's letter as they replayed. *He said he thought it was* Da Hah's villa. *Said he felt we were led together. Said his heart had been heavy, burdened. That today was the first day any girl had brought hope to his mind. I saw our children in his eyes, Manny. A dozen of them. Yet it was as if he already knew what would be. That I would say "no." His eyes were so sad. He said he understood, that he didn't have much to offer. I told him that was not the reason, but he didn't believe me.*

Rebecca placed both her hands on her face, shut out the window, the stars, the night, and the thoughts. "I'm not Emma," she groaned and was surprised at the silence that came. In the distance the faint howl of a dog rose, muffled through the closed window. She went back to bed and wept till sleep brought silence again.

Matthew's footsteps woke her at chore time, the clock she forgot to set the alarm on showed five thirty. Her head swam when her feet landed on the floor, but she forced herself to get dressed. The chill of the early morning air was not broken by any warmth from the floor register. Mattie rarely started a fire in the kitchen stove once late spring was past.

Out in the barn, she was thankful Matthew seemed lost in his own thoughts. Back in the kitchen her mother didn't operate under similar conditions.

"My," Mattie said, "you are a wreck."

"I had a hard night." A tear ran unbidden down her face.

Mattie paused, a plate of eggs in her hands. "What was in that package? If it was something awful, then I won't have Mennonite men coming around here again. Won't tolerate it."

"Letters from Emma. It's not his fault," Rebecca assured her mother.

"Oh…Emma." Mattie seemed satisfied. "It can't be too bad then."

The question still hung in the air, so Rebecca answered it. "I'm afraid Bishop Martin will stop the wedding."

"And you'll end up like Emma?"

"Without John," she said, another tear on her cheek.

"My, this is a mess. And your father wants to talk with you tonight."

"I had forgotten. Is it something bad?"

"I think he'd better talk with you and John together," Mattie said, as if she had suddenly decided.

"It's something awful." Rebecca gave up on all pretences, and the sobs came in great waves.

CHAPTER THIRTY

Reuben had to make a trip into town. He said so at the breakfast table, and Rachel watched him drive out the lane. The weather couldn't have been better for her plans, and now the coast was clear. Not since the time she planted the ferns had there been a chance for a return visit.

She considered the project to be her hope for the future. Rachel was aware it was a project of death but death for a reason, for a purpose. The thought lightened her days, comforted her nights, gave her an expectation of a brighter future when they would live in plenty.

That Reuben supplied a little extra money already with his goat project, well above what they were used to, seemed a thing to reduce to nothing because it held her back from the vision she was determined to attain. Her father had left an inheritance, which was hers by right of birth, and no goats would impede its return.

In failure Reuben would regain his senses, stop refusing the money, and acquire sanity again. Of this she was certain. That sanity was what she once hated in Reuben gave her no pause. His lack of motivation, his desire for the mundane, and his satisfaction with little now seemed a blessing to be sought out.

By destroying his goat herd, she would find the answer. With the last rattle of Reuben's buggy wheels, she went to the bedroom and removed the carefully hidden papers. She knew what they said but wanted to read them again to make sure but even more to enjoy the words.

Her child moved within her, as she settled on the bed. Even with

Reuben gone, she felt safer here. She read the papers in the shelter of her bedroom walls, hidden from imaginary eyes. She had hid them under her black funeral and communion dress.

How right, she thought. The two went together. The death of Reuben's goats and the death of her fellow man. She felt a kinship with both.

The child moved again, and she felt anger at its presence, at the intrusion of its life inside her. She comforted herself with the thought the inheritance would dull the pain, soothe the inconvenience to come, and give this child's life the worth it deserved.

She read the page. "Bracken fern is common to most areas."

This is good she told herself again, easily explainable if found, especially after the goats ate it.

"Can be consumed directly by animals." Goats ate anything. She knew from observation. "Signs of toxicity may take some time to develop." She smiled. This was good.

"Hemorrhages resemble anthrax in cattle. In sheep symptoms can be confused with pregnancy toxemia, pinkeye, or cataracts. There is weakness and fever. Symptoms in goats are as yet undocumented." She smiled. Then so much the better. The veterinarian would not know what to do.

"Antibiotics and blood transfusions are rarely successful as a cure." Rachel smiled again and replaced the papers carefully under the black dress. She made sure no white paper showed, even if one were to open the drawer abruptly. Not that Reuben would do such a thing, but all eventualities needed to be taken into consideration.

Just to be sure, she checked. Sharply she shut the drawer. Wood snapped against wood. When she slid the drawer open again, no white showed under the black cloth. Satisfied she returned to the kitchen and finished the last of the breakfast dishes. There was no sense of haste. Time seemed to be plentiful.

Luxurious thoughts flitted through her mind. They rose and fell with the swish of her washcloth in the soapy water. As she set each clean dish to dry on the metal rack, she saw the days ahead of her. They too were washed of unpleasantness, cleansed of Reuben's foolish ideas and efforts.

Their lives would be made new, prepared as fresh plates cleaned of raw usage from hungry mouths. Much of her existence now felt used, rough, and uncouth, but it was soon to change. Her hopes lay with the green plants in the swamp.

With the dishes done, Rachel got her coat and set out. The walk would look normal enough if someone noticed. The goat farmer's wife had gone to inspect the pastures. Her face grimaced, set in anger. It would not be long before this too would change.

Before her the lower pasture lay, its grass green, brought on by the recent spring rains and now summer's warmth. At present the goats had no access to these grounds, only the cattle, but Reuben would use them later for that purpose. He had said so.

The fences looked well kept, the wires taut. Rachel glanced at them as she walked, anger rising again. Reuben had never kept such fences, not when there were only cattle to keep in. Cattle brought good prices at the meat market but obviously not good enough for Reuben. At least they never gave him inspiration, motivation, energy to repair his fences. Only goats—filthy, stinky goats were good enough for him.

Back then cattle would regularly drift into the swamp, walking through fences in disrepair. From this had come the idea she now implemented. If cattle could break through fences, then goats could too—with or without her help. Reuben would think he had missed a line, a relapse to his old ways perhaps.

The black cattle looked at her with interest, their heads raised. Once they determined she carried no food for their consumption, they ignored her. She studied them though. This was what she would replace the goats with. Cattle—hundreds of them, well fed and gracious—were objects for which one held no shame. They were signs of prosperity and affluence.

Did not the Lord own the cattle on a thousand hills? Reuben

had read the Scripture the other Sunday. The words rolled out of his mouth like he fully enjoyed the reading. Let Reuben then enjoy it when she owned perhaps not a thousand but a hundred cattle on her own farm.

The green grass would bear them all. She would raise the best cattle. Buyers would gather around when Reuben took them to market. That they already did for his goats, she was unaware and would have been angry had she known.

Ahead of her lay the swamp, just beyond the barbed wire of their property line but within easy reach of any wandering goat. A movement caught her attention, a body among the trees, and she wondered what wild animal might be abroad, perhaps even a threat, but decided there wasn't any danger. This was Indiana, not the land of bears or cougars.

Rachel stood by the fence, her gaze fixed on the swamp, when a hand waved, and then her neighbor walked out from the trees, a pump strapped to his back, a spray nozzle in his hand. He was an *Englisha*.

"Howdy," he hollered. "Out to inspect the fences?"

"Reuben's gone," she said and smiled.

He approached. "It didn't spread toward your line. Can be thankful for that. It's my third spraying. Been working on it for a while. Think I got all of them."

"What didn't?" Rachel asked, fear gripping her heart, her knees weakening.

"The bracken fern," he said. "Haven't seen any in these parts. Not in years. Could happen anywhere, though. Good thing I checked. Need to turn the cattle in here next week."

"What's wrong with a fern?" she asked, despair in her soul.

"Bracken fern?"

"Yes."

"Poisonous to cattle," he said chuckling. "Do them in good, if they find it. Seems like they always do. Had it happen to me once. Two cows years and years ago. I've always checked the swamp since that happened."

"Sounds bad," she said and smiled.

"It is. Reuben keeps his fences up good," he said grinning. "Likes those goats of his. I saw he got good prices last market day. Wouldn't have believed it myself. Might have to consider goats."

"Don't," she told him.

"You don't like them?" he said laughing.

"No," she replied making a face.

"Smells like money to me."

"So did you get all of them? The ferns?" She let the words lightly out of her mouth and looked hopeful.

"Yep." He was confident. "Checked twice today again. If I missed any, I'd be surprised. I'll check again before I let cattle in next week."

"I better get back," she said, feeling light-headed, her hand on her stomach.

"Another one? Congratulations. You Amish are the salt of the earth. We could use more of you. Seems like us Protestants are determined to die out. We have children, one, maybe two, and then it's over. Wife and I had three, but our children have none. God knows when they'll start. All of them are over thirty and married, but nothing."

"That must be hard," she said.

"It is. Makes me wish I had a dozen children like you folks do. Chances of having grandchildren might be higher," he said laughing heartily.

"It's only our second."

He shook his head. "Not by choice, I'm sure. I know you folks better than that."

"That's true," she agreed and echoed the right words. "By the Lord's will."

He raised his cap at her words. "A right way to live. I must be going. The best to Reuben's goats."

"He'll be glad to hear that." She forced herself to smile as he turned to go.

On the long walk back to the house, she felt the agony of her plans destroyed. Not given to tears, which she considered a sign of weakness, she held back. The burden she carried inside became heavier with each step. The child was silent, as if it sensed her trouble and thought it best to be still.

Once in the barnyard, the sight of the house, the goats, the used buggy in the driveway, the certain knowledge that this could go on for years, unchanged and unbroken, became too much. She stepped inside the barn, lest someone pass by on the road and see her. There, seated on a straw bale in the company of goats, whose noses stuck through the wood partitions of their pen, she wept great swelling sobs.

Hope denied, her tears fell. Bitterness grew in her soul.

A goat bleated, a right hopeful sound, as if it looked to her for good things. The child in her leaped, and she hated both it and the animal that called. She knew the end of the road had come. There were no more exits or bypasses. *Da Hah's* hand was against her, apparently, and she was to be broken, condemned to a life she did not want.

That *Da Hah* would do such a thing didn't surprise her. She had always expected it, as if He delighted in such torment. With the knowledge her heart hardened and became like stone.

When he arrived home, Reuben must have noticed that something was different about her. "The goats are doing real well," he said, in the hope his news would bring cheer. "If prices stay as they are, we might even be able to paint the house this summer."

"It needs it," she said, her face set. "And supper's ready."

He turned away, pain on his face, but she didn't care.

CHAPTER THIRTY-ONE

W hy is Rebecca crying?" Matthew wanted to know. He was just in from his chores, seated at the breakfast table, his eyes on the food.

"I'm not," Rebecca told him.

"You were." He looked at her face again.

"She had a hard night," Mattie informed him. "Leave her alone."

He made a face, "That's why I'm not dating. No girls. Just me, my farm, and the land. Happy as a lark."

Mattie chuckled. "You wish."

"I don't," he retorted. "This boy will get it done."

Rebecca laughed, distracted in spite of herself. "You are entertaining."

He snorted loudly. "Love is nothing but trouble. Look at you all teary-eyed."

"It could be something else," she informed him.

"Like what?" Matthew gave an evil chuckle. "Love, love, love, that's all the trouble in the world."

"He'll get used to it," Mattie said. "Go get the girls up, Rebecca."

A soft call from the foot of the stairs got immediate results. If it hadn't Rebecca would have climbed the stairs to rouse her sisters.

They have always been decent about responding, she thought. It was a good thought on a dreary morning. At least her family was pleasant to be around, even if the world was rough at present.

Lester let the screen door slam as he came in and went to the sink to wash up. The thought of what her father had to say gripped her.

It must be horrible news if she was to need John's presence. Did her father know news from Milroy, which perhaps spelled disaster? Her heart throbbed with fear.

Yet, she brought her emotion under control, brushed her stray hairs back under her *kapp,* and composed her face. Whatever it was must be taken in stride, with the faith that God meant all things for good. Was that not their faith? Her faith? John's faith? Would it not sustain her?

That it would she didn't doubt, even in this moment, and felt the knowledge bring strength and courage to her soul. Her father would be gentle, whatever the news. She smiled at him when he appeared, his face red from the scrub, water droplets still on his beard, the towel still in his hand.

His eyes took in her face and searched her soul, she thought.

"*Druvvel,*" he said, "did the Mennonite man bring trouble in his package?"

"Letters from Emma," she said. "The troubles are my own."

"That's what we need to talk about. Tonight maybe?"

"What is it?" she asked.

"We had best have some time." He wiped the towel down the length of his beard. "With matters of the heart, one should not rush through them."

"Is the news awful?" she said, trying to press back the tears, but they ran down her face anyway, one right after the other.

"Rebecca." His hand touched her shoulder. "It's not evil, and it's not news. My heart hurts for you and John. I wished only to speak with you about how best to resolve the matter."

She nodded, but the tears wouldn't stop.

Apparently Mattie had heard because she appeared in the kitchen doorway. Behind them they heard the sound of footsteps of small feet coming down the stairs.

"You need to talk with them together," Mattie whispered. "Really, Lester, you must. It would be best. Now dry your tears, Rebecca. The girls can't see you like this. They are not to ask questions about this."

Rebecca nodded and moved toward the washroom. The stair door opened behind her as Lester whispered, "That's fine. I only wanted to talk with her. If John is there, that would be good."

Their voices faded out, as they moved into the kitchen and she stepped into the washroom. Rebecca knew her mother would have her younger sisters in tow, would distract them lest their lives become overloaded with burdens too heavy for young shoulders.

They are too heavy for my shoulders, she thought, but apparently *Da Hah* had other ideas. She gently washed her face, dried it, hopeful no marks of her tears would stay behind.

Lester led in the morning prayer. As heads bowed around the table, he praised the Almighty for His works, for the breath He gave to human bodies, for grace He gave souls. Lester asked for the aid and comfort of heaven, gave thanks for the food and the multitude of blessings they received each day, asked for forgiveness for their sins, and forgave those who sinned against them.

Matthew wasted no time. Taking the egg plate, he helped himself before passing it on.

"He's hungry," Mattie said.

"I'm sorry," Matthew muttered. He reached for the biscuit plate but gave it to his sister first. She took one, then passed it back to him.

"That's better," Mattie told him.

Matthew only grunted but waited patiently for the gravy to reach him.

Rebecca, relieved no one seemed to notice her red face, figured they were just being kind. Either way, breakfast proceeded without discomfort. The schoolchildren then scattered to prepare for school, and she helped Mattie with the kitchen.

"Not much on the list today," Mattie told her. "If we get the children off to school, we have the day to ourselves."

Rebecca nodded, thankful.

"You still look like you could use it. Your father will talk with you and John Sunday afternoon. You think John can bring you here?"

"We had planned on it."

"Good then."

"Is it something awful?"

"He just cares," Mattie said, her eyes soft with concern. "Missing communion is a serious matter. Now John's in this too. He's the preacher's son."

"I know."

"It'll be okay. Surely *Da Hah* will open up a way. You're a good girl. We both know that."

Rebecca nodded and pressed back the tears. This time she succeeded.

Mattie went upstairs to the girls' bedroom to help urge them on in their school preparations. Rebecca laid the lunch pails out and had sandwiches made and food packed by the time Matthew brought the horse up.

With lunches in hand, the girls climbed in, and Matthew took off. The old horse slowly picked up speed till it reached a tired trot.

"They grow up so fast," Mattie said. "I guess your leaving makes me aware of it."

"But...I'm still not married," Rebecca ventured.

"You will be. Something will work out. Now shouldn't you get some sleep? Your eyes look swollen."

"What if someone catches me sleeping in the middle of the day?"

"Are you afraid John will drive in?" Mattie said chuckling.

"No, but what a *shohnt* that would be."

"He'd get over it."

Rebecca smiled. "I suppose so. The mailman just went. I'll get the mail."

"You expecting something?"

"No, just the mail. That reminds me I need to mail Emma's letters back."

"Today?"

"Soon. The sooner the better. They really belong to the Mennonite man."

"The first person who goes to town can drop them off," Mattie said, as Rebecca left for the walk down the driveway.

Summer was almost here. The air had that heavy feel, the preparation for warmth. She walked briskly, feeling the refreshment of the outdoors awaken her. She almost regretted her mother's instructions for sleep in the middle of the day, but the tiredness, she figured, would return quickly.

Mail time was usually pleasant, a touch of the outside world, the breeze of news from their fellow brethren near and far, whether contained in *The Budget* or *The Pathway* papers. Today she expected nothing different. Sometimes there was even a surprise, a letter from a relative, news worthy of joy.

Rebecca wondered if today was such a day, then shivered with the feel of impending tragedy. With how last night and this morning had gone, great loss was more likely than news of comfort. With weakness in her knees, she approached the mailbox and eyed it as one would an enemy about to strike.

A tremble in her arm, she reached to open the flap. She almost retreated but knew her mother would not appreciate a trip back down simply because she feared to face the unknown inside.

The opened mailbox revealed the expected items—*The Budget*, some flyers from the *Englisha* stores in West Union, and a letter. The address on the letter was written in the round feminine scrawl she knew well. Aunt Leona had written to her sister.

Rebecca removed the items with care, barely touching the letter, fear gnawing at her. She told herself Leona wrote of good things, regular news from her family, things around which they could all gather and laugh, but she was certain it wasn't so now. After last night, aunt Leona wrote to share grave news.

On the walk back to the house, she tried to hurry, but her legs refused. They felt like the rest of her, exhausted and at the limit of human endurance. It was all she could do to keep from collapsing into sobs by the side of lane and sinking into the green grass. She sought anything to ease her apprehension but found none. She would take the letter to her mother. To read it herself was beyond her powers.

Mattie's eyes widened at the sight of Rebecca's face.

"What?" she asked.

"There's a letter from Leona." Rebecca sank into a kitchen chair.

"Is there bad news?"

"Don't know. Didn't open it."

"You could have."

"I know, but I couldn't." Rebecca lifted her face to meet her mother's eyes.

"You're not imagining, are you?"

"I don't know. I think it's bad news."

"Dear...your nerves are shot." Mattie opened the letter, her eyes scanning the page. "She's coming to visit this weekend. Late Saturday most likely. Oh, my. The house. We don't have any food. At least the wash was done yesterday. Oh, Rebecca, we have to get busy right now!"

"Why is she coming?" Rebecca wasn't convinced.

Mattie read some more. "Oh...they do want to talk. See if they can help."

"John and me," Rebecca said. A weariness swept over her, but the fear left.

"She says there's a lot of talk out there. Oh, my. We really have to find a solution to this thing. How wise of your father to work on this. I wonder if Sunday is soon enough."

"Leona will be here," Rebecca said sighing. Her aunt's visit produced none of the joy it should have—like so much of her life lately. It was as if a thief had come and robbed her house till it was empty.

"That's right. She will be. We must talk with John before that. Maybe something can be decided before Leona arrives. It has to be. We can't tell her nothing is being done about it. She'll think we are rotten parents."

"You are good parents. Both of you. I'm the one in trouble."

Mattie ignored her. "There's the food. We're almost out of bread. With them coming, it won't last the weekend. I had planned to bake on Monday. We have to bake rolls and pies. Leona likes apple and, of course, pecan. It's her recipe from when we were girls. Oh, my. We have to start now."

"Yes, Mother." Rebecca's mind was as weary as her body, but duty called, and both would respond.

"And John. He has to come tonight."

"Tonight?" A flush of emotion ran through Rebecca. She sat upright in her chair.

"Yes. That's the only time available. I will drive over and tell Miriam. She will understand. I'm sure they'll appreciate our concern. Get your package ready, and I'll drop it off at the Unity post office."

"Will John understand? He'll think I'm behind this."

"I'll make it clear to Miriam it's Lester's doing."

"What if it doesn't suit John?" Rebecca tried again.

"He can make it suit. He wants to get married, doesn't he?"

Rebecca nodded.

"Then get your package. I'm going to Miriam's first. You can start the rolls while I'm away. The yeast for the bread can be started too."

Rebecca nodded again and went upstairs, the house silent around her except for the sound of her mother rushing around the kitchen.

Chapter Thirty-two

The sight of Emma's letters, tucked into the brown envelope, brought back the waves of emotion Rebecca felt while she read them last night. Still shaken about Emma holding such secrets, Rebecca felt fear rise. Surely everyone around her wasn't like that—presenting one face in public and another in private.

Yet Emma hadn't lied, Rebecca told herself and restored some of her shattered faith. Emma had tried to live her faith. She reached for a notepad, and sat down to write the Mennonite man a quick note.

Dear Manny,

I have read the letters and was quite shaken. I can't imagine how you must feel. You never told me whether you married. If not, then your sorrow must truly be immense.

Please don't think me rushed by this quick reply. I mean no disrespect. In fact, it is Emma and her memory that drive me. No one must see these letters. Please keep them secret even from the most innocent eyes.

Emma was a dear person. I can see why you would have loved her and, after having met you, how she would have returned that love. What I feel about the rest doesn't matter, but it all seems such a shame.

Please tell Atlee it's over between us. I say that not for the reasons Emma had. I am not Emma. Perhaps you find that hard to believe, but it's true. I love John for my own reasons, and they are great and deep.

Then about the money. I suppose you think I will keep it. The problem is that there is plenty of trouble right now about it. I couldn't go along with communion. John stayed back too. I don't want the money and have said so, but no one believes me—especially those who matter most.

My mother thinks things will work out okay, and my father cares enough to try to help me. If by some miracle of the Almighty, we are ever married, that is John and I, I will sign the money and property over to Emma's family.

If you doubt that, as I don't blame you, I can only tell you that in this regard I am like Emma. I do what I believe to be right. My love for John is real, and returning the money will be right also.

Yours truly,

Rebecca Keim

She folded the letter and carefully slid it into the package. Pieces of scotch tape went on the envelope and over the edges. Not a foolproof method if someone wanted to get inside, but Rebecca knew her mother would respect the obvious message. Private.

"You coming?" Mattie asked from the bottom of the stairs. "I have to get going."

Rebecca answered by stepping into the hall and shutting the door. Mattie waited and reached for the package when Rebecca arrived on the last step.

"They sell larger packages at the post office. Perhaps you could put this into one and make it easier to mail."

Mattie nodded. "Should work. His address? Oh…it's here on the envelope."

"Yes. Manny Troyer."

"I didn't know he lived in Holmes County."

"That's where the offices of the mission are, I think."

"You won't be further entangled with him?"

"No." Rebecca shook her head.

"It might not help anyway. This may already have caused big problems."

"I hope not," Rebecca said as Mattie left. Apparently she had let Lester know because he already had the horse hitched to the buggy and waited in the yard, his hand on the bridle. Rebecca watched for a moment, as her parents exchanged words, then Mattie climbed in and took the reins. Her father let go and stepped aside. As Mattie left, he looked for a second like he would come into the house, then seemed to change his mind.

Rebecca sighed, a great weariness rushing over her at the sight of her father's stooped shoulders as he walked to the barn. This had all become too much for any of them to bear. She prayed that God would help them, would spare them from further suffering.

How that could be, she had no idea but felt relief flood her soul, as if heaven had heard and would surely answer. Her mother was headed to talk with John's mother. Perhaps Isaac would be there. At this time of the day, she doubted it, but she remembered his kind face and his gentle eyes when John had been injured last year.

Isaac had seemed to understand when others might have blamed her for their quarrel before the accident. Perhaps God would use Isaac to answer their problem. The hope sprang up unbidden. Was not Isaac a minister, and did he not have powers with the bishop?

With a lighter heart, she returned to the kitchen. She warmed water and prepared the yeast mixture. Then she wiped the table before bringing out flour and other ingredients she needed. By the time Mattie rattled in the lane again, an hour and half later, the bread had already risen for the first time and she had cinnamon sprinkled on the rolls, ready to bake in the oven.

"I hadn't planned on staying so long," her mother gasped rushing in. "We got to talking."

Rebecca nodded, her attention on the task before her.

"It's even worse than I thought," Mattie said catching her breath. "*Da Hah* must have moved on your father. That's all I can say. With us making the first move like this, it helps make things look much better. Miriam said Isaac has already had a hard time explaining all this at the ministers' meetings. But don't go telling anyone that. It was said in private to encourage us. Isaac is on our side. I'm sure that's why Miriam told me."

"Is John coming?" Rebecca felt the weariness settle on her shoulders again.

"Yes. Miriam said she would send him. He's at work, of course, at Miller's, but Miriam should know if he can come."

"What time?"

"After supper. I asked Miriam to work it into John's schedule. She said it wouldn't be too late."

With the hope from earlier gone, Rebecca asked, "What made things worse?"

"The deacon's wife saw you talking with the Mennonite man, Manny Troyer."

"I thought it was her," Rebecca said.

"You shouldn't hold it against her," Mattie said, her voice firm. "You must say it looked out of order. Thankfully the letters are out of the house."

Rebecca nodded.

"Would they have made things even worse?"

Rebecca nodded again. Her eyes stung, as the tears came.

"I thought so." Her mother's hand came around Rebecca's shoulder, as she drew her close.

Rebecca wiped her eyes on her sleeve. The bread needed to be punched down. She slipped out of her mother's embrace and washed

her hands before she kneaded the dough. Her arms soon ached from
the effort, and her mind spun.

"Did Emma have secrets?" Her mother's voice reached her.

"Yes."

"I thought so. Did they shake your faith?"

"Maybe." Rebecca glanced up. Her eyes found her mother's, and
she smiled in spite of the tears. "I'm not Emma, though."

"You are wise beyond your years sometimes. You'll make John a
good wife."

"Don't say that," Rebecca gasped. The tears came in a flood.

"Let me do that. You'll have the bread all soaked in tears."

"Wouldn't Matthew complain about that."

"What he doesn't know won't hurt him," Mattie said chuckling.

The rest of the day passed in a blur of action, with seconds too short
and hours that seemed to contain less minutes than the day before.
Rolls filled the counter, while the bread still baked. By the time the
timer went off, white powdered sugar frosting had been spread and
the soft cinnamon rolls were all tied in plastic bags, the air gently
pressed out.

When the schoolchildren came home, the pies were still baking
in the oven. Supper became soup, simple and easy to make. It turned
into a chore to make everyone eat soup with the abundance of sweets
on all sides.

Portions of pie were soon cut out, given with care, and eaten without
much talk. Although Mattie forbade any seconds, she gave in after
listening to Matthew's tender pleadings. Lester pronounced himself
satisfied, rubbed his stomach, and then took a third thin slice of pie.
This provoked a rush on the cinnamon rolls by the children.

Mattie, apparently thinking all order had been lost, rescued the
rest of the rolls from the table, slid them into the pantry, and bodily
stood by the doors. Lester laughed heartily and told her the danger
had passed. When Mattie was convinced they really could eat no more,
she returned and sat down to eat her own piece of apple pie.

The rattle of buggy wheels brought Rebecca to her feet and made her rush to her room upstairs. She was not about to let John see her in her soiled apron. While she changed, Mattie welcomed John in and organized the younger girls in the kitchen. When Rebecca came downstairs, Mattie left the girls to join Rebecca, John, and Lester in the living room.

Rebecca felt a shyness creep over her at the sight of John. She hoped her teary face didn't show. He looked so strong and determined tonight, sitting there on the couch as if he would take her in his arms if all else should fail. She felt weak, from the exhausting day and the emotions of the moment. With a smile, she sat beside him. Her hands trembled.

"I'm glad you could come," her father said, nodding in John's direction.

"Anytime," John said but offered nothing more.

"Keep your voice down," Mattie whispered.

"Yes," Lester said. "Do you think the girls should go upstairs?"

"They have to finish the dishes," Mattie told him. "Can we wait?"

"We shouldn't keep John waiting," Lester said.

"That's okay," John assured them.

"If we talk quietly, it should be okay," Mattie said and smiled in John's direction.

"I think so," Lester agreed and cleared his throat. "I wanted to talk to you and Rebecca about... Well, you know what, of course. We want to see if anything can be done. I'm not a minister, but perhaps... maybe something could be done."

"Do you have any ideas?" John said, moving forward in his seat.

"Your mother said the deacon's wife saw Rebecca with the Mennonite man."

"Oh." John looked toward Rebecca, a question in his eyes.

"Your mother just found out today," Mattie said.

"I was down at the bridge," Rebecca told him because he still waited, his eyes on her face. "The man brought me some letters. Emma's. He's the executor of the property. Emma wanted me to read them."

"Were they written to you?" John asked.

"No," Rebecca said and paused. "They were written to him, but she wanted me to read them."

John seemed satisfied.

Lester cleared his throat again. "I have thought of something."

John turned in Lester's direction, his face serious. Rebecca felt hope rise in her heart.

"Perhaps if the two of you separated—maybe till after fall communion—it would help calm things down a bit."

"You're not serious," John said.

Rebecca gasped, her hand on her face.

"Lester," Mattie told him, "that's really not the correct approach. It would just make them look guilty for sure—like they had done something wrong."

"I…really…I can't do that," John said. "I'm sorry."

"Mattie's probably right. It was just an idea," Lester told him. "I wasn't trying to make things worse."

"I have a better idea," John said, but Rebecca felt only despair, her heart still pounding.

"We should get married this fall—before communion," John said, his voice firm. "I had suggested this earlier to Rebecca. Now perhaps, I'll talk to my father. I really think it could be done."

"Spunky fellow," Lester said chuckling.

"This fall." Mattie's breath came sharply. "That's soon. How in the world would we get ready? Oh, my…I just knew something like this would happen."

"Do you think you could convince your father?" Lester asked.

"I do," John said.

"Would you really?" Rebecca asked.

John turned to look at her. "Yes," he said, his eyes glowing. "I would."

"Then I could give the money back before next communion." Rebecca felt like she could breathe again. The room faded away, and she saw only John, as hope rose strong and vibrant in her heart.

"Good enough with me," Lester grinned.

"Have we got time?" her mother asked.

"Sounds like you'd better start planning," Lester said chuckling again.

"That was wonderful of you," Rebecca whispered thirty minutes later. She stood beside the buggy. John stood with her, ready to climb in.

He said nothing, but his fingers lightly traced her lips in the darkness. Then he was gone. She listened as the sound of his horse's hooves lingered long on the night air.

CHAPTER THIRTY-THREE

John drove east, his buggy rattling across the Harshville covered bridge, the noise rolling out into the darkness. *So it comes down to this,* he thought, a rush of emotion filling him. He would marry Rebecca not in the spring but this fall, ahead of schedule.

He slapped the reins. Did not the preachers say many times that *Da Hah* works out all things for good. The stress of the past few months oozed out of him. He took deep breaths, as the night air moved across his face.

Rebecca had been so close. He let his thoughts dwell on the earlier moments, but then he always had to leave—had to go away from her presence, from the joy she stirred in him. Soon it would not be so. He would no longer go home without her.

The lights in Unity were already shut down. Because only a few of the home windows had lights, he thought it must be late. He searched his watch pocket, found the watch, and held it up close to his face, as he passed one of the lit homes. It was only nine twenty. His father and mother would still be up. He slapped the reins to keep his speed up the incline of Wheat Ridge.

Isaac and Miriam would be glad to hear the news. He was sure of that. His mother liked Rebecca, as did his father. They had told him so, and nothing, he was sure, had changed their minds. Even this fuss over communion hadn't. He pulled left into the driveway, unhitched his horse, took the harness off, and slapped the horse on the rump to send him out through the barnyard gate.

The door opened quietly, as he stepped inside. He returned his mother's smile, then sat on the couch. She paused in her knitting because normally he would have gone upstairs for the night.

"Everything go okay?" Miriam asked.

"I think so," he said, taking a deep breath.

"I'm glad to hear Lester got involved. Things are getting serious." His father dropped the page of *The Budget* to his lap, the crinkle of the paper loud in the silence.

John paused but decided his father was just concerned. "I think we've found a solution."

"Oh." Isaac looked relieved. "Did Lester come up with it?"

"Ah…no, I did."

"You did?" Isaac's eyes went to Miriam's face. "I hope it was a good one."

"Let him tell us," Miriam told him. "We can just be thankful for anyone who has ideas right now."

Isaac sighed. "I suppose so. What's the idea?"

"You don't think my ideas are okay?" John made no attempt to keep the hurt out of his voice.

"You are a good son." Isaac smiled. "I have no complaints. You love the girl. A lot, I think."

"Is there something wrong with that?" John asked.

"No." Isaac smiled again, but his eyes were weary. "It tends to cloud the judgment."

"Don't be too hard on the boy," Miriam spoke up.

"He stayed back from communion," Isaac said.

"I wasn't going to let Rebecca stand alone. It wasn't right to begin with. You know that." John half rose off the couch, then sat down again. His pleasant memories from moments before now gone.

"Perhaps," Isaac spoke slowly, "if it was up to me, I wouldn't have asked her to stay back. She's a decent girl, and I trust her. It's just that we can't expect others—those who don't know her as well as we do—to feel the same, not when things look the way they do."

"But there were reasons," John insisted. "Rebecca explained herself."

"I know. And I believe her," Isaac said. "But we are not alone. We must work with the church. Our people have always done so, even in difficult times like this. It may be hard, and others may be wrong. In the end, though, it cannot be any other way. We act as one people. This is our unity."

"I'm the one who loves Rebecca," John said.

"We know," Miriam told him. "Believe us. We like her."

"Then why this fuss?" John asked.

"That's what I said," Isaac said. "You are in a poor condition to judge or decide the matter. Believe me, son, it would be best if you let cooler heads handle this. That's why I hoped it was Lester who came up with the idea—the plan you talked about."

"What did you decide?" Miriam asked.

"Lester agrees with it," John said, his eyes on the darkened front window. The light of the gas lantern lit the ceiling behind him. An early summer fly, lately awakened from his winter sleep, popped into the glass shade. Stunned, it fell to the floor and loudly buzzed his complaint to the world.

"But what?" Miriam's eyes sought his face.

"We want to marry this fall," John said. His eyes didn't leave the windowpane.

"That's what I was afraid of." Isaac's voice was weary.

"You could help." John looked up, his gaze desperate. "I know you can. You can persuade Bishop. He respects you. If we marry by fall, before communion, Rebecca can give the money back before pre-communion church. It's the only answer."

"It's too late now," Isaac said. "I wish it wasn't, but it is."

"Why?" John rose off the couch again, then sat back down.

"There's just too much going on. I don't know how to explain it. This and that, and then even more piles on, so it seems. Now there was a Mennonite man who stopped in to see her. It just looks bad, John. We can't blame the others for being concerned."

"Let us marry. Then we can show them Rebecca is telling the truth."

Isaac sighed again. "It's not about Rebecca anymore. Really, John, it isn't. It's about…well…the concerns of how this affects the others. We can't allow just anything to happen. Mennonite men show up. Rings, promises, money from inheritances. Lots of money, I must say. Please understand, son."

John rose to his feet, lifted by a force outside of himself. He felt anger, disappointment, hurt, all mixed together and rolled up. "I don't understand," he said much too loudly.

"John," Miriam said, "you are speaking to your father."

"I know," he said. "That's why I wanted help from him—because he is my father. Lots of good all this has done for me. Haven't I been faithful to you, to him, to the church, to God? Haven't I upheld all that has been required of me? Haven't I?"

"You have, son. I know that," Isaac said. "I don't blame you for being angry."

"Then I will talk to Bishop myself."

"It won't do any good," Miriam told him. "It really won't. Either for you or your father. Can't you see that?"

John sat down. "Then I will tell him we're leaving."

"Leaving?" Miriam leaned forward on the rocker.

"Yes, leaving. We'll go to some Mennonite church somewhere. Makes no difference. Maybe Holmes County. They'll marry us. That will take care of the money problem. Rebecca can't receive the money if she marries outside the faith. Then perhaps we'll come back, and perhaps we won't."

"Oh, no." Miriam dropped her knitting on the floor. "Rebecca wouldn't go with you."

"You want me to find out?" John asked.

"No," Isaac told him, his voice soft. "I'm sorry to hear you say this. I never thought you would go there, even think of going there. Surely you wouldn't be tempted by what the Mennonites have to offer?"

"It's not right that Bishop won't marry us. We're not to blame," John said.

"I know," Isaac told him. "Can you find patience? Wait maybe?"

John was quiet, then turned to face his father. "I'm sorry, but I can't," he said. "I'm going to talk with Bishop this Saturday. Lester agrees with the plan. That ought to count for something. If Bishop doesn't agree, then I will tell him what I just told you."

"And you are serious?" Isaac's eyes searched his son's face.

"Yes," John said meeting his gaze, "I am."

"You know what this will cost you?"

"Yes." John turned back to the windowpane again.

"These things are not easily undone. Your words will not be forgotten."

"I know," John said.

"You think it's worth it?"

John stood to his feet again. "Rebecca is worth it all—whatever it may cost."

Miriam gasped.

"I'm sorry," John said. "I love her."

"You must love God more," Isaac said. "Don't forget that."

"I do, but it's not God who separates us. It's other people's selfish reasons."

"You must be patient with them," Isaac told him.

"I will stand with Rebecca," John said. Then as if he couldn't believe his words himself, he turned and went upstairs. The door shut quietly behind him, the sound of his sobbing mother filling his ears.

He reached the top of the stairs and the door to his room stunned. His blood pounded in his ears, the resolve in his heart strong. Rebecca would be his wife because he loved her and because she was worthy of his love. To leave her alone in this storm was beneath him.

But join the Mennonites? The sound in his ears of his earlier words throbbed in his head. This was something he had never contemplated, a thought that never had crossed his mind before. Where did it come from? He had no idea nor did he seek to find out. He would simply follow it. That was all he knew, and Rebecca would be with him.

He lit no light and undressed in the darkness. He slipped beneath the covers, but sleep eluded him. *A Mennonite.* The full impact flooded his mind. *Me, John Miller, a Mennonite.*

For a short time, he told himself, *then we'll come back. Is that possible?* The thought troubled him. Would excommunication be in store? He wasn't certain. His resolve shook, but he pressed on. They would be together in a world where things were fair, where men believed you, where they didn't stop marriages for someone else's doubt and unbelief, where they didn't question the goodness of your soul.

He tossed and turned. The moon rose outside his window, its bright round orb flooding the outdoors. Reluctantly he got out of bed, drawn by the light from this night sun, this ruler of the darkness. It hung golden on the horizon, seemed to reflect his agony, the torment of his soul.

"Help me. Oh Father of heaven and earth," he prayed, "I am but dust, made from the soil under my feet. How can I bear this burden, this sorrow of the world? Love has come to my heart, given by You, and man would take it from me."

"Do You blame me for caring, for standing by Rebecca? Do You judge me for choosing love? Am I to trust in my people or my heart? Great Ruler of the universe, can You answer my cry? If You can make the sun, the earth, and the moon, can You make a way for us to be together—Rebecca and I?"

He paused, his face close to the pane. His heart ached. His eyes studied the ridges on the moon, their gentle shadow so close he felt he could touch its mountains. "You will not leave or forsake us." he prayed and paused to wait, finally comforted.

Sleep came, his face toward the light in the window. His dreams were of fields strewn with fall leaves, of lines of buggies gathered, of women in white aprons, of food, long tables of it, and of her face drawn with delight, the bishop as he held their hands together in blessing.

The alarm didn't wake him, as the first dawn crept into the sky. It was the voice of his mother, her cry desperate in the stairway. "John! Your father! Come quickly!"

CHAPTER THIRTY-FOUR

Instantly he swung his feet to the floor and dressed in quick motions.

"John." Her urgent voice came again.

"Yes," he said, already at the door. His mother stood at the bottom of the stairs, the flickering kerosene lamp in her hand, the light framing her tense face.

"Your father," she said. "Come."

His bare feet made little sound on the steps, as he took them two at a time.

Miriam had already turned to go, when he got down. "What's wrong?" he asked.

His mother said nothing, her steps quick. He followed her to the bedroom, the door already open. The form of his father, laying motionless, came into focus.

Miriam held the lamp low and shook Isaac gently. John came closer, chills of fear ran through him. *Did Father die in the night? Had my words last night cut this deep?*

Isaac moaned and moved his left arm slightly. He seemed to struggle but then lay still.

"He's been like this since I woke," his mother said, her voice shaking. "He's breathing but little else. I think it's finally happened, what I've feared."

"I'll go call from the store."

"The neighbor's phone would be faster. Maybe we could hire their van."

"No, Mom, we can't move him. It takes the ambulance."

"But it's your father, John."

"It's the fastest way," he insisted, galvanized into action by fear and guilt. "Stay with him till I get back."

"Isaac. Isaac," his mother called gently, as he found his keys to Miller's Furniture and ran out into the early morning chill without his coat. He took the shortcut across the field, ignoring the rip of cloth when his pant leg caught on the barbed wire fence.

His hands fumbled but found the right key. He rushed indoors. A chair clattered sideways off his foot. Apparently he'd left it out of place the night before. His fingers found the phone and dialed the numbers by the dim battery-powered nightlight.

"Yes, it's my father," he said. "An emergency. We just woke up. He's not responding."

He listened to the questions.

"No, he moved a little. Moaned. Couldn't talk."

The voice took the address, said help would be on the way. John hung up with a thank-you and moved slowly outside. Behind him the door clicked shut, and he remembered to turn back and lock it.

In the parking lot, he heard footsteps behind him on the gravel.

"What's wrong?" The question came from his uncle Aden.

"Dad. Mom got me up. He's not responding. I called the ambulance."

"Is he gone?"

"No. Moved a little. Mom's with him."

"I'll go back with you," Aden said, as he matched John's steps. They stayed on the road, the need to return not as urgent.

At the house Aden opened the door. Miriam met them inside.

"Is help coming?" she asked.

"I called," John told her. "They are sending the ambulance."

"Shouldn't we try taking him in ourselves? With Aden here now."

"I don't know," John said. "Has anything changed?"

"It might be best to wait," Aden said. He put his arm around

Miriam's shoulder. "Can we see him? It's in *Da Hah's* hands anyway. He will do what's best."

"I know," Miriam said, but her voice caught. "He's in the bedroom."

John hung back as Aden led his mother there. The two of them stood before the bed, Miriam's hand on Isaac's arm. His father made as if to respond, even opened his eyes.

"Aden's here," Miriam said. "Can you talk to him?"

The only sound was a soft moan.

"I've feared this so long," Miriam said. "His heart must have finally given out."

When the sounds of sirens were heard in the distance, the first hard waves of remorse hit John. Surely he had caused this by his words last night. If this illness was his father's heart given out, as his mother supposed, what reason could there be but their conversation from last night. It must have been the thought of his son joining with the Mennonites that had done this.

John wanted to take his words back, plug the spoken words back into his mouth, say he was sorry, and change all this. Yet he knew it wouldn't change anything. He stood back in the flurry of the action that followed. Two attendants wheeled in a cart, their movements rapid, and placed an oxygen mask quickly on his father's face.

Aden told him he would take care of things at the store, said he would notify the people who needed to know, and would come down to the hospital later with Esther. John, blame heavy on his shoulders, went with the ambulance, seated on the opposite side from his mother, his father between them. At his father's head, the attendant sat, her face intent.

"Will his heart make it?" Miriam whispered.

"It's not his heart, ma'am," the attendant said. "Looks like a stroke to me."

The siren was still now. The churn of the engine beneath them combined with the rhythmic beep of some machine in the ambulance. The sounds reminded John of the strange world he suddenly found himself in. At home the early chores would have been done by now. Breakfast would have been on the table, his place in the world secure. His father would have been seated at the head, waiting to bow in prayer.

Here he didn't belong—watching his father's face behind that mask and his mother, her hands clutched in front of her. Outside the little window, the first houses of West Union could be seen, and the siren began its wail again. It warned his heart to get prepared, as it warned those ahead to give them room to pass. There were questions that needed to be faced, answers given for his actions.

"We can't lose him," his mother whispered.

"I know," he said, his burdened eyes meeting hers. "We'll be there soon."

"Your father loved you. Remember that no matter what happens."

"Dad will make it," he said, but the doubt hung in the air. "I'm sorry about last night."

"It's not your fault. You shouldn't think so. I've been afraid of this for a long time."

"I'm still sorry," he said.

She nodded. "I hope something can be done."

"There will be," he said, not certain where the strength of the answer came from.

Their arrival at the West Union Hospital caused another rush, in which John stayed close to his mother. The cart with his father on it disappeared rapidly. They signed papers, answered questions, and soon faced a doctor, whose face looked familiar.

It was the young Dr. Wine from last fall. He made no comment about their past acquaintance, a fact which didn't strike John as strange. They both had more important things on their minds at the moment.

"Mrs. Miller," he said, "your husband has had a stoke. Do you know when it began? When did you first notice any signs of his impairment?"

Miriam shook her head. "When I got up, he already was so. Is it bad?"

"I'm afraid so. The clot is in his basilar artery. Large. Two doses of t-PA haven't helped. You don't know what time this happened?"

"I just don't know," Miriam said.

Dr. Wine paused, seeming to hesitate. "There's another procedure we can do. Cincinnati has an advanced stroke care center, and they might be able to intervene. We can life flight your husband in."

Miriam was quiet, her face drawn. "We have no insurance, doctor. Do you know the cost involved?"

"You really shouldn't think of the money," Dr. Wine told her. "We don't have much time. There still is a chance, if we act quickly."

"We should do it," John spoke up. "I'll help pay."

"It's a lot of money, I'm sure." Miriam said glancing at him.

"The church will help," he said.

A slight smile crossed her face, and John realized what he had just said. He had appealed to the entity he had said last night he would leave, and his mother drew comfort from his instinctual reference, likely hoped his words last night had been forgotten.

"We will do it then, doctor," she said.

John stayed with his mother until the helicopter came, like the swoop of a bird over the horizon. It disappeared just as quickly back into the sky with his father and mother on board. Alone and with no way home until his uncle came, John returned to the hospital waiting room. The thoughts of regret began again, burning through his mind.

Had he been wrong last night? Would he have to give up now and turn back on his intention to persuade Bishop Martin? Was he to blame for his father's illness—a stroke, he now knew, which came the night of his rebellion. He could think of no other name. It had been rebellion. It rose up, as sure as the hidden blood clot had risen in his father's body, and struck at his heart.

Waves of guilt and remorse filled him. He must abandon his quest, he told himself. The certainty of it gripped him. There was no other choice. His mother had every right to hold this action against him for the rest of her life, even if she tried not to. With his father injured, his body destroyed for life, the reminder would be there each day.

If he turned back, forgiveness would follow him, not just the forgiveness of his mother's words, but the forgiveness of his own heart. There would be comfort, knowing he had done the right thing.

He reached for the familiar, the habit of a lifetime, and then knew what it meant. Rebecca. If he allowed things to drift, to go with the current of the community, they might well be separated. The church council would act slowly at first, then the final cut would come. He could see it all, as clearly as the sunshine outside the hospital window.

His old fear returned but died out because of his resolve. There would be no turning back. Any talk with Bishop Martin without his intention to see this through would only prove disastrous. His voice would betray him, his tone saying what his words didn't. He simply was not willing to compromise, take the easy way out, nor allow others to decide his fate. On this, the question could no longer remain.

People came and went around him, but he didn't notice. He was just an Amish boy, his hat left at home, forgotten in the rush of the morning. He was a young man seated on the *Englisha's* steel chairs, wrestling with the question of the ages—is love worth your all?

He decided it was. The decision was made in the face of his father's fall, in the knowledge of his mother's sorrow, and in the certainty of his bishop's words. He would go all the way with what lay in his power to do. Any less would be unworthy of her, of what she meant to him, and of the life they would live together.

They would be together. His mind struggled with the concept. Even if they never married, they would walk the same earth. That was reason enough, he decided, to do what was right. Not the right of others, but the right of his own brain.

A nurse came through the doorway. "Are you Mr. Miller?" she asked.

He nodded.

"Your father just arrived at the hospital in Cincinnati. They have taken him into surgery."

"Thanks." He smiled, grateful for the courtesy.

He gathered himself together, ready to face what lay ahead, even the death of his father. There would be a time to mourn, a time to weep for what had been, a time to explain if he could, but there was no longer a time to turn back. His heart was fixed.

An hour later, after he had called his sister, Bethany, with the news, Aden arrived with his wife, Esther. John filled them in on the details. They pondered what to do, asked questions of each other, and decided the best route was to return home until further news reached them. John rode along in the backseat of the buggy. They talked about his father, his life, and the man he had been.

Chapter Thirty-Five

The hired van pulled into the Keim driveway at around eleven o'clock, while Rebecca and Mattie were feverishly preparing another batch of pies. Several loads of wash were also underway. The driver halted the van in front of the sidewalk, and the door slid open.

"Looks like you surprised them," Stephen said chuckling. He got out and began to remove their luggage from the back.

Leona grinned from ear to ear at her accomplishment. She had baby Jonathon along, as well as her two youngest, James and Leroy.

"It's Leona?" Mattie exclaimed from the kitchen, both hands in flour.

"She would do that." Rebecca had her ear tuned to the washer downstairs, but now all was forgotten in a rush for the front door.

Mattie brushed off her hands as she crossed the yard and embraced her sister. "You naughty thing," she gushed.

Stephen grinned. "I guess her life was getting a little boring."

"I just had to do it," Leona replied. "You know I don't mind whatever you're in the midst of."

"We are in the middle of a mess," Rebecca told Leona, shaking her hand, then Stephen's. Leroy and James just stood there, looking her over.

"Come on, boys. You haven't forgotten Rebecca already," Leona told them.

They shook their heads, and Leroy finally said, "Hi."

"You want to play in the barn?" Rebecca asked. "There are all kinds of things to explore."

"After they change," Leona spoke up.

"Well, come on in then." Mattie shook her apron. "But welcome to the mess."

Leona laughed heartily.

Stephen excused himself to talk with the driver, after he asked Leona whether she still wished to leave on Monday morning. "If your sister doesn't throw you out first," he said chuckling.

"Don't pay attention to him," Leona said.

"I should throw you out," Mattie said, then asked, "Does the driver need a place to stay?"

"She has relatives in the area," Leona assured her. "You don't have room anyway."

Mattie nodded. "Edna does, though. She'd be glad to take her for a few nights."

"Oh, my wash!" Rebecca suddenly remembered her duties and rushed off.

Leroy and James grinned at the sudden departure.

"Your room is upstairs," Mattie told them all. "The large bedroom. The boys can sleep in Matthew's room."

"Take the suitcase up, right away," Leona instructed Stephen, who hoisted the luggage on his shoulders. "The boys can change."

Mattie led the way into the house and returned to the pie dough, while Leona ushered her boys up the stairs behind Stephen. A few minutes later, they were back down, out of their travel clothes, and ready for adventure.

"Be careful," Mattie told them. "It's a strange barn."

They nodded vigorously and disappeared out the door at a run.

Moments later Rebecca heard the rattle of buggy wheels in the driveway. Usually they saw a buggy before it came this close to the house. Curious, she glanced out the small window to see John tie up his horse at the hitching post.

"Well," she said, "that's strange." She thought to call up the stairs to her mother, but decided not to. Her arms around the hamper full of wet clothes, she went outside, a smile bright on her face.

John's face looked drawn, tense, she thought, and she sobered. He must be the carrier of serious news, which would explain the mid day visit.

"What's wrong?" she asked, setting the hamper on the grass.

"Dad," he said. The words simple, his voice sad. "He had a stroke last night. We took him to West Union. They couldn't do anything there, so they used the life flight and took him to Cincinnati."

A thousand pictures raced through her mind. "When?"

"Mom found him this morning. She woke me up early."

"Oh, my. I'm so sorry. Is it serious?"

"He wasn't moving much. Just moaned."

"Do they expect...much hope?"

John shrugged. "You know doctors. We saw the young one, the one who took care of me. He's good, but said he couldn't do anything more in West Union. So it must be pretty serious."

"Your father..." Rebecca felt the tears come. Visions of Isaac's kind face passed in front of her.

"Yes..." John seemed to struggle with his own emotions. His lips parted as if to speak, but no sound came out.

She took his hand and squeezed it. "What's happening now?"

"He's in surgery. Some intervention. That's what the doctor said. Aden brought me home. There didn't seem to be any use waiting in West Union when we can wait here."

"What's happened?" Mattie called out, as she and Leona came across the yard.

"Isaac had a stroke," Rebecca told them. "He's in surgery now."

"Your father?" Leona asked.

John nodded, his face etched in pain.

"How is he?" Leona asked. "What a wonderful man your father is."

"We don't know. We're waiting for news. Mom's with him. I just wanted to let Rebecca know," John answered.

"*Da Hah* will watch over him," Leona said, her voice strong, certain, as if she knew something the rest didn't.

"We can only wait," John told her, and Rebecca thought he looked like he wanted to say more. She wondered how the evening had gone last night. Had John talked with his father? Had there been time before this happened? She pushed the thoughts back. It was selfish of her to even think of such things with John in such obvious agony.

"We will send someone over. Maybe Lester can go tonight," Mattie said, "to see how things are. Surely your father will be out of surgery by then."

"I hope so. I really have to get back," John said. "Aden needs help at the store. Sharon tried to run things this morning by herself, while Aden and Esther drove to the hospital. I think business is backed up."

"You do that," Mattie said patting his arm. "We all know how hard this is, but *Da Hah* knows best."

Rebecca decided to walk with John back to the buggy. The wet clothes would just have to wait. Her mother saw her hesitation and gave her a look that said she understood. Leona must have seen their exchange because she promptly grabbed the hamper and headed toward the wash line.

She heard her mother tell Leona, "You didn't come all the way out here to work," as she walked with John. Leona's response was gentle but firm. "I'm going to help."

At the buggy John hesitated and then said, "I talked with Dad last night. He took some things I said pretty hard."

"You don't blame yourself, do you?" she asked.

"I do," he said, "at least in part. But it couldn't be helped."

"Surely your mother doesn't feel so." She searched his eyes for the answer.

"I have to do what has to be done," he said and seemed on the verge of saying more but dropped his gaze to the ground.

"Does your mother think…that it's your fault?"

"I don't think so," he finally said. "I told her I was sorry. She has been afraid of this happening for quite some time."

Rebecca breathed deeply. "Maybe your father will be okay."

"I don't know," he said and put his foot on the buggy step, obviously preparing to leave. "Regardless, I have to do what is best for us."

She wondered what that meant but figured there was time later to speak of it. "I'll be thinking of you. There might be good news. Leona seems to think so." Confidence in her aunt's opinion rose up in her heart.

John smiled and climbed up onto the seat. She stepped back as he took off. The last of his buggy disappeared around the river bend when she thought of her wash again. Quickly she ran to the clothesline. Leona was already done, the empty hamper in her hand, and on the way back to the house.

"That's too bad," Leona said. "You two do have it rough, don't you?"

"Don't say that," Rebecca chided her. "You'll make me cry."

"That's good sometimes."

"I'm about cried out," Rebecca replied. "Now this happens."

"He'll be okay. Isaac will be," Leona said, with confidence in her voice.

"How do you know?"

"He's a good man."

"That doesn't always help."

Leona nodded. "I know. It's not just that—not all of it, really. I just feel he will."

Rebecca took a deep breath. She thought of spilling all her news—of last night and the letters, but she held back, especially what she learned about Emma. That ground seemed forbidden, as if she had been a spectator to sacred things that were unspeakable.

"I really need to talk," Leona said, "with you and Mattie."

"About me and John?" Rebecca asked. "You said something in the letter."

"Yes. Maybe we can talk over the lunch hour. Stephen's gone back to the fields with Lester, I saw."

"We did decide something last night." Rebecca held the front door open.

"I hope something is done and soon. People are really talking out there."

"It's not my fault," Rebecca informed her aunt. She knew she sounded too intense, but the feelings just rose up in her.

"I think we'd better talk right now. Let's help your mom with the pies."

"I have another load of wash to do," Rebecca told her.

"I'll help you when we're done." Leona led the way to the kitchen. Jonathon cried from the floor when she passed, and that took a moment to get him satisfied again.

Rebecca waited. She enjoyed the sight of her nephew as he kicked on the floor, his blanket firmly under him again.

"He'll be okay," Leona said. "It's a strange house for him, but he gets used to those things quickly—like a boy." She made a face as she finished her statement.

"Where are you two?" Mattie hollered from the kitchen.

"Coming," Leona said. "Jonathon distracted us."

"Leona wants to talk," Rebecca told her mother, "while we work."

"I suppose so. If it's about John and Rebecca, I'm about talked out on that subject," Mattie informed them.

"But something has to be done. It's all over the place out there. Can't something be done?" Leona spun the opener on a can of cherries, as both she and Rebecca found their places in the pie-making process without instructions.

"You surely didn't come all the way out here just to say that," Mattie said.

"Not really. I guess I wanted to visit. But can't something be done? I hate to see Rebecca's name dragged down like this. Everyone thinks she's marrying for money. Emma never did anything like that. It's all just a shame, the way things are turning out. How Emma got the money from her brother, I don't know. But now everyone thinks Emma must have found out about Rebecca and Atlee and that she's trying to do a good deed with the money, of course. She's just trying to keep someone in the faith."

Rebecca cleared her throat, but the words wouldn't come. Her heart felt tied up, obligated to an honor, a loyalty to her former teacher. She couldn't violate it even to defend herself.

"I'm going to give back the money," she said instead.

"That's good to hear but hard to make anyone believe," Leona told her. "Do the ministers around here believe you?"

"Mom and Dad do," Rebecca told her.

"Yes, we do," Mattie agreed. "Lester and John talked last night. Well... all of us did. They want to be married before next communion."

"Oh!" Leona'a eyes lit up. "And you and Lester agreed?"

"We did," Mattie said.

"Then that would solve the problem for Rebecca and everyone."

"I think so," Mattie told her.

"So you're getting married. And early." Leona turned to face Rebecca.

Rebecca felt a flush rise up her neck. "The bishop has to agree yet. John had hoped to speak with his father. He did last night, John said, but now this has happened."

"*Da Hah* will help you," Leona said, her voice firm. "I just feel it. Emma was such an honorable person. She wouldn't do anything without the blessing of the Almighty on it. This cannot but turn out well."

"We hope so," Mattie said. "Turn on the oven, Rebecca."

"It will," Leona said. "Love is in the air. My, my, isn't that good."

"You sound like a schoolgirl," Mattie told her. "Acting like one too. Scaring the wits out of us, coming early."

Leona laughed heartily. "It's the best thing I've done in a long time."

Rebecca smiled, caught up in their emotion. Leona left with her a few minutes later for the basement and the final load of wash. They chatted about Milroy and the news from there. The hours passed quickly.

A full supper was started about three, and the children were welcomed home from school at three thirty. After handshakes and hugs were exchanged, it was time for chores. Rebecca left to help Matthew, while Leona and Mattie stayed in the kitchen.

After supper her father, filled in on the happening of the day, left with Stephen for Wheat Ridge to see if there was news about their fallen minister.

CHAPTER THIRTY-SIX

Rachel called for Reuben to come. Supper was ready. He lowered *The Budget*, glanced at her, and then lay the pages on the floor. Rachel, already seated at the kitchen table, sighed. Her days had grown long, filled with drudgery and weariness. She felt tired most of the time. Reuben told her cheerfully it was the expectant child and she would feel better once it was born. Rachel knew the reason wasn't the child but couldn't really say so without too much being said. She had given in to despair.

Her antics with the ferns remained her secret and would stay so, if she had anything to say about it. A lecture from Reuben, combined with the disappointment of her plan's failure would be too much to bear. To her the plan would always remain sanctified, an attempt at a noble effort.

She had now remained without a new plan for weeks and supposed things would continue so. Her strength had simply come to an end, her efforts thwarted at all turns. The inheritance lay beyond her grasp, her life condemned to poverty, she had concluded. God, as well as man, seemed to be against her.

Reuben wanted her to help in the barn tonight after supper. The "goat barn" he called it. She couldn't bring herself to do the same. To her it was the barn, as it had been before the goat venture, before the building was associated with the lowly critters Reuben cared so much about.

Reuben sat down across from her. She was large with child, and he was deep in his own thoughts. They bowed their heads together in prayer.

"Luke's coming home Saturday night," he said, as he reached for the nearest bowl of food.

"I know." She really had no interest in the subject. Since the ferns were gone, the attempt to stay on Luke's good side held no purpose. Plus he would bring along Susie or talk about her. Susie was just another reminder of so many things gone wrong.

"You don't look well," Reuben said searching her face. "Is the child too much?"

"I'm not having problems," she told him.

"It's a late pregnancy," he said. "Neither of us are spring chickens anymore. I guess no one could blame you."

"I'm just weary. Tired of life."

He smiled, "It's *Da Hah's* gift, the child, His mercy in our old age."

"A cross," she muttered.

"It bears the mark of righteousness," he said. "Children are a great blessing."

"Perhaps the inheritance would make it easier," she said. Not that she expected her words to change his mind, but she couldn't help herself.

"God has already provided. Your father's money can just stay where it is. That Rebecca girl will get her things straightened out in time. Sooner or later, I might even speak with Bishop about it."

"About what?"

He glanced at her. "I heard she was having some trouble with the church. She stayed back from communion, at least that's what I heard. I think it's correct. It's all kind of silly. Let the girl have the money. Bishop might be able to clear things up with Milroy."

"So she can marry Amish?"

"Of course. Then the problem's solved."

"What about us?" She gripped the side of the chair.

"*Da Hah* has blessed us with a prosperous business. We are well supplied for. As the good book says, if you have food and raiment, be content. That we have and more. I've never felt younger. We're about to have a child in our old age like Abram and Sarah. Let the girl have the money. It never did your aunt much good."

"How can you say such a thing?" She felt the food catch in her throat.

"It didn't," he insisted. "Look at Emma, the life she lived. Sure she was a good schoolteacher, but others could have taken her place there. What did she miss out on? A husband, children, grandchildren, many blessings. Every woman should experience them."

"I would have taken her place," she said.

He glanced mildly at her. "Sometimes you worry me. You will meet *Da Hah* someday face-to-face. What will you tell Him then? Money won't do any good. He might even have problems with you, with how much you love money."

"I obey Him same as you," she said but avoided his gaze.

"We must love Him with all our hearts. Do you love Him?"

"Of course I do. How can you ask that?"

"It troubles me," he said. "I think about it at night sometimes, the day that's to come. Like a great dawning it will be. Angels will come with Him. He'll be brighter than the sun. That terrible sword will be in His mouth. Trumpets, loud, will awake the dead. Do you love Him, Rachel?"

"You read too many Scriptures on Sunday," she said with a tight smile. "You don't have to be a deacon at home. I'm your wife. You don't have to preach."

"I wasn't trying to preach," he said, but his eyes looked sad. "It's your soul, Rachel. You are the one who will have to give answer for it."

"You shouldn't think such things. You're my husband. I'm okay. I'm married to a deacon."

"You have been a good wife." His words caught her by surprise, as he reached for a second helping of potatoes. "I have no complaints. We have a good son. He will stay in the faith, I think. Now another child, one who will comfort us in our old age. I couldn't ask for more."

She said nothing but studied his face. He was such a simple man, so easily satisfied. He had interested her at one time, drawn her in, but that was a long time ago. To satisfy him now meant little to her. She already knew where his standard lay. It was well below the mark that mattered to her.

Reuben pushed his plate away, the last of the food scraped off. "I'm ready for help in the goat barn."

"I need to do the dishes first." She rose too.

"This won't take long. I really need help right now. I can finish by myself then."

She assented silently and followed him outside. He pulled his boots on, while she did the same. Apparently whatever he needed help at would require boots. On the way out, he stopped for a stepladder and then his tool belt. She held the door of the barn open for him, as he passed through sideways with his tools.

Goats greeted them. They came from all corners of the barn, heads uplifted, bleating cheerfully. Some bounced around, butting each other. Reuben chuckled with delight, pushed them aside with his foot when they came too close.

"Where do you want help?" she asked. Every moment spent here would be too long.

"We need to fix those boards." Reuben motioned with his chin toward the ceiling. "They're broken and falling down."

"What am I supposed to do?"

"Hold the stepladder and hand me the boards." Reuben pointed again toward the side of the barn. She saw the boards lined up there and went to get one. The sooner this was done, the sooner she could get back to the kitchen.

Reuben set the stepladder in place. The goats crowded around.

"Why don't you put them out?" she asked.

"There's no gate on the yard," he said and smiled.

"There used to be."

"They knocked it down."

She bit back her retort. That Reuben didn't fix things too quickly was old news with her.

"I'm going up," he said and took the first step.

She set the board down a little distance away and got ready to grasp the ladder, once his legs were high enough.

"I'm going to push," he said, then moved up higher. She saw him reach for the ceiling boards, straighten them out, and then let go again.

Apparently he saw the question in her eyes. "I have to nail these first. Then I'll need a board."

She watched, her neck bending upward as Reuben produced a nail from his pouch and gripped the hammer. His arm extended, he took another step higher. Out of the corner of her eye, she saw the commotion. Two goats tussled, their heads together, their hindquarters bouncing skyward, their bodies coming toward her.

Rachel told herself later, told herself a thousand times, that she had hung on tightly, had grasped the ladder with all her might as the two goats plummeted into the legs of the stepladder. The impact was too much. The ladder went sideways, and Reuben went airborne, his arms extended, his hammer arched skyward.

She had lost her own balance. Her knee had struck the stepladder, causing a stinging pain all the way up her leg. Behind her, she had heard Reuben land, the thud dull in her ears. Expecting a rebuke, she had turned, pulled the ladder upright, then waited.

It took a moment to realize that Reuben didn't move. With a hesitant step forward, the area now clear of goats that had fled the falling human bodies, she approached him. She touched his shoulder. He moaned once, seemed to move his arm, and then there was silence.

"Reuben," she called. Then louder, "Reuben."

A man simply didn't die so quickly. She was certain of it. Yet Reuben was not one to tease her either, especially in matters such as this. Gently she moved his head and noticed, for the first time, the board she had set on the ground. Its upraised edge cut across Reuben's neck. She knew then, without being told, that Reuben was dead.

Her instincts screamed that Reuben must be moved, taken out of this horrible place, but she overpowered them. In the midst of reaching for his arms with the intention to pull him with all her might toward the door, she stopped.

Will I not be blamed for this? There were *Englisha* people who would come. They would ask questions. They would investigate and be suspicious of her. Reuben would have to stay where he was, so they could see what had happened, that she had not caused this.

She left him surrounded by goats. Shuddering at the sight but driven by necessity, she ran across the road to the neighbor's house. She and Reuben never went there to call—Reuben didn't want to be a bother—but in his death, there was no choice.

Her knock was answered, her breathless pronouncement noted. "I'll call right away," Mrs. Henderson said, and Rachel ran back to the barn.

She kept the goats away, drove them back with a vengeance, and that was how they found her. She stood near his body, her face dry of tears, her soul in shock. They asked questions as she knew they would, and she answered them in detail, and then said it all over again to someone else.

They seemed satisfied. The ambulance soon left with the stretcher, the white sheet over his body. She told them what funeral home the Amish used in Rushville. Then Luke arrived, his horse foamed at the mouth from the hard drive, followed by Ezra and his wife. Word quickly reached the corners of the Amish community. Men and women left what they were doing to be with those who suffered.

It was Luke who asked the remaining police officer about the cause of his father's death.

"I'm not medical, son," the officer told him. "I suppose the doctor will give you his final report. The first responders thought his neck was broken up in the C4 range. Spinal shock. Your father fell on the edge of a board."

Luke stood there, tears streaming down his cheeks.

"Sorry, son," the officer said. "You'd better stay with your mother. Make sure she doesn't go into shock. She was there when it happened."

Luke nodded numbly and walked toward the house. Buggies pulled into the yard all around him. Rachel sat inside on the couch, as the tasks of her house were taken over by others. Already women washed the supper dishes, their voices hushed. She made a place on the couch for Luke when he came in.

Luke sat beside her and took her hand. The tears came down his cheeks, as if they never would stop. Rachel pulled him toward her, her son, her firstborn, and held him tight. She saw before her eyes the days that would come—the funeral, the burial, and the loneliness she would experience without Reuben. She knew she should feel sorrow, yet she watched in horror as joy rose in her heart. Reuben no longer stood between her and the money.

She bit her lip fiercely and leaned her head against Luke. She told herself she was evil, that Reuben shouldn't have died, but the pleasure wouldn't go away. Inside of her the child was still.

CHAPTER THIRTY-SEVEN

I n Miller's Furniture store the phone rang, its shrill sound filling the empty building. The phone rang a dozen times, and then was silent. In the living room across the fields, John waited, a calm hush in the house. Bishop Martin and Aden had come over for the evening with their wives. The two women were in the kitchen, preparations for a simple supper under way. Since this was an illness of a minister, more visitors might be expected. Those already there would eat when supper was ready and feed any others as they arrived.

John noticed Lester and his brother-in-law Stephen driving their buggy into the driveway. John thought at first Rebecca might have decided to come. He jumped up from his chair but saw by the time he stepped out into the yard that she had not. He then told Lester the news.

Isaac had come out of surgery a little after twelve. The surgeon hoped for the best because the blood clot had been removed. Aden had called the hospital in Cincinnati at six again, but nothing had been definite. He had also updated John's sister again by leaving a message at the neighbor's house she used for emergencies. Miriam had said she saw a lot of color in Isaac's face and that he seemed to have recognized her for the brief moment she was allowed in his room.

Lester thanked John, and the two left again.

Inside the house Aden's wife announced that supper was ready. The bishop and Aden motioned for John to go first. Because no other visitors had come yet, they were to sit around the table apparently. John took his place and was surprised he could be so hungry. Under the circumstances he expected otherwise, but the warm vegetable soup, its rich aroma rising to his face, drew him in.

Bishop Martin led the group in prayer, giving thanks for the goodness of God, for being with them that day, and for helping the doctors during Isaac's surgery. When he was done, another buggy came up the driveway, and another one arrived after that. They both pulled up to the hitching post and tied up.

John, already on his feet and prepared to go outside, was told by Aden to sit down.

"I'll take care of them," his uncle said. "You need to eat."

"I suppose so," John said, his smile weak.

"Your mother taking this well?" the bishop asked, when Aden had left.

"Seems to. She's often worried about something like this happening," John told him.

"Ya, we all do," the bishop said nodding. "Old age comes. *Da Hah* has seen fit for us to drink that cup."

John thought about blurting out his regrets regarding his disagreement with his father, but he would have to include the reason why. He must wait, he had decided earlier, until Rebecca could be present. It would be better that way. Rebecca could hear and decide for herself when the moment came. If he spoke to her beforehand, she might be persuaded against her better judgment.

The bishop ate his soup slowly, the spoon rose and fell the full length of his beard. John wondered what the bishop's reaction to the disagreement would be. Would he be shocked, astonished that Isaac's son thought about joining the Mennonites? No doubt he would, and John had doubts again about the wisdom of his plan. Perhaps it might be better to wait, let the matter blow over. He pushed the emotions aside and resolved to do what he felt was right.

"I need to speak with you sometime," he said, his voice low. Outside he could see Aden talking with the two couples who had just arrived. They then made their way slowly toward the house.

"Oh?" Bishop Martin said raising his eyebrows.

"About Rebecca and me."

"Yes. That might be good. We have time tonight, maybe when the others leave."

"I would like…for Rebecca to be here."

"You are wise," the bishop said nodding his head. "It's a serious matter before us."

"I know," John replied. Aden came in the front door, pausing to hold it as the others walked through. They came over to shake hands with John and Bishop, and then went to get plates for themselves.

The evening wore on. The conversation ebbed and flowed around stories of others who had suffered strokes and the hope of Isaac's recovery. Aden went to call the hospital from the furniture store, just before everyone left, and came back with a good report. Miriam said the doctor had been in to see Isaac and was satisfied.

John didn't think the look on Aden's face matched the news he brought and so was not surprised when Aden continued, "A call came through from Milroy just as I was ready to leave. Reuben Byler died this evening."

The mood in the room changed instantly. "How?" Bishop asked. "He was not an old man."

"In a fall in the goat barn. Off a stepladder. Rachel was with him, holding the stepladder, they thought. I guess the goats acted up, and Rachel couldn't hold the ladder. The funeral's on Monday."

"We will have to go," Bishop said. He glanced at his wife beside him on the couch. She nodded her agreement.

"Two things in one day," Aden said. He sat down on a chair brought in from the kitchen. "At least the news about Isaac is good."

"*Da Hah* takes, and *Da Hah* gives," Bishop said, his voice soft. "He has perhaps seen good to spare us a good man. Your father is that, John."

"I know," John said in agreement.

"We should be going," Aden spoke up. "Perhaps we should go to the funeral too. They are relatives."

"It'll be a large one," Bishop said and got to his feet. To John's surprise he motioned for him to follow. Outside the bishop's wife, as if by some secret signal, walked on past them and climbed into the buggy.

The bishop cleared his throat, the light from the gas lantern playing on his face. "I thought perhaps we should talk now—about you and Rebecca."

John wasn't sure what to say.

"I know you wanted Rebecca to be here, but we will be gone over Sunday. This matter has dragged on long enough. It would be a great relief to my mind…to find an answer to the problem."

"I would like that." John cleared his throat, his jaw tense.

"Has your father's stroke anything to do with you and Rebecca?"

"We spoke last night," John said but decided to offer no more. He still didn't think it wise to get too far into this conversation, lest he have to reveal his final intentions. But one didn't rebuff a bishop's interest.

"Isaac told me how much he was burdened down with this. You are his only son, John, and have always been in the church standard. I must say this has troubled both of us plenty."

"Rebecca has only spoken the truth," John said. "She will return the money after the marriage. There is no other way to do this."

"I know," Bishop Martin sighed. "I must say this has gone on long enough. There is just nothing good coming out of all this. If we keep going on, with how people feel about this, soon we'll have to do things we don't want to. We'll have to take steps—steps for which there is no real reason. What did you speak about to your father last night?"

"Of my talk with Lester and Mattie," John said because he had to answer the question.

"Oh…" the bishop said showing interest.

"Lester asked me over. We talked with Rebecca and Mattie."

"Did you come to any conclusion?"

John thought he shouldn't but then blurted it out. "That we marry this fall—before communion time. That way Rebecca will have time to give back the money."

"And Lester agreed with this?"

"Yes."

"And your father? Did he think it would work?"

"No," John said. "That was when I said some things. But I wanted Rebecca to be here for that."

"He's a good man." The bishop smiled in the darkness, the living room light casting shadows on his beard. "So he thought it wouldn't work?"

"Yes," John said, surprised where the conversation was going.

"Then perhaps I should surprise him," the bishop chuckled. "Relieve his mind. Especially now that *Da Hah* has spared him from a stroke."

"But the deacon?" John caught his breath.

The bishop smiled again and lay his hand on John's shoulder. "You leave the deacon to me, son. He's the deacon. I'm the bishop. You two just go ahead and plan that wedding. Get it over with in time for communion. You won't let me down, will you?"

"No," John choked.

"You can tell your father. It might help him get better faster. I must attend the funeral. We'll drive out tomorrow, I suppose. Keep us off the roads on Sunday."

"Thank you," John said.

"Don't worry about it." The bishop turned to leave. "Just take care of that girl." Then he was gone, his walk slow. John thought he saw a limp in his step on the way to the buggy.

John struggled with his feelings. With the suddenness of their arrival, relief and guilt ran through him. He turned to go back into the house and thanked the two couples who had come. They were on their way out. Inside Aden and Esther were on their feet.

"There are leftovers," Esther told him. "We left them for later. We'll let you know if any calls come in on the answering machine."

"Thanks," he said again as they left.

Alone the reality of the bishop's words came back. Relieved by the good news of his father's health, he let the joy rise up. He was to be married—married to Rebecca—and he didn't have to make good on his threat. He didn't have to see his parents' teary eyes or Rebecca's. No decisions needed to be agonized over nor hearts broken, rather the path ahead was straight and smooth.

Then the knowledge that the purchase price had been partially paid by his father's stroke came to him. It bothered him, but then he let the thought go. He couldn't control everything. What was said needed to be said. Had it not turned out okay in the end?

True, Reuben Byler had died the same day, but he figured that was another matter. Tragic, yes, and sad, but he now had a full plate of responsibilities in front of him. He was to be a married man, a man with a wife and a home to support. And if *Da Hah* willed it, children to raise.

Upstairs he lay on the bed and let the wonder of it sweep over him. A gate, which he had often figured would never open, had opened. Not only had Rebecca agreed to marry him all that time ago, she had stayed with him and sorted out her feelings and desires that drew her to the past.

It didn't seem fair that she had to go through so much in the past months. First, she had to deal with his jealousy, the accident, the uncertainty of whether he would walk again, then Emma's passing. That had been the last trial. So suddenly it had come. So out of the blue, and yet Rebecca had weathered the storm.

Not only had she made it through, but more than that, she had seemed to grow more beautiful with each difficulty she survived. He could not be more blessed, of this he was certain. *Da Hah* had seen fit to bless him with a truly wonderful girl.

He closed his eyes, but sleep didn't come. There were so many things needing to be done. The renters on his place would have to be notified. Thankfully there was a clause in his contract where a thirty-day notice could be given.

He decided it would be given right away. Even if a little early, they needed plenty of time to clean and repaint the house. Rebecca might even want to change some things, and he could only imagine them as wonderful changes. If he could afford it, they would be made.

Sleep came much later, but all night he dreamed—dreams awash with Rebecca, the house on the hill, the stream that flowed behind it, and the beauty of her face in his hands.

CHAPTER THIRTY-EIGHT

Morning brought another phone call from the Cincinnati hospital and a request from Miriam for taxi transportation home. The doctors, she said, expressed great delight in Isaac's progress. Apparently Isaac's stroke had not set in till the early morning hours, and so the clot had been removed in time. His recovery was nothing less than dramatic. By that evening Isaac would be able to walk, Miriam said, so there was no need for a special handicap van.

His joy at the bishop's news nearly exploding inside him, John had planned to visit Rebecca that evening after his duties at Miller's Furniture, but this trip to pick up his father took priority. The news, he figured, would be none the worse for its late transmittal. Rebecca would understand.

Aden's wife, Esther, rode along. They hired Mrs. Coldwell, who lived in Unity. She often drove her van on taxi trips for the Amish. John sat on the first bench seat. Esther sat in the front. He listened as Esther filled Mrs. Coldwell in on the details of Isaac's illness and recovery.

"They have quite the techniques for stroke victims," Mrs. Coldwell commented when Esther was done.

"We are thankful," Esther told her. "It would have been awful to see Isaac struck down in his old age."

"Comes hard enough already," Mrs. Coldwell agreed. "You folks don't have insurance."

"No." Esther shook her head.

"Expensive. That treatment has to be," Mrs. Coldwell said glancing sideways.

"I know," Esther replied nodding.

John remembered the conversation at the hospital, forgotten in all the rush of things. There would be a bill to pay—a right big one. For a brief moment, he thought of Rebecca's money. It would be easy to use some of that, pay off the bill and unburden his parents.

As soon as it came, he rejected the thought. It would be dishonest, a betrayal that would only open the door to even greater ones. He could imagine the hurt on Rebecca's face, if he were to even ask for such a thing.

When they arrived at the hospital, John walked in with Esther, while Mrs. Coldwell waited in the van. She said she would pull up when she saw them come out. Miriam had Isaac already checked out and in the front waiting room. John approached them, emotions strong in his chest. He knew they had been spared a great tragedy.

"I'm so sorry about the other night," were his first words after Isaac's embrace.

"You shouldn't say such things," his mother said from beside them.

"It was not your fault, son," Isaac assured him. "I had this coming a long time. I guess your mother was right."

"Of course I was," Miriam said, but tears brightened her cheeks.

"It is good to see you and so well," Esther told Isaac and shook his hand.

"I'll be eating rabbit food from now on," Isaac said chuckling. "Miriam got the list. Doctor's orders."

"You've heard that before," Esther told him. "This time you'd better listen."

"He will." Miriam's voice was grim.

"Oh, well..." Isaac said sighing, "there will still be pleasures in life, I suppose."

"Having you around in good health will be one of them," Miriam told him. "You have the van outside?"

"Mrs. Coldwell is waiting," Esther said, as she moved toward the door.

On the drive back, John sat in the second seat back and listened to the questions about his father's hospital stay and surgery. Isaac obviously remembered little of it.

"The first thing I remember is waking up and my head hurting," Isaac told them. "That must have been after the surgery."

"That's how bad it was," Miriam said, her face still drawn.

"I guess *Da Hah* had mercy on me," Isaac said and chuckled.

"We needed to hear you preach again," Esther told him.

"Oh…he is a preacher," Mrs. Coldwell said as she remembered.

"Don't take Esther's word on the preaching," Isaac informed her.

"Don't take his either," Miriam said. "He's good. I'll take him any day."

"Now…now," Isaac said, taking her hand in his. "*Da Hah* has been good to us."

It was already late by the time they got back. John had entertained thoughts of a trip over to the Keim place yet but decided against it. He followed his father's slow steps into the house and helped him into his chair.

"Bedtime for me," Isaac said grinning. "Real soon."

"You're eating something first," Miriam informed him. "The stuff they feed you at hospitals—it's frightening."

She brought him a slice of leftover meat loaf, from last night's food preparation, and lettuce. Isaac made a face but ate it. John sat with his father but knew he wouldn't last too long. Tiredness swept over his body. The events of the last few days, he thought, had sapped more of his strength than he had been aware of.

"You must talk to the bishop tomorrow," Isaac said. "Perhaps he will understand."

"He won't be here," John told him. "There is a funeral in Milroy."

"Oh, no," Miriam said from the kitchen. "I forgot to tell you Reuben Byler died. He fell off a stepladder."

"Reuben," Isaac said, his voice quiet, "he wasn't that old."

"No," Miriam agreed and came into the living room to sit beside him. John sat with them in silence. The light of the gas lantern hissed above their heads.

"*Da Hah* does as He sees best," Isaac said. "His ways are above ours. He leaves some and takes others."

Miriam stroked his arm, her eyes full of tears.

"I wish you could speak with Bishop soon," Isaac told John. "This thing weighs heavy on me."

"He already spoke with me," John offered, now that it seemed appropriate.

"Bishop did?" Isaac said looking up.

"Yes. He said Lester's plan would be okay."

John saw joy leap into his father's eyes.

"*Da Hah sei lohb,*" he said. "He is worthy."

"What made Bishop change his mind?" Miriam asked.

"I don't know for sure," John said. "I suspect it was Dad's accident."

"Really," Miriam said, "you think so?"

"Then it was worth it all." Isaac reached out to grip John's arm. "It was the right thing for Bishop to do. I am so glad. Now you are..." Isaac's voice choked. "You will be with us, the way it ought to be."

"You weren't serious, were you?" Miriam asked him. "About going Mennonite?"

John was silent. He hadn't expected his mother to ask the question.

"He was," Isaac said.

Miriam raised her eyebrows, so John nodded.

"But...Mennonite. Not really. You wouldn't now, would you?" His mother's eyes pleaded with him.

"No." John shook his head. "I never did want to. It just wasn't right the way Rebecca was being used. I thought I had to do something."

"*Da Hah* respects an honest heart," Isaac said. "You are a good boy. We can be thankful you received help."

"You can say that," Miriam said. "Mennonite. You don't think Rebecca would have gone with you?"

"I have no idea," John told her. "I wasn't going to tell Rebecca till together we talked with Bishop."

"The follies of youth." Miriam sighed. "Are you ready for bed, Isaac?"

"More than ready," he told her.

John watched as his mother helped his father toward the bedroom. His face looked tired, his body weary, but underneath John knew his father's heart was full of joy—joy that his son had found the right answer to his problem, joy that the faith they believed in had stood the test, joy that though so much had depended on the actions of men and women, vessels made of clay, things had turned out okay.

Tomorrow John would see Rebecca, and he would tell her the good news. Sleep came easily for him, and he dreamed no dreams all night. He woke with the alarm clock, since even on Sunday mornings, chores had to be done. Both his parents would stay home from church, he figured, and his mother told him at the breakfast table his assumption was correct.

To leave early had no purpose, but John still drove out of the driveway ten minutes ahead of time, such was his eagerness to see Rebecca. Perhaps, he figured, he could catch a glimpse of her when she arrived. The family would likely come in the buggy, with Rebecca's aunt in the van they had hired. He doubted whether the Keim buggies could hold both family and visitors.

He parked his buggy and shook hands down the line of men and boys, then took his place and waited. His face must have showed his excitement because Will, who stood beside him, teased, "You'll see her in church."

John jumped.

Will must have put his imagination in high gear immediately. "You're not being published today, are you?" he asked John.

John's voice caught. "No," he said, but Will still looked suspicious.

"Just good news," John told him, in the hopes Will would be satisfied.

"She already said the good word, didn't she?"

"Yes." John couldn't help but grin. "Just more of the same."

"Okay, be mysterious." With that Will turned to speak to the boy beside him.

John got what he waited for a few minutes later. The van carrying the Keim visitors pulled in first and parked off to the side. Lester, in the surrey, came in soon afterward and stopped by the front walk. While Mattie and her younger girls climbed down, Rebecca appeared with her aunt from the van.

Together the shawl-wrapped women walked up the concrete walk. John thought he saw Rebecca glance his way but couldn't be certain. Ten minutes later, when the line of men and boys moved indoors, he caught Rebecca's eye. The hint of a smile played on her face. He sat down on the hard bench and held himself back from a steady stare in her direction.

When the songs started, he was asked to lead in the praise song. He gladly agreed, even though he wasn't that good at it. The energy came more from his heart than his ability to stay on tune with all the ups and downs of Amish German hymn singing. Nothing could dim his happiness today though, even when he stumbled on the second line and had to receive help from the song leader.

After the last line was sung, he dared to glance at Rebecca and saw her eyes twinkle with mirth. He felt as if his heart could hold no more joy. By the time the service was done and dinner was eaten, he could hardly contain his news either.

"What are you grinning about?" she asked him, when she climbed into the buggy. "You really shouldn't try to lead songs."

He ignored the remark. "Bishop talked with me."

"Oh…" She settled down on the seat beside him. "He did?"

"Yes. We can get married this fall."

"Oh, John," she said, reaching for his arm, "did he really?"

He nodded and knew his face glowed with his joy.

"Such good news. Oh, John. And right after your father's illness. Do good and bad things always happen together?"

John slapped the lines. The horse in line behind him was impatient, its nose already tight against his back.

"One may, in fact, have had something to do with the other. I think Bishop wanted to give Dad good news."

"Then all thing do work out."

"Seems so. Are you happy that we can marry sooner?"

"Yes," she said but avoided his eyes because of the tears on her cheeks. "It seems almost wrong to be so happy."

"I'll talk to the renters tomorrow," John told her. "I can hardly believe it myself."

"Leona wants us to come to our place for supper tonight. They're leaving tomorrow."

"Miss the singing?" John asked.

"Yes, it's worth it. Leona doesn't visit too often. Plus, we're almost old people now. Singings are a thing of the past."

"Not quite," John said chuckling, "though not soon enough for me."

He put his arm around her and pulled her close, as they drove across the Harshville covered bridge.

CHAPTER THIRTY-NINE

L eona and her family left at dawn on Monday morning. Rebecca got back in from chores in time to sit with her aunt for a few minutes at the breakfast table. Mattie had prepared a separate breakfast for her sister's family to give them an early start.

The goodbyes were happy ones, hopes high for a soon reunion at Rebecca's wedding. As a sister of the bride's mother, Leona would have a favored seat all day. She pronounced herself excited at the prospects of a wedding in which she had no work to do.

In many ways Leona's departure triggered the beginnings of the wedding plans. Before that something always seemed to disrupt them. To Rebecca Leona's visit would always remain the dividing line between uncertainty and the sure knowledge she was to be a bride.

The wedding dress came out of the closet. That was where she had stored the box of cut material when she had realized what Emma's actions might mean. She figured there would be plenty of time to work on it but had never found the heart to sew the dress. Now that things were settled, the energy returned with a rush.

After Matthew left with the other schoolchildren, Rebecca laid the material on the kitchen table. Mattie must have forgotten what she purchased because her mother's breath caught when she came up from the basement.

"It's beautiful, Rebecca. So you really are getting married."

"Yes. Bishop said so."

"Then I'd better get busy. I still have Leona's visit on my mind, I guess."

"I'm so glad she was here this weekend."

"Next time we'll be ready for her the day before she arrives," Mattie chuckled. "So let's see. My...my head's just spinning, but we should be able to handle everything."

"It's not your first wedding, at least. I'm thankful for that."

"The others didn't have as many bumps in the road," Mattie said making a face.

"To a smooth sailing from here on out!" Rebecca made a flourish over the kitchen table, the scissors in her hand. They slipped and flew across the room, the arch high, but missing the kitchen table and wedding dress. The point thudded into the bench Matthew had left pulled out before they clattered onto the floor.

Mattie raised her eyebrows. "Don't count the chickens before they hatch. There are always rough spots in the road."

Rebecca felt a little pale, as she went to pick up the scissors. "I guess I'd better watch what I say."

"Be happy," Mattie assured her. "This one should be about over soon. Now, let's see. Why don't you work on the dress? A week's time should be enough, don't you think? Then next week we'll start on the meal menu and the guest list."

Rebecca took a deep breath. "It's really going to happen."

"The more time you spend dreaming, the less time there is for work," Mattie told her, as she left for the basement. But Rebecca saw the smile on her face.

Her gaze went back to the cloth spread on the table. Its light blue sheen glowed in the morning light. She ran her hand across the length of a piece and imagined the day she would wear the dress. It would be beautiful, as lovely as the day when she and John would be man and wife.

Now, though, there was work to do and plenty of it. She lifted the first two pieces and took them into the living room to begin. By lunchtime she had the upper part of the dress done and stopped to prepare sandwiches. Mattie wanted help cleaning the rooms upstairs, where

Stephen and Leona had stayed, so that took most of the afternoon. Since she still didn't want her sisters to see the dress, it all went back into the box before three thirty.

On Sunday John told her the renters would leave next month. He wanted Rebecca to come over to pick out paint colors. She told him the house was just fine, just as long as he was in it. That brought a smile, but John wouldn't be persuaded. The whole house would be repainted in whatever colors she wished. He still had the paint samples in his room but didn't want to work on the project today. They set a time when Rebecca could come over during the week.

On Wednesday the dress was done, and Rebecca tried it on, alone in her room, and then dared show it to Mattie.

"John will like that," Mattie told her.

"Do you like it?"

"It's beautiful."

"Really?"

Mattie grinned. "Quit preening now. We have lots of work to do."

Rebecca laughed in the sheer delight of the moment.

"I'm glad this is working out for you," Mattie told her. "Both your dad and I are. You don't know how much."

"I'll put it up right away," Rebecca said and raced back upstairs. There she folded the dress carefully, placing it in the box and sliding it back on the top shelf of the closet. To leave it hang would invite her sisters to visit her room for quick glances and soon quick touches, she figured. The dress would stay here, only to be taken out of the box and ironed the night before the wedding.

Each day followed the other in quick procession. Some longer than others, but all were full of work and plans. John and Rebecca got down to the subject of witnesses a few weeks later. It was on a Sunday night. They had again chosen to stay home from the singing. A habit, John said with a tease, he was used to already.

They were at John's place, upstairs in his room. Rebecca suggested they go down and consult with Isaac and Miriam, especially about John's choice for a witness.

"You don't trust me already," he protested, but his eyes twinkled.

"I'm just saying it might be better to get your parents' opinion on this," Rebecca told him, to which he agreed.

Downstairs Isaac was on the couch, his Bible open in front of him. Miriam still had the supper dishes to finish in the kitchen but came out when she saw they meant to stay.

"Rebecca thinks we ought to ask about my choice of witnesses," John informed his parents.

"She's a smart girl," Isaac said chuckling. "Anyone who wants my opinion is smart."

"I thought about that," Miriam said ignoring Isaac. "You don't have any near relatives to choose from, and Bethany's children aren't old enough yet."

"You see the problem," John said. "So I have come up with a solution I like."

"And?" Isaac said.

"Luke Byler," John said.

"Luke?" Miriam sat up straight. "Don't you think that's pushing it? Rachel will be sore enough the way it is—probably thinks she'll never get the money now."

"It would be a good way to show her that we mean to do what's right," John said.

"You like him, don't you?" Isaac asked.

"Yes, from what I know of him," John said.

"Then ask him," Miriam told him. "He's got a girlfriend, doesn't he?"

"I think so."

"Bishop's wife said he did," Miriam offered. "She told me after they came home from the funeral—Susie's her name. I don't know her."

"Then that's it," John pronounced with a smile. "We'll ask him."

"What about your side?" Miriam asked with a smile. "Do you have something of the same problem?"

"I do," Rebecca agreed. "Both Lloyd and Margaret's children are too young."

John waited beside her but didn't look too interested, Rebecca thought, so whatever she decided would likely be okay.

"What about Wilma?" Rebecca suggested. "That's done sometimes. Ask your friends, if you don't have relatives."

"Is she dating?" John asked.

"Just started," Rebecca told him. "A boy from Holmes County, James Wengerd."

"She should be thrilled." Miriam smiled in agreement, and so it was decided.

John took Rebecca home around ten. He went inside but soon left. She watched his buggy leave. The lights seemed to linger along the road even after the sound of his horse's hooves could no longer be heard. She went upstairs to her room and, for the joy of it, peeked into the box. The blue color of the wedding dress danced in the light of the kerosene lamp.

They made plans to paint the rental home, after Rebecca picked the colors. Miriam and Esther offered to help, and Mattie said she could come for a day. John planned to clean the house on his own, now that the occupants were gone, but the task quickly became more than he bargained for. He *man cleaned* he said. Rebecca told him it was good enough until she could get to it, which would be before the women began the paint job.

She then spent a whole day cleaning the walls and ceilings, before she asked for help from her mother. Mattie and Rebecca spent a better part of another day before they were satisfied. The next time John saw Rebecca, he protested the extra work this caused, but Rebecca told him that what needed to be done needed to be done. John smiled and said he figured he might as well get used to her ways. She assured him he was a wise man.

The paint work began in earnest the next week. This time it was the women who needed help. John convinced Aden the need was serious and came down for the rest of the week. With drop cloths spread thoughout the house, the hardwood floors well protected, paint rollers and brushes moved all day long. Rebecca was thrilled when they completed the work by Friday after lunch.

She had painted most of the home a gentle gray. The bedroom, though, was painted a light blue, as close as she could get to her wedding dress, but John didn't know that yet. He had asked twice already, and she had told him he would have to wait. The morning before the big day would be soon enough.

John turned off the electric power. He said he didn't even want them to get used to such conveniences. Rebecca had no objections, even when John had to pull the water pump and change over to an air pump. She figured it needed to be done sometime anyway. Early was fine with her. In the back of her mind, she also hoped to make the best impression on Bishop that was possible. Only a small way to repay him perhaps, but this was something that would mean a lot to him.

Time seemed to slow down the closer the date came. There were invitations to prepare and mail. Rebecca drove into West Union to have them printed. She spent another Sunday afternoon with John to prepare the out-of-town wedding guest list. Rebecca made sure Rachel got one, not just because Luke had agreed to be a witness but because she hoped Rachel would come. Perhaps on the day of the wedding, she could assure her that the money would be returned.

Then the baking began—a mighty rush the week before. Cherry, apple, and pecan pies and date pudding would have to be prepared right at the end. The chickens were thawed, and the potatoes peeled and mashed. Vegetables were obtained, most of them fresh because the local markets still carried them. The official cooks arrived the day before, a duty considered a privilege even with the heavy workload.

Rebecca went to John's house to drop off food items and make final preparations to move in. She arrived and left during the middle of the day to avoid John. It seemed more fitting, now that the time was so close. They would stay the night of the wedding at their own house instead of staying at the bride's home, as was the custom. Mattie had suggested this, and Rebecca quickly accepted.

Leona and Stephen arrived in the afternoon, and Lester gathered the whole family around the kitchen table that evening, his face joyful.

"It's our last night here with Rebecca," he told them all. "She'll be married tomorrow. She has been a good daughter. We wish John and her the rich blessing of the Lord."

Rebecca had expected something of the sort but still choked up. "You don't have to, Dad," she told him.

"She'll be back soon," Mattie said with a smile.

"Girl stuff," Matthew muttered under his breath, but Rebecca was certain he would miss her too.

Lester led in a prayer of thanks for the food and for a blessing on the new home about to be established. After supper and dishes, they gathered in the living room and sang songs for thirty minutes. Rebecca hadn't planned to cry but couldn't keep back the tears when she saw the shine of wetness on her mother's cheek.

They had prayer again, then settled into silence. The girls headed to bed twenty minutes later with their cousins. Rebecca left too, as she wasn't needed downstairs. The kitchen work had been done quickly with all the ready hands.

With the kerosene lamp lit, she stood by the window. Just over the horizon, the new moon seemed ready to slip down for the night.

"To us," she said. The words hung softly on the night air. "To our life together. May it be more than even I can imagine."

CHAPTER FORTY

Rebecca awoke before the alarm and went out to chore one last time. Matthew knew she didn't have to. He was certainly able to handle things by himself but grinned when she walked in. She handled the milkers for one round of cows and knew she would miss even this when she was gone.

Leona was up when she returned to the house. She and Mattie were deep in conversation in the kitchen.

"Don't even think about helping with breakfast," Leona informed Rebecca. "Sit right down here. This is your day."

"I still want to help," Rebecca said.

"There's plenty of time for that later. Some other day." Leona was firm.

"I would say so," Mattie joined in. "Breakfast will be ready soon. You can eat early. It's going to be a little scattered anyway."

"Who's driving you?" Leona asked.

"Matthew. He insisted," Rebecca said grinning. "And I want to get there before too long."

"Eat. Then you can go change," Mattie told her. "I have enough eggs done so you can start. The oatmeal is almost cooked."

"I'll toast the bread." Leona got up and expertly ran two pieces of bread over the open flame of the gas stove.

Rebecca ate, took deep breaths, and smiled, as the butterflies began to turn in her stomach. Leona saw her face and insisted she finish what she had taken. That done, they shooed Rebecca upstairs. She took the dress out of the closet and put it on. Freshly ironed, it fit even better than she remembered.

By seven thirty, Matthew had eaten and hitched the horse to the buggy. Leona and Mattie came out to watch her walk through the living room, big smiles on their faces. Stephen and Lester were still in the kitchen, finishing their breakfasts, and could wait to see her until church time. Matthew let out a low whistle when she stepped outside.

Matthew dropped her off at the front sidewalk. He handled his horse as if he were already with the young folks and knew his way around girls. The wedding was to be held at Aden's house, with the meal served in his large pole barn out back. Already buggies were parked in a long line out by the barn. Cooks were hard at work preparing the noon meal.

With a glance around to see if anyone would come out of the house, she waited until Matthew drove forward, then walked to where the cooks worked. A few of the table waiters, paired or dating couples, were around too. They seemed surprised to see her but had little time to pause in their work other than to say "Hi" as she passed.

Rebecca knew it was time to go upstairs before too many people saw her. John would join her there, along with the two witness couples, until it was time to walk downstairs to their assigned seats in the front row.

Aden met her with a smile at the front door and motioned for her to come inside. Esther came from the kitchen and told Rebecca, "Second bedroom on the right." Around them the living room was filled with church benches—the overflow went well into the kitchen and main bedroom. "I'll send the others up when they arrive," Esther added.

Rebecca nodded and climbed the stairs. The bedroom Esther directed her to was furnished with six chairs for the three couples to use until they were to go downstairs. John arrived ten minutes later. From the look on his face, she was glad he came before anyone else was there.

"You're beautiful," he said and took her face in his hands and kissed her.

Rebecca knew she blushed bright red and that more people could arrive any minute. "Quit it," she told him and pushed him away.

He grinned and took a chair. She sat down beside him, her knees weak.

Luke and Susie came up next. Rebecca knew Susie from her time in Milroy and greeted her warmly. She found Luke grave, though— troubled almost. At first she thought it was the money but decided against that conclusion. It was unlike the Luke she knew.

"I'm so sorry about your father," she said and knew from his reaction this was the cause of his sorrow.

"It was hard," he said. "Dad's in a better place now."

"It must be rough," John told him. "My dad just went through a rough spot."

"That's what I heard. Is he okay now?" Luke asked.

"Almost normal," John told him. "We are blessed."

"I wouldn't have missed this," Luke said, with his first smile. He sat down beside Susie, and Rebecca could see how comfortable he was with her.

Wilma arrived with a blast of good cheer and changed the whole atmosphere of the room. Her boyfriend in tow, a stranger to the community, Wilma introduced him all around. It looked as if Wilma had everything under control.

At five till nine, it was time to go downstairs. Silently Luke and Susie led the way because the bridegroom's party was to go first. John and Rebecca followed. Wilma and James came at the end. Rebecca's heart pounded as they walked in front of the packed house and took their seats in front of the ministers' bench. Six chairs had been set out, three lined up facing the other three, boys on one side, and girls on the other.

The song leader announced the song, and the service began. As they all sang the second verse, Bishop Martin got up and, followed by his fellow ministers, walked up the stairs. Rebecca watched John's feet, and when they moved, she slowly stood too. They followed the ministers up the steps.

Bishop Martin cleared his throat when they all had settled down in the bedroom. Isaac was seated beside the bishop. Two visiting ministers and their home minister sat to Isaac's left, the deacon to the right of the bishop. John and Rebecca sat directly across from Isaac and Bishop Martin.

"It's good this day has come. I'm glad for it," Bishop said smiling. "I will let the others express themselves first."

Isaac glanced at Bishop Martin and received a nod, which meant he was to go first.

"I am glad to be here, in more ways than one," Isaac said. "The Lord has spared my health, for which I am thankful. John has been a good son, faithful to God and to the church. I wish him and Rebecca nothing but the best—grace for their trials, joy in the good times, and above all a gracious and full end to their married lives, which they are to begin today."

The home minister said much the same, and the two visiting ministers said that, while they didn't know the couple well, they trusted God's blessing would rest on their union.

When Bishop glanced at the deacon, Rebecca thought he looked uncomfortable, but he bravely said what he had to say. "There have been storm clouds—many of them—gathered around Rebecca and John. This was not their fault entirely. Others were also to blame. I also wish God's blessing on this union. John has never made trouble for us. Nor has Rebecca. They have been up-building church members. We trust this will continue. May God grant us all grace, as He extends that same grace to them."

Rebecca was certain a smile played on Bishop's face, but he cleared his throat again and said, "There is one question we need to ask. We ask all our young people this because it is important that marriage begins in God. It's also important that the foundation of marriage be laid in God's laws. Have you, John, and you, Rebecca, conducted your courtship with honor? Are you *frei* from each other?"

Because she hadn't quite expected the question put so bluntly, Rebecca felt red creep up her neck, but she nodded along with John.

"I am glad to hear that," Bishop said, but Rebecca was certain he didn't look surprised. She had heard lectures from Bishop before on the dangers of courtship. Bishop was not a man who expected his words ignored.

What followed were further instructions on how a man and wife needed to communicate and share everything. Finances were explained in detail, from sharing a joint checking account to consulting together on business decisions great or small.

"A man is the head of his home," Bishop said, "yet he is not so without his wife. Women often see dangers men cannot see. A wise man will listen to what his wife has to tell him. I hope you two get along."

Rebecca saw Isaac grin at that comment but hide it when Bishop looked his way.

The others took their turns, addressing much of the same information, adding their own stories of battles fought and battles won. When they were dismissed, the ministers stayed upstairs, while John and Rebecca walked back downstairs and took their seats again. Around them the singing continued until the line of ministers appeared at the top of the stairs.

Preaching seemed to go on forever, Rebecca thought, probably because she sat in front where everyone could see the slightest move she made. John looked tense too, his hands clasped in front of him. The two sets of witnesses on either side seemed in a little better shape, but then they weren't the ones the people looked at.

Finally, twelve o'clock came, and Bishop got to his feet.

"If these two are still willing to be joined as man and wife, will you, John and Rebecca, come forward."

Rebecca hoped she wouldn't faint, as she stood to follow John. They moved toward Bishop.

The bishop looked upon the young couple's faces, and then he asked, "Do you believe, John Miller, that this, our sister Rebecca Keim, is given to you by God to be your wife?"

John said, "Yes."

"Will you take her hand in holy matrimony, to be your helpmeet in sickness, in health, in tragedy, and in joy? To stand by her, as Christ has instructed us, until death parts you?"

"Yes," John nodded.

Bishop turned slightly to face Rebecca. She had a flash of fear. Could someone stop this yet? Perhaps Bishop would be unable to say the words and change his mind, but his voice reached her with the same questions. She said "yes" to them all.

Then Bishop took their hands, laid John's hands on top of Rebecca's, and said, "To the will of God, I now commit these two, our brother and sister. May they be blessed with the abundance and grace of the Most High. May His most Holy Spirit dwell in their home, and may you both, with us, find an end in that heavenly dwelling on high. You are now man and wife."

Bishop let go of their hands, and they sat down as the last song was sung. When it was finished, John got up first and led the way, Rebecca at his shoulder. The two pairs of witnesses followed. Out in the yard, two robins and their young took off, with a quick flutter of their wings. Rebecca had mist in her eyes, as they approached the pole barn and entered. They walked slowly past the tables laden with food—baked chicken, mashed potatoes, brown gravy, dressing and noodles, veg-etables, cole slaw, pies, date pudding, and sheet cake. Bowls of canned fruit and celery sticks served mainly as decorations.

At the corner table, John slid in first, followed by Rebecca. He held her hand briefly under the table. "You are my wife," he whispered, but she could only nod as she met his eyes and pressed back the tears.

On either side, the witnesses sat down. The guests slowly made their way in and sat down. Only soft whispers rose from the tables until prayer was announced, and then the conversations grew louder.

John glanced at Rebecca and grinned. "Now I'm a rich man."

"Not in money," she said, pretending to glare at him.

He laughed, "No...just in the kind that lasts. A wonderful woman."

"We'll see how long that sweet talk lasts," she said and made a face at him.

"All of our life together," he declared and sliced his fork through the piece of pecan pie. "Completely all of it."

CHAPTER FORTY-ONE

Rachel spent the day in agony, not just physical because her time to give birth had come but of soul. She wouldn't have gone to the West Union wedding anyway. This handy excuse just made things easier. How had Rebecca dared to ask Luke to be a witness at her wedding? Sure, she knew it was for John's side, but Rebecca had something to do with it. Rachel was certain of it.

In a twist of fate she hadn't expected, the goats were still on the farm. After Reuben's funeral she had gone over the books just to be sure, but already knew the answer. She would have to keep them out of financial necessity. They were the largest income producer on the farm, and she needed income.

So the thing that Reuben had kept at a distance now needed to be handled daily. It was an affront to the depths of her being. Luke came by often, out of compassion she figured or for the sake of his father's memory. Either reason rankled Rachel.

They never spoke of the inheritance, Luke for his own reasons she could well imagine. She had simply given up any hope of ever receiving it. News of Rebecca's wedding, apparently approved by the bishop, had reached her even before Luke was asked to be a witness. Protest was useless, Rachel knew. She determined to bear the burden given her in silence.

When her labor increased that morning, Rachel drove herself to the midwife's house. With no husband to take her, Rachel didn't waste time on self-pity. It was just the way things were. On the way she stopped in at Ezra's house to let him know she needed someone to do the chores because Luke was gone. When she arrived at the midwife's home, she was ushered right in to a room that had been prepared for such purposes.

The midwife didn't seem surprised when Rachel showed up. "Is Luke at the wedding?" she commented more than asked.

"Yes," Rachel said.

"How close are the contractions?"

"Ten minutes apart."

"Sit down on the couch, then. I'll take you back soon."

Rachel did as she was told, and the afternoon dragged on. She hated every moment of this. While she birthed Reuben's baby, Rebecca was enjoying her wedding meal. She was, no doubt, full of delight at the thought of her abundant life ahead—a life with plenty of money in it.

It was after two when the hard work began, and the afternoon and evening dragged on. Not till after ten did the midwife hold the child in her hands. Rachel could see, in spite of exhaustion, the child was a boy. She lay back, glad it was over.

Soon the child would be in her arms, and her heart leapt in anticipation, in spite of herself. *But we have no money,* she thought and felt the sorrow of her lot. *I'm alone with no husband and now a young child to raise. Yet I like him even if I'm poor,* she thought in amazement.

The silence soon startled her. Rachel raised her head. The midwife had her back turned and seemed focused on the child, as if she had forgotten Rachel.

"Is something wrong?" Rachel asked.

The midwife didn't turn around or answer.

Rachel tried to sit up but was too weak. "I hear nothing," she said.

The midwife turned slowly, the child in her hands. "He never breathed," she said, "not even for a second. I'm sorry."

Rachel felt the pain swell up with great waves and crash into her heart. The pain was greater than that of childbirth. She cried aloud from the agony. Her mind couldn't comprehend the news, and her body felt as if it had been torn apart.

"It is *Da Hah's villa*," the midwife said. Her voice was gentle, but the words passed through Rachel like arrows.

"He's taken my husband. He's taken our money. Now He's taken my son," she screamed, her head falling back on the pillow, her face contorted with passion. "How can He do this. What have I done to deserve such treatment? Have I left the faith? Have I been unfaithful to my husband? Have I so sinned?"

"It is none of those," the midwife said, quickly laying the still child on the table and turning her attentions to Rachel. She ran her hand across Rachel's forehead, the fingers gently moving her hair out of the way. "You must not say so. It's not your fault. Of course you lived your life…obeyed Him."

"Then why?" Rachel asked. "Why must I suffer so?"

"Now…now. You didn't mean any of that." The midwife ran her hand across her forehead again. "I'll send Norman to tell Bishop Mose in the morning. I doubt if he'll want a funeral."

Rachel stared out the window and tried to compose herself. Life must go on, even when it becomes too hard she told herself.

The midwife wrapped the child in a white blanket and took him across the hall to the other bedroom. Rachel heard her footsteps go out to the kitchen, then return. She proceeded to clean up the room and make Rachel comfortable.

"I've got soup warming," she whispered. "It will do you good."

Rachel nodded, surprised she could be hungry, but she was. The bowl of vegetable soup brought a measure of comfort. She ate it quickly and handed the bowl back to the midwife.

"You sleep now. I'll take care of things in the morning."

Rachel lay in the darkness when the bedroom door shut, the pain still stung in her chest. She didn't want to think, to wonder what lay ahead of her. Sleep was a welcome guest at the moment. A wave of loneliness overwhelmed her, and she wept until sleep came.

Bishop Mose and his wife both came in the morning and spoke what words of comfort they could. They said the child would be buried that day beside Reuben, that their sons would dig the grave, but there would be no funeral. Bishop's wife brought the white wrapped bundle in for her to see and asked whether she wished to be at the gravesite. Rachel, after she lifted the blanket, shook her head.

While they attended to her, the midwife left for town to register the birth certificate. Bishop and his wife had to leave before she returned. Rachel watched them go. The white bundle lay on the back seat of the buggy.

She felt nothing. Her whole insides were frozen, as if great sheets of ice had fallen on them. By noon the midwife came back and fixed lunch. Rachel felt well enough to travel, and the midwife hitched the horse to the buggy. She insisted she take Rachel in her buggy. Her husband would pick her up when he was done with chores, she said.

Rachel felt this was all a waste of time and said so to no avail. She was driven home, then ushered into the house before the midwife unhitched and fed the horse. Ezra came by later to tend the goats. He came into the house, when he saw the buggy.

"So what is it?" he hollered, apparently in an attempt at cheer.

"He was stillborn. Bishop's taking care of him," the midwife told Ezra.

Rachel, from where she lay in the bedroom, heard the shock in Ezra's voice. "Not again."

"There was nothing we could do," the midwife told him. "I'm fixing something for supper now."

"So that's why there's no help here," Ezra said. "I wondered."

"She had the Burkholder girl lined up, I think. But we didn't stop in. I guess I should have let her know. She's probably wondering."

"I'll send someone," Ezra told her. "We'll be here for the night, then."

"It would be good. She took it pretty hard."

Rachel heard footsteps, then Ezra stood in the bedroom doorway.

"You must not blame yourself," he said. "It is all in *Da Hah's* hands."

"They're all gone," she said. Tears stung her cheeks. The vast emptiness of the house pressed in on her.

"Elizabeth and I will come back," Ezra said. "Elizabeth can stay with you part of the day tomorrow. It might help."

"Nothing will help me," Rachel whispered.

"You must not talk so. I'll do the chores. We'll be back." And then his footsteps faded away.

The midwife brought in a plate of food for her but had to leave when her husband came. They left before Ezra and Elizabeth returned. Rachel got up and walked around a while. Her gaze fell upon the checkbook, and she wondered how she would continue to exist. Goats and more goats stretched out into her financial future, as far as she could see.

Ezra and Elizabeth returned around nine and found her still at the desk, bills and checks lay all around. Elizabeth made her go right back to bed.

"You'll have plenty of time for money problems later," she told Rachel.

Sleep came sooner than she expected, the weight of her body's weariness simply overwhelming her.

Ezra did the chores in the morning, while Elizabeth fixed breakfast and served Rachel in bed. They left with a final promise to keep tabs on her, after Elizabeth cleaned the kitchen and Ezra made one final check on the goats.

So began her existence again. Rachel would always remember those days, especially because of what came a few weeks later. A fancy *Englisha* car drove up the driveway late one Thursday evening. The day had been like most of her days, filled with goats, goat troubles, and goat chores. Rachel brushed her apron off and went out to see what this old man wanted. He came out of the car, moving slowly, as if he wanted to get a good look at the place.

"Are you Rachel Byler?" he asked as she approached.

"Yes," she said, her face puzzled.

"Emma Miller your aunt? The Emma who never married?"

"Yes. And who are you?"

"The executor of Emma's will, Manny Troyer," he said. "This is now yours."

She looked at the papers in his hand but made no attempt to take them.

"Why would you have something for me? Rebecca married Amish."

"Yes," he said looking pleased, a smile playing on his face. "She knows what to do with money. She's a good girl, a great catch for that John of hers. This is your share."

He held the papers out again, and she took them this time.

"All of it, except what the lawyer and I got paid. The rest is divided equally among the four of you. Hope you enjoy it." And then he got back in his car and, without a backward glance, drove out the driveway.

Numbly she walked into the house and sat at her desk. The papers fell open in front of her—a deed to the old home place and a checkbook, which contained an account balance with commas in it.

She expected joy to leap in her heart. Many times she had imagined what the light of this day would be like, had thought this worth anything her life contained. Now the numbers on the checkbook swam before her eyes, and her arms trembled. With the goal in front of her, her hands around the prize, she laid her head on the desk and wept bitterly.

Book Group Discussion Questions

1. How does John handle his fears? For those who have read the first two books in The Adams County Trilogy, describe how John's attitudes have changed since his accident.

2. Why do you think Rachel's brothers' opinions about the inheritance had no effect on her?

3. Do you think the exuberance with which Ruth wrote the article for *The Budget* is typical of the average person writing about a personal cause?

4. What reasons did Manny Troyer give for never marrying? Do you think those reasons were genuine? Justifiable?

5. Did Isaac, as John's father, do everything he should have to protect John and Rebecca from the accusation—that Rebecca is marrying John for money—noted in the card John received?

6. What do you think drove Rachel to such extremes in her quest for the inheritance?

7. Do you think Manny Troyer should have contacted Emma during their latter years?

8. Was John being loyal to Rebecca when he threatened to leave his faith and join the Mennonites?

9. Do you think Rebecca's wedding day was all she had hoped for?

10. Did Rachel change her ways in the end?

About Jerry Eicher...

As a boy, **Jerry Eicher** spent eight years in Honduras where his grandfather helped found an Amish community outreach. As an adult, Jerry taught for two terms in parochial Amish and Mennonite schools in Ohio and Illinois. He has also been involved in church renewal for 14 years, and has preached in churches and conducted weekend meetings of in-depth Bible teaching. Jerry lives with his wife, Tina, and their four children in Virginia.

To learn more about books by Jerry Eicher or to read sample chapters, log on to our website:

www.harvesthousepublishers.com

HARVEST HOUSE PUBLISHERS
EUGENE, OREGON

Acknowledgments

Thanks, first of all, to the good people at Harvest House, who I am still getting to know. They are the ones who took the risk and welcomed me into the real world of publishing.

Thanks to the editors I work with, Nick Harrison and Peggy Wright. Terry Glaspey—the great mediator extraordinaire—you are good.

In the world outside Harvest House, there is a man to whom I cannot fully express my gratitude—Mr. John Gerber, the executive director of Choice Books of Midwest. It is no exaggeration to say that without him there would be no Jerry Eicher who writes Amish fiction. The dream would have died with the self-published memoirs of my childhood memories.

On that Saturday afternoon in the summer of 2005, I visited with Lavina Hostetler at her home, where I had boarded some twenty-three years prior as a parochial school teacher. That meeting was the last stop on what my wife, Tina, called my "book tour." A sort of pitiful affair, but I was trying. I had by then given up on the book but showed it to Lavina anyway.

She said, "You have to talk to John Gerber from Choice Books. You know him from your school teaching days."

I said, "Ja, I know him, but I also know Choice Books. They turned me down at the main office."

"You have to talk to him," she insisted and picked up the phone. Fifteen minutes later Mr. Gerber walked into her living room, sat down across from me, and cast his steely eye on my book.

"We need this kind of literature," he said, "but this is all done wrong."

"Okay," I said. At least the man seemed willing to give me information.

What followed was rapid-fire information about the world of publishing, all highly classified and not to be disclosed here . . . just kidding. He took me down to the local Choice Books offices at Metamora and gave me the full tour.

I left with his promise that if I changed the cover he would test market ten copies. I did, and he kept his promise. On such a small thread hung my destiny as a writer. I think I sold six copies in two weeks—and I was in. From there he pushed me into writing romance, a place I would never have gone on my own. I only had mystery, suspense, and that sort of thing in mind.

Thanks, John. You have been a friend indeed.

THE ADAMS COUNTY TRILOGY

By Jerry Eicher

REBECCA'S PROMISE

The Adams County Trilogy, book one

Rebecca Keim has just declared her love to John Miller and agreed to become his wife. But she's haunted by her schoolgirl memories of a long-ago love—and a promise made and a ring given. Is that memory just a fantasy come back to destroy the beautiful present...or was it real?

When Rebecca's mother sends her back to the old home community in Milroy to be with her aunt during and after her childbirth, Rebecca determines to find answers that will resolve her conflicted feelings. Faith, love, and tradition all play a part in Rebecca's divine destiny.

REBECCA'S RETURN

The Adams County Trilogy, book two

Rebecca Keim returns to Wheat Ridge full of resolve to make her rela-

tionship with John Miller work. But in her absence, John has become suspicious of the woman he loves. Before their conflict can be resolved, John is badly injured and Rebecca is sent back to Milroy to aid her seriously ill aunt Leona.

In Milroy, Rebecca once again visits the old covered bridge over the Flatrock River, the source of her past memories and of her promise made so long ago.

Where will Rebecca find happiness? In Wheat Ridge with John, the man she has agreed to marry...or should she stake her future on the memory that persists...and the ring she has never forgotten? Does God have a perfect will for Rebecca—and if so how can she know that will?

New Amish Books
from Harvest House Publishers

THE POCKET GUIDE TO AMISH LIFE *by Mindy Starns Clark*

As Amish fiction continues to appeal to a huge audience, *A Pocket Guide to Amish Life* gives you a glimpse into an obscure, fascinating world—what the Amish believe and how they live. Full of fun and fresh facts about the people who abide by this often-misunderstood faith and unique culture, this handy-sized guide covers a wide variety of topics, such as:

- beliefs and values
- clothing and transportation
- courtship and marriage
- shunning and discipline
- teens and *rumpsringa*
- children and the elderly
- education and work

Presented in an easy-to-follow and engaging style, this pocket guide to the Amish is a great resource for anyone interested in Amish life.

THE HOMESTYLE AMISH KITCHEN COOKBOOK *by Georgia Varozza*

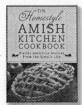

Just about everyone is fascinated by the Amish—their simple, family-centered lifestyle, colorful quilts, and hearty, homemade meals. Straight from the heart of Amish country, this celebration of hearth and home gives you a delightful peek at the Amish way of life—a life filled with the self-reliance and peace of mind that many long for.

You will appreciate the scores of tasty, easy-to-prepare recipes such as Scrapple, Graham "Nuts" Cereal, Potato Rivvel Soup, Amish Dressing, and Snitz Pie. At the same time you will learn a bit about the Amish, savor interesting tidbits from the "Amish Kitchen Wisdom" sections, find out just how much food it takes to feed the large number of folks attending preaching services, barn raisings, weddings, and work frolics, and much more.

The Homestyle Amish Kitchen Cookbook is filled with good, old-fashioned family meal ideas to help bring the simple life home!

RACHEL'S SECRET *by BJ Hoff*
The Riverhaven Years, book one

In *Rachel's Secret,* Hoff introduces a new community of unforgettable characters and adds the elements readers have come to expect from her novels: a tender love story, the faith journeys of people we grow to know and love, and enough suspense to keep the pages turning quickly.

When the wounded Irish American riverboat captain, Jeremiah Gant, bursts into the rural Amish setting of Riverhaven, he brings chaos and conflict to the community—especially for young widow, Rachel Brenneman. The unwelcome "outsider" needs a safe place to recuperate before continuing his secret role as an Underground Railroad conductor. Neither he nor Rachel is prepared for the forbidden love that threatens to endanger a man's mission, a woman's heart, and a way of life for an entire people.

WHERE GRACE ABIDES *by BJ Hoff*
The Riverhaven Years, book two

In *Where Grace Abides,* the compelling second book in the series, Hoff offers her readers an even closer look at the Amish community of Riverhaven and the people who live and love and work there. Secrets, treachery, and persecution are only a few of the challenges that test Rachel's faith and her love for the forbidden "outsider," while Gant's own hopes and dreams are dealt a life-changing blow, rendering the vow he made to Rachel seemingly impossible to honor.

Many of the other characters first introduced in *Rachel's Secret* now find their gentle, unassuming lives of faith jeopardized by a malicious outside influence. At the same time, those striving to help runaway slaves escape to freedom through the Underground Railroad face deception and the danger of discovery.

SHADOWS OF LANCASTER COUNTY *by Mindy Starns Clark*

Following up on her extremely popular Gothic thriller, *Whispers of the Bayou*, Mindy Starns Clark offers another suspenseful stand-alone mystery full of Amish simplicity, dark shadows, and the light of God's amazing grace.

Anna thought she left the tragedies of the past behind when she moved from Pennsylvania to California, but when her brother vanishes from the genetics lab where he works, Anna has no choice but to head back home. Using skills well-honed in Silicon Valley, she follows the high-tech trail her brother left behind, a trail that leads from the simple world of Amish farming to the cutting edge of DNA research and gene mapping.

Anna knows she must depend on her instincts, her faith in God, and the help of the Amish community to find her brother. She also must finally face her own shadows—and pray that she's stronger than the grief that threatens to overwhelm them all.

A WIDOW'S HOPE *by Mary Ellis*

A bright new voice shares a tender love story set in the rolling green fields of Ohio Amish country.

After the death of her husband, Hannah Brown is determined to make a new life with her sister's family. But when she sells her farm in Lancaster County, Pennsylvania, and moves with her sheep to Ohio, the wool unexpectedly starts to fly. Her deacon brother-in-law finds just about everything about Hannah vexing. When his widower brother shows interest in the young and beautiful widow, the deacon turns to prayer for guidance.

Hannah thought she could never love again, until she meets the strong, gentle farmer. Unfortunately, Seth Miller's only interest is in Hannah's sheep. He is content in his bachelor state and slow to recognize his daughter's need for a new mother. Yet God offers Seth the perfect solution to their problems if he could only open his heart again...and love.